ALSO BY SUSAN GABRIEL

Temple Secrets Trilogy:

Temple Secrets

Gullah Secrets

Tea Leaf Secrets

The Wildflower Trilogy:

The Secret Sense of Wildflower

(a Kirkus Reviews Best Book of 2012)

Lily's Song

Daisy's Fortune

Trueluck Summer

Grace, Grits and Ghosts: Southern Short Stories

Seeking Sara Summers

Circle of the Ancestors

TEA LEAF SECRETS

SUSAN GABRIEL

WILD LILY ARTS

1

VIOLET

The ancient oak that survived Hurricane Iris reaches across the Gullah cemetery like an ancestral grandmother protecting her descendants. Spanish moss clings to her limbs in the breeze, swaying like long, gray hair. Resurrection ferns wrap her body. Ferns that will remain a dry crackly brown until the next rain when the seemingly dead plants revive and turn a vibrant green. After her yearlong drought of sadness, Violet longs to resurrect, too.

Every Sunday morning, Violet visits her grandmother's grave. She usually comes alone. Today, however, her friend and half sister, Rose, asked if she could tag along, reminding her—as if Violet needed reminding—that it was the anniversary of when Old Sally left them to join her ancestors. A day that still feels recent. Merely days or weeks ago instead of a full year.

Violet places a handful of wildflowers tied with an indigo blue ribbon on Old Sally's above-ground grave. The small Gullah cemetery is on higher ground, with enough elevation to have escaped the worst part of the hurricane's storm surge two years before.

As Violet and Rose stand together at the gravesite, a comfortable silence settles between them. The half-sister part of their relationship came to light at Miss Temple's will reading when Violet was informed that her father was Mr. Oscar, Miss Temple's husband, and that Queenie was her biological mother and not Queenie's sister, who died when Violet was an infant.

Violet's family tree is as twisted as the old crepe myrtle that used to grow in front of the Temple mansion and is just as colorful, given Gullah and aristocratic Temple blood has been mixing and mingling for generations.

Violet's memories take her to the day that Old Sally died. She'd returned to the porch thinking her grandmother was napping in her rocking chair. Old Sally had looked so peaceful that it took several moments to realize she was gone. It was as though, in her last moments, Old Sally had glimpsed heaven and was pleased.

"You seem different lately." Rose's voice is soft and interrupts Violet's thoughts.

They have been friends since they were girls, and Violet sometimes glimpses the girl Rose once was. She sees her now.

"Different?"

"Sad," Rose says, looking down at her hands, which still hold the car keys.

"Sad? Me?" Violet stares at the horizon. If pressed, Violet would choose a different word. She is sad, yes, but not only that. Losing Old Sally was like having the ground disappear from underneath her feet. Even a year later,

Violet has been unable to find her balance. It reminds Violet of the missing railing outside of the lighthouse the night Hurricane Iris came ashore. One wrong step, and she would have fallen into the darkness.

"If you don't want to talk about it, that's fine," Rose says.

Is Rose being careful with me, her sad friend Violet, who is different these days?

"I'm glad you're here," Violet says. "I mean, I don't mind coming alone, but it's nice to be with someone, too."

Rose looks at her. "I'm not intruding?"

"Of course not," Violet answers, with a smile usually reserved for customers these days.

The stone ruins of the small Gullah church stand in the distance. The church is covered from floor to the remaining rafters with wisteria vines that once a year present a breathtaking burst of purple blooms. The founders of the church must have picked this spot for its beauty, as well as its slight elevation. As is the Gullah tradition, all the graves face east toward the rising sun and their homeland. Remnants of a one-room schoolhouse are beyond.

Awkwardness rides in on the steamy breeze, uncharacteristic of their friendship. It is not always easy to be seen by someone. Violet has managed to hide her struggle from Jack and the girls. Or she thinks she has. Maybe they have noticed the difference, too, and just haven't said anything.

The smell of the salty sea calms her thoughts. It is a sunny June morning, already eighty degrees, even with the breeze. An effortless sweat from the humidity dots her forehead. For some reason, the summer feels eventful, as though the heat serves as a pressure cooker—a pressure cooker whose lid is poised to whistle its readiness.

Before the storm, Violet often sat in this cemetery and imagined hearing her ancestors singing in the church nearby. She would listen to the ancient Gullah songs that Old Sally taught her. Songs that floated through the breeze and shook the brittle oak leaves. It gives her goose bumps, even now.

"Not a bad place to spend eternity," Rose says, as though overhearing Violet's thoughts.

Violet agrees. With another birthday on the horizon, she is reminded that she will rest here, too, someday.

"This tree would make a great painting," Rose says, looking up into the limbs.

Although Violet walks past the portrait Rose painted of Old Sally for the living room several times a day, she sometimes forgets that Rose is an accomplished artist.

Violet studies the vastness of the tree, as well, with its intermingling of sunlight and shade. "Would you like to sit for a while?"

They walk to the new bench under the oak, one of two in the cemetery that Jack and Max, their husbands, built from the remains of the tree that fell into Queenie's bedroom the night Hurricane Iris came ashore.

"How are you sleeping these days?" Rose asks.

Violet regrets that she told Rose about her bouts of insomnia over the last year. Now she asks about it nearly every time Violet sees her.

"I can't seem to turn off my brain," Violet says. "It doesn't help that Tia and Leisha are off to college soon. Tia, for the first time."

It is helpful to know that Tia's older, more responsible sister goes to the same school and will watch out for her. But it's still a huge change.

"I remember those days of being an empty nester." Rose reaches over and squeezes Violet's hand, an act of tenderness that somehow feels threatening. Violet is too fragile these days. Always on the verge of tears that never fall. Her life also seems smaller than it used to, a collection of meaningless routines.

Rose asks about the quarters on top of Old Sally's grave.

"It was a joke between Old Sally and me," Violet says. "I would ask, 'A penny for your thoughts?' And she always answered that it would cost me a quarter."

They exchange brief smiles.

Violet doesn't say that she would give all the quarters in her bank account to hear Old Sally's voice again.

"I miss her, too." Rose's voice softens as if a secret is passing between them. "She still hasn't spoken to you?"

Violet lowers her eyes. With all the preparation for Old Sally's passing—learning the Gullah secrets and honing their ability to speak to each other from the other world on what Violet called the Gullah airwaves—they have not communicated since her death. What happened to the opening she and her grandmother created between the worlds where their thoughts could get through? Was it all a lie? Did she imagine it? If this mysterious communication system of theirs had an answering machine, Violet would have left a thousand messages by now, asking Old Sally to please pick up the phone.

At times, the absence of Old Sally and all she brought

to Violet's life feels unbearable. Violet has never felt so removed from her grandmother and her ancestors.

Rose leans in, and their shoulders touch. "Is there anything I can do?"

"Not really." Violet sits straighter and remembers how Miss Temple, Rose's mother, insisted on good posture whenever Violet worked at the mansion. But Rose isn't anything like her mother, and this certainly isn't the mansion.

"I'm a good listener," Rose says, with a hint of pleading.

"You are," Violet says, "and I promise to tell you when I need someone to listen."

Rose holds out her hand to pinkie swear as they did as girls. Violet laughs a short laugh, and they link fingers. Yet Violet isn't so sure she can keep this promise. The more sadness she feels, the harder it is to put into words, much less share it. But Violet knows Rose means well.

"Do you think the dead speak to the living?" Violet asks.

"Sure," Rose says. "I grew up in Savannah, remember? It's famous for ghosts."

Violet nods. The Temple family mansion was full of the spirits of former residents.

"I can't imagine Old Sally as a ghost, though," Rose says. "It wouldn't be her style. But Mother was certainly good at it."

Violet agrees. "Old Sally used to say that Miss Temple had unfinished business, and that's why she was always hanging around, but Old Sally didn't have any of that. She went eagerly and knowingly into the next life." Her sigh is like a period at the end of the sentence.

"I want to die that way," Rose says thoughtfully. "At peace. Ready to go home."

"Don't we all," Violet says.

She thinks about how important it was to Old Sally to pass on her ancestors' wisdom before going home. It fell to Violet to be the person who recorded this knowledge to preserve the Gullah traditions. But without Old Sally here, their rich culture now seems destitute.

Along with the wildflowers and quarters on Old Sally's grave sits a small stone box, as well as Old Sally's favorite teacup and saucer. In the Gullah tradition, items belonging to the deceased are placed on the grave, like in Egyptian tombs. The objects have meaning for the person who has died and are thought to be used in the afterlife. The stone box contains an old photograph of a dark man playing the fiddle. A small square of pink fabric sits beside it, embroidered with an *A* for Annabelle, who died at six days old. The elegant white china teacup and saucer, made the year that Old Sally was born, was a gift from Violet after she opened the tea shop. Faded purple flowers encircle the cup covered with tiny veins of age.

When Violet first placed the teacup on Old Sally's grave, she imagined they could have tea together on their Sunday mornings together and talk. It seems foolish now.

A pair of Old Sally's worn sandals also sits atop the crypt to take walks together, having conversations the way they had planned.

Life doesn't always respect plans. Perhaps death doesn't, either.

Rose stands and invites Violet to take a walk on the beach. When Violet says she wants to stay, Rose gives Violet one of her worried looks. A look that reminds Violet how most people generally don't understand grief or know what to do with it.

Alone again, memories rush forward of Old Sally's funeral. Most Dolphin Island residents came, as well as many people from Savannah and neighboring states. It was astounding how many people Old Sally had touched in her long life, and how many of them wanted to pay their respects.

The sound of Gullah spirituals lifted to heaven that day as the service went long into the night. People sat in lawn chairs around a bonfire on the beach and told stories of their time with Old Sally. The tales seemed endless. Many were ones Violet had never heard before—instances of great kindness where Old Sally nursed friends or encouraged people to make their ancestors proud. Or times when Old Sally talked for hours to whoever showed up at her door. When Violet was a girl, her grandmother got ready for work some mornings without having a bit of sleep because someone had needed her the night before.

How could this same person, who showed up so often in life, abandon Violet in death? She scolds herself for thinking this way, but she can't seem to stop.

After everyone except the family left the service that night, they gathered for a final ritual with lit torches at the gravesite. Sally Rose, Rose's granddaughter and only a year old, was gently passed over Old Sally's grave. Violet handed her to Queenie, Violet's mother, who then gave her to Rose. Thankfully, Sally Rose wasn't frightened and allowed them to do it, at times laughing as if it was a game between them. This Gullah tradition supposedly protected Sally Rose from following Old Sally into the other world, given their fondness for each other.

Pelicans fly low near the water in formation and bring Violet back to the present moment. Gentle waves break on the shore. Her ancestors rest here on sacred land, thousands of miles from home, enslaved to work in a strange land for wealthy Southerners before finally finding their way to this island.

History is everywhere. A history that Violet still struggles to make sense of, as well as claim. She is lucky compared to her ancestors. Not only is Violet the owner of a lovely tea shop in downtown Savannah, but she is also no longer a servant for the Temple family. Miss Temple—may she rest in peace—has been gone for four years now, and her surprise generosity in leaving the Temple mansion to Violet changed her life forever. When Edward, Miss Temple's son, burned the mansion to the ground, probably out of spite, it was the first time Violet realized there might be more to fate than she thought. Oddly, it feels destiny is calling her now, and she hasn't been willing to listen.

When Rose returns, Violet is relieved to get out of her thoughts. Rose places a white sand dollar on the top of Old Sally's grave. As girls, they collected sand dollars to hang on the tree in the Temple garden. A tree very similar to the one they sit under now.

Violet has also collected hundreds of entries in the Gullah Book of Secrets. Somehow, it seems a waste that Old Sally would give Violet all this information not to use it. Fate tugs at her again as if to remind her that it's not too late. But Violet feels too powerless to answer its call.

Violet looks at her watch and then at Rose. It will be getting busy at the tea shop, and she needs to relieve Queenie and Spud. She tells Rose they need to go. But before leaving, Violet places her hand on the top of the grave. She leans over and kisses the cold stone as she used to bend over and kiss Old Sally's cheek whenever she left the house. The warmth of her grandmother's cheek is one of a thousand things that Violet grieves. Violet tells her she loves her and then waits. The hot, humid breeze carries no reply.

2

QUEENIE

Q ueenie returns to the counter after cleaning off tables, and Spud gives her a quick kiss on the cheek.

"We're a good team, Queenie Temple."

"I agree, Mr. Grainger."

After two years of marriage, they aren't the newlyweds they once were. Since she has never been married before, Queenie wonders if this is normal.

Last night, to rekindle their ebbing flame, Queenie suggested they watch *Young Frankenstein* by Mel Brooks on the television in their bedroom. They had both seen it in the 1970s, long before they knew each other existed, but Queenie remembered it had some funny, sexy bits and thought it might be good for them. After the movie, when they were in bed, Queenie sang a boisterous rendition of the Madeline Kahn song featured when she and Frankenstein took their first roll in the hay. Spud was startled at first —Queenie never sang in bed—but they laughed so hard afterward that Queenie made a joke about wishing she wore Depends. Laughter is a good tonic, but it didn't lead to anything else, which caused her to worry.

"What are you grinning at?" Queenie asks Spud as she makes a pot of English breakfast tea for Table 2.

"Ah! Sweet mystery of life ..." Spud softly sings the song from the movie.

Queenie laughs a short laugh, gives him a half-hearted *not here* look, and tells herself to stop being so concerned.

Now and again, Queenie remembers how she used to drive Iris Temple to see Spud at the Piggly Wiggly. Spud was not only the butcher of the exotic meats Iris always ordered, but also her ex-flame. It seems a million years ago now, yet it still nags at Queenie that Spud was with Iris first. Those weekly flirtations with Iris over the meat counter are imprinted in her memory. Memories she wishes she could forget. At least Iris and Spud's time together was brief and amounted to no consequence. If it had been a long affair with more substance, Queenie isn't so sure she could have moved past it.

Much harder to reconcile is the fact that Queenie worked for thirty-five years as Iris's assistant, which required spending an eternity in that drafty old mansion with Iris and the Temple ghosts. Sure, Queen ran errands and attended the occasional meeting where privileged white women sat around eating finger sandwiches and drinking tea with their pinkie fingers up. And Violet bustled around, keeping the mansion clean and Iris and Queenie fed. Yet, a busy tea shop suits Queenie much better.

It makes Queenie dizzy sometimes how much their lives changed after Iris died. Queenie is forever grateful that Violet forgave her for keeping that stupid secret all those years that Violet was Queenie's child, not Queenie's sister, Maya. She wonders now how she could have been so misguided. In her defense, secrets have all sorts of fear and shame wrapped around them, a fortress built to keep out the truth. Sometimes it takes years to break through that fortress. Sometimes decades. She imagines some secrets never see the daylight.

Queenie isn't the type to reminisce, and yet today she has allowed herself this indulgence. A year has passed since she lost her sweet mother. Violet went to the cemetery this morning, but Queenie just couldn't bring herself to tag along. Thankfully, Rose opted to go. Every time Queen visits Old Sally's grave, she throws a full-fledged pity party and has a hangover for days afterward. People grieve in different ways. Queenie's method of avoiding the pity party is to stay busy and carry on. Otherwise, she fears she might stop carrying on at all.

Queenie returns her attention to Spud, who chats with one of their regular customers. Everyone loves him—even strangers. By the time they began to date, Queenie had given up on love. Even her fantasies of Denzel Washington had fizzled. Romantic love, she had decided, just wasn't in the cards for her. Until, well, it was.

Never say never, Queenie tells herself.

Meanwhile, two weekends ago, she and Spud celebrated their second wedding anniversary and drove up to Charleston for two nights at the Omni Hotel. Unfortunately, Spud's allergies were acting up, and most of the time he was miserable or pretending not to be. Their plans for being amorous didn't work out that weekend, either.

After all those years of being single, Queenie still pinches herself when she remembers that she is married and to an accidental millionaire at that. Queenie looks at the simple gold band that matches Spud's, trying not to think of the article she recently read in *Cosmopolitan* about the steps to take to keep your husband happy. An article that convinced Queenie she was failing at many of them.

Two middle-school girls are next in line, one black and one white. They order breakfast croissants with ham, egg, and cheese, and two hot chocolates. They remind Queenie of Violet and Rose when they were girls. In the 1960s, a mixed-race friendship was unusual. Forty years later, could things finally be changing? She is not in the mood to get her hopes up.

Spud makes the hot chocolates, and Queenie puts together the breakfast croissants and then carries everything out on a tray with two napkins and two forks. Of the friends, one is more boisterous than the other. Queenie is reminded of the Sea Gypsies, the club she, Rose and Violet created as girls. Deemed their Queen, she kept the nickname of Queenie because her given name, Ivy, never seemed to fit her. Of the three of them, Queenie was, of course, the boisterous one.

Her mind wanders to wanting to teach Sally Rose about the Sea Gypsies someday and to extend membership to another generation. Katie and Angie, as Sally Rose's parents, would surely encourage it. To Queenie's great pleasure, she and Sally Rose are close, spiritually and physically. At two years of age, Sally Rose follows Queenie everywhere. Even up the stairs, if one of her moms doesn't stop her. Sally Rose takes one careful step at a time and then scoots back down the steps on her bottom. Sometimes Queenie will do the same, even though she is a bit hefty to scoot these days. But in some ways, being around a two-year-old has made her feel young again.

"I hope Violet's okay," Spud says, looking at his watch.

In the last year, they have voiced their concerns for Violet, who seems preoccupied and unhappy.

Queenie sometimes wonders if Violet has second thoughts about opening a tea shop. The baking alone is a massive undertaking, as is keeping up with supplies. Not to mention having to have someone here every day the shop is open. Yet Queenie has never heard Violet complain.

The bells jingle on the door, and Queenie glances up as she always does.

"Uh-oh," Queenie says, causing Spud to ask her what is wrong.

"You don't want to know," Queenie says, straightening the countertop as if a team of health inspectors has entered the premises.

"Tell me, gingersnap." Spud's endearments always make her hungry.

She gently elbows him out of the way and whispers, "Later," as two of Iris Temple's wealthy, silver-headed friends approach.

They must be slumming it today, seeing how the other ninety-nine percent of us live. Queenie dons a fake smile.

Two white women, richly dressed, have expensive handbags slung over their shoulders. One is tall, the other much shorter. They reek of entitlement and costly perfume. Queenie's nose twitches as she remembers her former training.

"Well, if it isn't Queenie Temple," the shorter woman says.

Wealthy people in Savannah know Queenie from her

days as Iris Temple's assistant. More than once, these two wore fragrances that Queenie had to ask them to wash off in the restroom because of Iris's sensitivity to smells. A request that did not make Queenie popular with either of them.

"I thought you moved to Dolphin Island," the taller woman says.

"Yes, I did," Queenie says, not offering any other details. Due to the resilience of the Savannah grapevine, they undoubtedly know the entire story of the departure from Savannah. They just aren't letting on.

"Poor Iris," the shorter one says, looking at Queenie as though she is part of a fallen empire.

Restless from the effect of being looked up to physically, but down at as a person, Queenie doesn't comment. In the same book that told her to gird her private parts, she is not supposed to throw her pearls before swine. Queenie is pretty sure this applies to pearl-wearing swine, too.

Queenie felt lower than the graveyard dirt Old Sally used to keep in that time-worn flour bin during those days of working for Iris. The last few years, living with Spud and the others has raised her confidence. But seeing Iris's friends again is like a magnet pulling Queenie into the dirty past.

"Fallen on hard times?" the taller one asks, looking around at the tea shop.

"Excuse me?" Queenie straightens her backbone, contemplating giving the woman a quick slap to wake her up to such rudeness.

Spud steps in as if to stop Queenie from getting jail time. "Don't take this personally," he whispers to her. "She's showing her ignorance."

She is showing her ass, is what she's showing, Queenie wants to say.

Queenie takes a deep breath to calm herself as Oprah taught her. "My daughter owns this tea shop," Queenie begins. "And my husband and I help out here occasionally because of our love for her."

They take turns glancing at Spud as though a former butcher from the Piggly Wiggly requires no respect, even if he is currently a real estate tycoon.

"Iris always complained about how arrogant you were." The shorter woman narrows her eyes. "Always getting above your station."

"Arrogant?" Queenie's voice rises. It's a good thing the countertop is there, or she might launch over it and grab that pig by her pearls.

The taller woman nods in agreement about the arrogance and says something about Iris's unending patience with her servants and how badly they treated her in return.

Queenie's face grows hot, and she can feel her blood pressure rising. Is Iris sending Queenie a message from the grave by way of her friends?

Spud steps in front of Queenie. "Sweetheart, let me take it from here."

Hearing Spud's voice breaks the spell, and Queenie takes a step back, feeling prickly heat climb her spine.

Then Spud smiles in the direction of the two women, and with a businesslike tone, he takes their order. Meanwhile, Queenie excuses herself to go into the back room where she can seethe in private.

Every day that Queenie lived in the mansion, Iris artfully put Queenie in her place. Dead for years, Iris is doing it again and using her friends as messengers. Yet

Queenie knows these old biddies were never friends to Iris. Iris had no *real* friends. Only people who thought they could benefit by knowing her.

The two women order their fancy coffees and then wait impatiently at the counter before taking them out to the courtyard.

"They're gone," Spud says, coming to find her in the back room.

"Sweet God in heaven, what did I do to deserve that?"

"Absolutely nothing," Spud says.

Queenie huffs. "I mean, who died and made them judge and jury?"

"Exactly," Spud says with a brief and uncharacteristic frown.

"I sometimes forget what a pain Iris was," Queenie says. "This is a nice reminder of how lucky I am now." She squeezes Spud's arm, suddenly wondering if Iris ever said anything to him about her when they were together. Queenie never caught on that Iris had a boyfriend back then. She was just grateful that she had more time to herself.

As soon as Queenie returns to the front, Violet arrives, hugs Queenie, and asks how things have been.

"We had a rush around ten, but things have calmed down again." Queenie doesn't mention Iris's friends, who just left, even though her face still feels hot from the encounter. Violet seems to have enough to worry about for now.

Spud returns to the counter and hugs Violet, too. She tells them to go home and that Tia and Leisha will be here in fifteen minutes. Violet's girls have been working on weekends to earn spending money for college.

"I don't know how to thank you," Violet says to them, offering a rare smile these days.

"How was the cemetery this morning?" Queenie asks Violet. "Any word from Mama?"

"Nothing." Violet busies herself as if not wanting to think about it.

Like Violet, Queenie assumed that Old Sally would be in touch from the other side. Before her mama passed, they often practiced their Gullah magic, communicating without ever moving their lips. Queenie has missed her mother, too. Fiercely at times. But she could never speak to spirits as Violet does.

"Well, don't give up," Queenie says. "I imagine she had a long line of ancestors to greet her once she arrived. That could take some time."

Violet nods and refills the bin with artificial sweeteners while Queenie and Spud go into the back to gather their things.

"She looks so sad," Queenie says, putting her name tag in her purse.

"Should we try to talk to her again?" Spud asks.

"What an excellent father you would have made, Mr. Grainger."

Spud's cheeks blush pink. "You think so?" A look of longing crosses Spud's face that Queenie has never seen before.

When they return to the front, Violet rearranges the pastries in the case next to the cash register. No customers wait.

"I'm worried about you, sweetheart," Queenie says to her.

"I am, too," Spud says. "You seem out of sorts."

Violet turns to look at them, and her face softens. "Oh my, I must not be hiding it very well. Rose said the same thing this morning."

"You've been like this since Old Sally died, sweetheart." Queenie says this as gently as she knows how. "What can we do to help?"

"Honestly, nothing," Violet says. "Or maybe everything? I wish I knew."

Violet pauses as Queenie wonders if all those tears Violet has been holding back will finally fall.

"You guys go home. I'm fine," she says.

But Queenie doesn't believe Violet is *fine* at all. She knows when her daughter is suffering.

Violet gives them each a hug goodbye and thanks them again for helping before walking them to the door. Once outside, Queenie and Spud exchange a look of helplessness. Old Sally would know what to do. But while her mother is keeping mum in the Gullah cemetery, Iris's friends seem to be announcing her return for the last hurrah.

3

ROSE

Rose sits at the cottage kitchen table with stacks of papers in front of her. One pile is for documents to toss. One is for pieces to save in the family vault, and one is for donations to the Georgia Historical Society in Savannah. Another stack contains photographs of the Temple mansion and the surrounding square taken in the previous century. Pictures before and after Savannah became "the Forest City." A time when city planners planted trees for shade, as well as beauty: live oaks, palmettos, magnolias, dogwoods, crepe myrtles, and gum trees filled the squares.

Rose thinks again of Violet and their trip to the Gullah cemetery. Nothing Rose said or did helped her friend, whose grief at times still seems raw. Thankfully, they will have a joyful reason to gather tonight. It is Sally Rose's second birthday. Two candles will grace the cake Violet has prepared. The grown-ups plan to wear party hats, and balloons will fill the kitchen. Rose imagines Max, her husband, will take pictures while the proud moms, Katie and Angie, will be all smiles.

But before the festivities, Rose goes through papers that she found the last time she went to the bank vault. She has been slowly emptying the documents and brought a box home, along with an old accordion file that was tucked away in the back.

Rose picks up a receipt written in Chinese, with a notation in English that the object purchased is a diary. Diaries have always fascinated Rose, but the Temples have never been diarists. They were more prone to document business transactions and Savannah secrets to help maintain power. Rose imagines her ancestors might consider a diary a dangerous thing in the wrong hands.

Regardless of the unlikelihood that one exists, she searches through the latest pile, questioning where her grandparents might have put a diary purchased in 1935 during one of her grandfather's overseas trips—judging from the date of the receipt.

"You still at it?" Max steps into the kitchen.

"Afraid so." Rose doesn't look up from the papers.

"It smells like an attic in here," he says, pouring himself a glass of cold water from the fridge.

"Old papers," Rose says. "I've got just a few more to go. Now I'm trying to find something that I found a receipt for."

"You ready for the party tonight?" he asks.

"Yeah. It should be fun." Distracted, Rose searches through another stack for the diary.

"Well, I'll leave you to it."

Rose doesn't answer as she grabs an old accordion file tied with a brown string to keep it together. She has found several of these organizers over the years. Rose unties the string and opens it, getting another stale whiff of history.

Shuffling through more papers, she finds a small book with an Asian design on the cover.

Rose smiles. It is almost as if the diary wanted to be found, and that's why it was so easy. She opens to the first page like a curator observing an ancient manuscript. Her eyes widen, and she gasps upon seeing the handwriting in the first entry. She quickly closes the book again. The diary didn't belong to one of her Temple grandparents as she imagined, but her mother. Rose stares at the book like its pages might carry a rare debilitating disease. It's surprising that her mother didn't destroy it. Iris Temple wasn't someone who wanted to be *known*. Her mother was private. Closed. Unavailable. At least Rose thought so.

A bit disoriented, Rose stands. She takes the diary to her studio and places it on the side table next to her reading chair. For now, just knowing it exists has thrown her, and she can't imagine reading it.

LATER THAT EVENING, their makeshift commune gathers at the big house, a remodeled, enlarged version of Old Sally's small beach house with a cottage in the back where Rose and Max reside. Spud and Queenie live upstairs in the big house, as well as Katie, Angie, and Sally Rose. Downstairs is Violet's family. Old Sally's bedroom now sits empty.

Sally Rose, a sweet cherub of a child with blond curly hair, sits in her booster chair at the head of the table. Katie wasn't blonde when she was Sally Rose's age, so Rose imagines the light hair and curls have passed from the mysterious side of Sally Rose's genetics via the unknown sperm donor. At least unknown to Rose. Given the Temple family's attention to bloodlines, it is sometimes hard for Rose not to worry about the unknown ancestors. However, this doesn't in any way take away from Rose's love for her granddaughter.

A rousing round of "Happy Birthday to You" has Sally Rose clapping and staring at the two burning candles on her cake. What must she be thinking? Who are these silly folks? Rose looks around at the family and friends she cherishes more than any of the Temples she grew up with and tries not to think about her mother's diary on the side table in her studio.

While Queenie and Spud help Sally Rose blow out her candles, Violet arrives with plates and forks and cuts everyone a slice, including a small one for the guest of honor. The evening progresses with gifts. As Katie and Angie requested, they were asked only to contribute one present per family unit given Sally Rose already has a room full of toys from this many quasi-grandparents.

Tiring of playing with her new toys, Sally Rose climbs into Rose's lap. The joys of being a grandmother have surpassed Rose's expectations. Max has embraced the grandfather role as quickly as he embraced living on the beach after being a rancher in Wyoming. He seems happier than she has ever seen him. Yet, a part of Rose can't seem to relax. A puzzle deep within her psyche needs to be solved.

Rose suddenly realizes she has thought about her mother more in this one day than in several years.

"Nana, swing?"

"Grandpa Max will do it," Max says, lifting the girl firmly onto his shoulders as Sally Rose giggles with glee at being taller than everyone else in the room. She waves at each person in the kitchen before going out to the swing set built for her in the back by Max and Jack, Violet's husband —last year's birthday present.

It is hard for Rose to imagine what their life was like before Sally Rose. She even has a daybed with a railing in the cottage so her granddaughter can sleep there whenever Katie and Angie need some time to themselves.

Everyone gathers on the back patio as dusk settles in around them. Sally Rose will go to bed soon and playing on the swing set is one of the ways she winds down.

"Big day," Rose says when Violet joins her.

"Sure is," Violet says. "Hard to believe that two years ago we were sheltering in a lighthouse and wondering if we would survive a hurricane."

With Old Sally's death and Sally Rose's birthday, not to mention finding her mother's diary, Rose forgot it was the hurricane's anniversary, too. Hurricane Iris. An uncanny synchronistic tribute to her mother, Iris Temple, who now, it seems, has left behind a surprise diary.

Rose hasn't told anyone yet about her mother's diary and isn't so sure she will. Not even Violet, who seems too distracted these days to solve puzzles. For all she knows, the diary may only contain a recounting of her mother's busy social calendar and be a treatment for insomnia.

"The cake was delicious," Rose says.

Violet thanks her.

From the sadness around Violet's eyes, Rose can tell that the day has worn on her friend, too. A day that seems to have come full circle, from honoring deaths to cele-brating births.

After the party ends and Rose helps clean up, she returns to her studio. The diary waits on the table by her chair. It surprises Rose how hesitant she is to peer inside. Both volumes of the Temple books of secrets were about prominent people in Savannah. Old secrets are useless with age. Her mother's diary feels different and of more consequence.

Rose sits in the chair and studies the red leather-bound book edged in gold with Asian etchings on the front. It is perhaps a half-inch thick. The paper is fine, probably linen.

Am I going to do this? Rose taps the cover as though knocking on a door of the past.

Rose's mother was a stranger in many ways. A woman whose prickliness and constant criticism pushed them apart —if indeed they had ever been together. To protect herself, Rose avoided her to the point of estrangement for twenty-five years. Rose never felt like she belonged in the Temple family, anyway. As a girl, a favorite fantasy was that she was adopted.

With the trepidation of someone preparing to open the Savannah version of Pandora's box to release demons into the world, Rose opens the book. The result is anticlimactic. The ink inside the front cover is faded and reveals her mother's name and the date, 1936. It is hard to imagine her mother young. She would have been a teenager.

April 1936

Daddy brought this diary back from Hong Kong when he was there last spring. He said that I am to fill it with my private thoughts. That way, I can look back at it when I am old and see how young I used to be. But I have never felt young. Not really. I mean, technically, I am young. Fourteen. But inside, I feel much older. I already know what is expected of me for the rest of my life. I am to sit up straight and be a good girl. I am to be seen and not heard and only talk to the right people from the suitable families who make as much money as Daddy does. As a girl, I am not to be ambitious. I am to be loyal. I am never to leave the house unless I am "presentable." I am to know how to throw a good party and get my picture in the Society section of the newspaper. Though I have a lot of money, I am never to talk about it, and I am wary of people who may take advantage of me. I am a Temple, and I am never to forget it.

I hate my life!!

Rose shudders, feeling like she just walked over someone's grave. She snaps the book closed. "Wow." The word penetrates the quiet room. She grew up with the same burden of expectations and never realized until this moment that they were multigenerational, and her mother had carried the same load.

With the act of reading her mother's words, memories rush forward of her mother's constant unhappiness. Her unwillingness, or perhaps lack of ability, to be flexible or spontaneous. The total lack of affection. Rose sifts through these memories like the old papers in the bank vault. It is midnight when she finally looks at the clock again. She hasn't moved in almost two hours.

When Rose gets into bed, Max is already sleeping. She turns off the small lamp on the bedside table and finds herself thinking about the Gullah graveyard where she started the day. Rose misses Old Sally much more than she does her mother. A fact that feels bittersweet. Everyone in their household has been grieving Old Sally's absence. But none of them more than Violet.

She yawns. The past has been everywhere today. Finding her mother's diary was like coming face-to-face with a ghost. A ghost who has stepped back onto the stage of the Temple drama to deliver a soliloquy that promises to change everything.

4

VIOLET

Driving over the bridge into Savannah, Violet lets her thoughts wander. It is Friday again. The weeks gallop by, and her days carry a certain sameness. Uncharacteristically, she takes the weekend off and relies on Ava to handle things at the tea shop. Violet and Ava met when Ava was a home health-care nurse before Miss Temple died.

The house is emptying for the weekend. Tia and Leisha left this morning for Charleston to visit friends. Katie, Angie, and Sally Rose are meeting Angie's mother in Myrtle Beach. And Jack, Max, and Spud drove to Hilton Head for a reunion of elderly musicians from New Orleans that Spud knows from playing saxophone in a jazz quartet for decades. That leaves Queenie, Rose, and Violet at home for what they are calling their Sea Gypsies weekend. Though they are far from being girls, Violet likes the idea of a bit of playfulness. Something she so desperately needs.

Violet will not have anything expected of her until Jack and the girls return on Sunday afternoon. She plans to spend a lot of time on the porch looking out at sea and rethinking her life. A life that from the outside might appear perfect, containing a husband and daughters who adore her, ownership of a shop in downtown Savannah, and good health. Yet a life filled with unsettled grief.

The familiar smell of the salt marsh fills the car as the bridge stretches into the distance toward Savannah. For most of her adult life, Savannah was Violet's home. However, returning to the island where she grew up has been good for her—a nice change.

Violet hums one of the old spirituals that Old Sally taught her and realizes how strange it is to hear her singing voice. When did she stop singing? Was it after Old Sally died? After the hurricane? She used to sing in the car all the time. Now she doesn't even play the radio. Her hum ends with a sigh.

Why can't I shake myself out of this mood?

But is it a mood, or has it become a new way of being? She has so many questions and no one to answer them. Violet depended on Old Sally. Not just for moral support but also to answer her questions.

Violet squeezes the steering wheel as if to get a grip on her life. She is approaching fifty and suddenly feels old. She reminds herself that not even half of her life was over yet when her grandmother was Violet's age. She was over one hundred when she died. Longevity is in Violet's genes. It is too soon for her to feel this tired.

Violet exits the bridge and drives toward the Temple mansion instead of the tea shop in a fit of absentminded-ness. Is she driving back to her old life? Violet turns around and reminds herself that she is no longer a Temple servant who must wear a maid's uniform, arrive promptly, and follow Miss Temple's orders. Violet owns her own business that becomes more successful with each passing year. She was even able to hire a baker for the early shift a few months ago, so Violet doesn't have to do all the baking herself.

However, a question nags at her: If she has realized her dream, why does her life feel empty? She needs something more.

Tell me what to do, Violet says to Old Sally.

A familiar silence follows.

Four customers wait in line when Violet enters the tea shop. Ava has been here since seven when it opened. It usually doesn't get busy until around 9:30. It is 9:15 now and already crazy for a Friday. Violet quickly puts her things in the back and steps behind the counter. Ava offers a grateful look.

Ava is five feet tall, with green eyes that match a green lizard tattoo that climbs up her hand. Her hair is black and often accented with a streak of green or purple. Today's accent is purple. Last year, Ava showed up at the coffee shop asking for an application. She wanted a different career path having burned out of working in the health-care system. Since Violet was looking for someone she could count on, she likes to think that they both got what they wanted.

Violet's mood lightens as she gets busy. She fills orders, makes coffee, and cleans off tables. Busyness is what saves her these days. The rest of the morning passes quickly, and another wave of customers comes in for lunch. Violet and Ava don't have time to talk until Ava gathers her things to leave at three o'clock. They chat about Ava's plans for the weekend and the new man she is dating.

"Are you okay?" Ava asks before leaving to go home.

"Why wouldn't I be?" Violet says. Three people have commented on her mood lately, reminding her again that something needs to change. If only she knew what that "something" was.

A few more customers trickle in and out, and Violet busies herself with setting up for tomorrow. At 4:30, the shop is empty except for one college student who has nursed the same cup of coffee for two hours while studying. She appreciates the company. At the same time, Violet looks forward to having fewer people in the house this weekend. Besides rethinking her life in this quiet she has to herself, she wants to walk up to the lighthouse that saved their lives during the hurricane. Violet forgets sometimes that she is lucky to even be here.

The door opens with a jingle, and Violet's thoughts scatter like birds taking flight. At first, she thinks it is Old Sally, and her heart races toward the possibility. However, the sunlight and shadows are playing tricks on her. It isn't Old Sally at all, but someone needing Violet's help.

5

QUEENIE

As Queenie sits on the top step of the front porch playing with Sally Rose, her mind wanders like a vine searching for sunlight. Just when Queenie thought her rocky days with Iris were over, two of Iris's wealthy white friends came into the tea shop and unearthed everything Queenie had buried. If anyone was arrogant, it was Iris. Her entire countenance was the definition of snobbery mixed in with an extra helping of entitlement. Suddenly, Iris is back in her life again. A ghost from the past rattling chains.

Don't let those old biddies get to you, she tells herself, but they already have. Queenie hasn't slept well for days. In the middle of the night, she woke up remembering how Iris used to say to her that she wasn't a true Temple, only a watered-down version. Or all the constant harping on how Queenie couldn't do even the simplest things right. Iris's daily mission in life for thirty-five years, it seemed, was to tell Queenie how much she didn't measure up.

After watching Oprah every day for years, Queenie

now knows that her self-esteem suffered from the experience. Worn down by her persistence, Queenie began to
believe Iris's criticisms, no matter how unfounded they
were. Iris did the same thing to Rose, and when Rose was
old enough, she left Savannah. Queenie missed her, of
course, but welcomed her back after Iris died.

Queenie has not missed her half sister, Iris, for one
minute. Missing Iris would be like missing a bad case of
hives. However, Queenie does continue to grieve all the
time she lost. Queenie spent thirty-five years of her life
catering to someone impossible to please. It still confounds
her that it rarely, if ever, occurred to Queenie that she
might have had a choice in the matter. Why in the world
didn't she just get another job?

Yet an absence of choices seemed to run in her family.
Queenie and Iris shared the same father, making Queenie
of mixed race. Her mother, Old Sally, only once hinted
about it. Nobody questioned it in those days; it was just
what happened. If your boss came on to you, your main
agenda was to keep your job. Complaining or quitting,
especially as a black woman, meant you might never work
in Savannah again.

"Sally Rose, you need to remember that you always
have a choice," Queenie says as they stack several blocks of
different sizes. "No matter what anyone tells you. You
hear me?"

Sally Rose glances at Queenie before stacking more
wooden blocks on the front porch. When her stacking is
complete, she stops and looks at Queenie full-on.

"Be big bad wolf, Key." Sally Rose has begun to form
complete sentences. A delightful development as far as
Queenie is concerned.

Key is what Sally Rose called Queenie when she first started to talk. Queenie is happy to be "Key" to this sweet girl. More than once, Queenie has wished she played blocks with Violet like this. Denying her baby is one of the few things in Queenie's life that she genuinely regrets— that and spending so much time with Iris.

As ordered, Queenie huffs and puffs and pretends to blow the house down while knocking the blocks over with a sly hand. Sally Rose bursts into giggles, and Queenie can't help but giggle, too, despite her turmoil about Iris.

With a smile, Sally Rose looks up and stares toward the ocean as though she hears something. Queenie looks where she's looking. "What is it, baby?"

Sally Rose closes her eyes and rocks herself as though a song is playing in her head. A piece she enjoys.

"You hear something?" Queenie asks.

Sally Rose nods.

"What do you hear?"

Sally Rose appears enraptured.

"O' Sal talkin'," Sally Rose says, smiling up at Queenie.

"O' Sal? You mean Old Sally?"

Sally Rose nods again, and Queenie gets a case of the shivers right then and there. How could Sally Rose even remember her? She was only a year old when Old Sally died.

"Mama?" Queenie says, looking at the rocking chair where Old Sally always sat. She glares at it as though sneaking a peek into the spirit world, but she sees nothing.

"What's Old Sally saying to you, sweetheart?"

Sally Rose grins like it is a secret, but a two-year-old is

too young for secrets. She goes back to playing with her blocks, but Queenie needs to know more.

"Are you sure it's Old Sally that's talking to you, baby?"

Sally Rose gives Queenie a glance before picking up more blocks. Maybe it's normal for a toddler to hear a deceased person talking to them during playtime. It doesn't seem to have hurt her in the least. Besides, Queenie likes the thought of her mama still being around.

While Sally Rose continues to play, Queenie looks past the dunes to the ocean and watches the waves break toward the shore. A young couple walks through the dunes. She notices them because they are dressed too warmly for a sunny day in June. Long sleeves, long pants, as well as hats and sunglasses. The man has a long beard that looks fake, like a prop from a high school drama class. Despite the low tide and the vast beach, they stay close to the beachfront houses. The high sand makes them look like they are walking in slow motion.

"What are they up to?" Queenie says, more to herself than Sally Rose. She squints in their direction.

Sally Rose hands Queenie a block, but Queenie is still distracted by that couple.

Queenie turns and pretends to huff and puff and blow the house down, which again gets more giggles.

If only Queenie could blow away that house of memories that contain Iris, then she might giggle, too.

Meanwhile, the couple stands near where Queenie and Spud got married and appear to stop to have a casual conversation. She will never forget that lovely day Spud emerged from the dunes playing "Here Comes the Bride" on his saxophone.

The couple pretends not to look toward the house, but Queenie can tell they are doing just that.

"Let's go inside, baby," Queenie says to Sally Rose, although she isn't a baby anymore. "Those people hanging out in the dunes are giving me the creeps."

Queenie gathers the blocks and the child and goes into the house where Katie is finishing up the lunch dishes. Sally Rose runs to Katie, who swoops her up and gives her snuggle kisses. The toddler asks for water and drinks from a cup by the sink. When Katie returns Sally Rose to the ground, she runs back to Queenie and hugs her leg as if hugging a palm tree during a strong wind.

"Thanks for playing with her," Katie says. "The front porch is her favorite place to play for some reason."

"The front porch was Mama's favorite place, too," Queenie says.

"They sure had a special connection that first year," Katie says.

Queenie doesn't know how to tell Katie that her daughter and Old Sally may still have that special connection. Queenie still has days where she hopes Old Sally will walk in from the beach, happy to see her. Now she wonders if her mama ever left. But that doesn't make sense. Wouldn't Violet be the first to know?

"You seem a million miles away," Katie says, wiping her hands on a dishtowel.

"Do I?" Queenie looks at Sally Rose, curious about what her mama and a two-year-old may talk about.

Katie got close to Old Sally that last year, too, but Queenie isn't sure she should mention that Sally Rose may be getting visitations. Katie can be a bit of a worrier. Perhaps she shouldn't mention the couple in the dunes, either. It is probably Queenie's imagination, anyway, or a result of watching too many detective shows on television.

Katie turns her attention to Sally Rose.

"You ready for an afternoon nap, sweetie?" she asks Sally Rose.

With the word *nap*, Sally Rose yawns. The two go upstairs, but not before Sally Rose says to Queenie, "Night-night, Key."

"Night, angel," Queenie says.

After they go upstairs, Queenie returns to the porch to see if the couple is still there, but they're gone.

I'm sure it's nothing, Queenie tells herself.

Then she turns and looks at her mama's rocker. Could Sally Rose hear Old Sally's voice? Queenie doesn't have the heart to tell Violet about this possibility in fear of adding insult to injury, as the saying goes.

"You're looking out for us, right?" she asks Old Sally.

She waits for a response, but all she hears is the crashing of the waves.

6

ROSE

Rose pulls up a stool and sits across from the painting she started working on after going to the Gullah cemetery with Violet. It is of the live oak with the bench underneath and the ocean in the background. Rose went back the next day to take photographs and started the painting. She looks at one of the pictures now and compares it to the image on the canvas.

Her mother's diary sits on the side table where she left it last night after reading the first entry. Already, she is seeing a part of her mother that she never knew. The diary pulls at her from across the room. She tells herself to save it for later. She has things to do this morning. If she picks up the book, she will lose the whole day.

"Focus," Rose tells herself as she looks back at the canvas.

After two decades of painting the arid landscapes of the West, upon returning to the southeast, her paintings have bloomed with trees and lush shades of green. What called to her most were the giant live oaks, with their wide branches and roots crawling along the ground. During Hurricane Iris many live oaks on the island were lost, and it feels healing to paint them. The old trees also remind her of Old Sally.

The first one she painted was the live oak that still stands in the Temple garden. A tree which, thankfully, the fire spared. Rose went back to visit several times with her easel and acrylic paints. It was odd to work in the garden of her childhood and sit where the mansion used to be. The painting sold quickly at the Savannah gallery that represents her work.

This latest painting will go up in Violet's Tea Shop, where Violet often graces a wall with Rose's work. But first, she must finish. She steps back to study it and then adds another layer of color.

The phone rings. Rose groans. How does the universe know when she doesn't want to be interrupted? She lets the answering machine pick up. She turned it up earlier to hear it from the studio. It is Kitty Tate from the Junior League, inviting Rose to attend their next meeting. After returning to the Savannah area, Rose has received many invitations to join boards and head fundraisers. Red Mason at the bank is the latest to pursue her for a board position. But the thought of following in her mother's footsteps makes Rose want to pour herself a glass of merlot. As anyone in recovery knows, this is a clear indicator that she shouldn't go.

Max stands at the door, having heard the phone message. "They're pretty relentless."

Rose agrees, not looking up from the painting.

Even though her mother's reign has ended, it has not lessened expectations that Rose might take her place. Rose is a Temple. In Savannah, being a Temple is like being a Vanderbilt in the northeast.

"I would never have the patience for that stuff," Max says. "But if it's ever something you want to explore, I'll support you."

"No thanks," Rose says, adding gray to the Spanish moss.

Lucy wanders over from her dog bed. Of their two border collies, Lucy is the one who is most connected to Rose. She always shows up when Rose is emotional. Sometimes Lucy arrives before Rose even realizes she needs her.

Rose never felt like she belonged in the Temple family. No matter how hard her mother tried to turn Rose into a miniature version of herself, she failed. Rose was not suited in temperament nor personality. Whether Rose failed on purpose or by accident, it was a clear indication that reigning over Savannah as heir apparent was not an option. She wasn't that much like her father, either. A sense of belonging was never there.

Max stops by her studio again, announcing that he is ready to leave for his weekend away. He carries a small duffel.

"Only a man could fit everything he needs for a weekend in a duffel," Rose says.

Max smiles. He is becoming better-looking with age, as men often do. His dark hair now has streaks of gray. "You know where to reach me?"

Rose nods.

They hug. Rose has been looking forward to having the cottage to herself all week. He is probably looking forward to having some space, too.

"You girls got plans for the evening?"

"Dinner in Savannah."

"Don't get in too much trouble." Max winks before leaving the cottage.

Like a cat getting the lay of the land, Rose walks into every room, experiencing the empty cottage. She puts a few clothes away that Max has left out in the bedroom, knowing that everything will stay the way she leaves it, at least until Sunday evening.

When she returns to her studio again, she glances at the diary. This time, she picks it up, takes it into the kitchen, and makes herself a cup of tea. Later this evening, Rose will meet Violet and Queenie on River Street in Savannah. Violet will come from the tea shop and Queenie from the beauty parlor. But Rose has a few hours before she must leave. She sits at the kitchen table, feeling cautious about what she might find inside the book. Rose slowly opens it, and her mother's voice returns.

August 1936

I hate this old house! It is a dungeon. I escape to my room when I can, but even that is oppressive. My bedroom is next door to Grandmother, who tattles on me like a little sister. She tells Mommy if I listen to the radio or talk on the phone more than she thinks I should. Sometimes she just makes things up!

Tonight, I have to attend a fundraiser for the man Daddy thinks should become the next attorney general of Georgia. Those events are always incredibly dull. Mommy is always watching me and telling me with her stern looks to sit up straight. I hate wearing those starchy dresses and matching ribbons in my hair. Why must Mommy and Daddy always parade me around like

I am Great-granddaddy's prize pig? Afterward, I will hear everything that I did wrong. I know it isn't ladylike to scream, but sometimes I would like to!!

As before, it feels like her mother is in the room speaking to her and confessing things that Rose never knew. No wonder she spent so much time in the sunroom. It was the least dungeon-like room in the house.

Rose stands, feeling the need to move, to take a walk on the beach to process what she has just read despite the heat of the afternoon. That her mother never liked the mansion is a revelation. Rose hated it, too. Given the different ghosts that lived there, creepiness was part of the decor. But if Rose ever voiced a complaint, her mother would tell Rose how ungrateful she was. Or "spoiled." A word Rose hates to this day.

On multiple occasions, her mother lectured Rose on the historical importance of the mansion. She often made Rose stand in the hallway and look up at the encased torch that General Sherman tossed to the ground in the yard because he didn't have the heart, so the story goes, to burn the mansion down. It only took her brother one hundred and fifty years to finish the job. Although, given her mother's hatred of the place, Rose is surprised she didn't burn it down herself. In terms of motive, Rose imagines that her brother would have rather seen the house turned to ash than pass to Violet, as her mother's will stated. But perhaps it was an accident. Unfortunately, no one will ever know.

Walking briskly, Rose breathes in the salty air. She has already worked up a sweat and looks forward to a shower later. Because of the diary, the past walks with her. She wonders if her mother's hatred of the mansion is why she traveled a lot when Rose was a child. Rose didn't mind her being away. It left her more time to spend with Old Sally. Sometimes Rose would even get to stay at Old Sally's house on the beach. These were the times she loved best of all. Rose imagines her mother wanted to be anywhere other than the mansion, and all that time, Rose thought it was because her mother wanted to get away from Rose.

At the lighthouse, Rose stops to pay respect to their sanctuary from the storm. The hurricane was the most dramatic event of her life. But finding her mother's diary feels dramatic, too. All the secrets of her mother's life have suddenly washed ashore. Secrets assumed to have gone with her to the grave.

After reading only two entries, Rose already has insight into what may have made her mother who she was. Her mother lived in an old mansion she loathed her entire life. It must have felt like a prison for her—a golden cage. And her diary documented her time there. What else might the book reveal?

Rose turns to go back to the house. Dark clouds gather to the south that she didn't notice before. She quickens her step to avoid the coming storm.

7

VIOLET

Marylou enters the tea shop. She has long been Violet's favorite customer, and now she is a friend. Marylou was the first customer who showed up from the prosperous old Savannah neighborhood nearby. Her endorsement went a long way toward Violet and her shop's acceptance in this predominantly white part of the old city. Violet feels a debt of gratitude in that regard. Today, it seems, it is Marylou who needs help.

When she greets Violet, Marylou offers a faint smile instead of her usual vibrancy. Although in her nineties, Marylou could easily pass for seventy. *Good genes*, she said years ago when Violet commented on her youthfulness.

As always, she has draped her perfectly postured dancer's body with a beautiful scarf around her shoulders. A celebration of greens and purples. Never without her silver cane, she approaches at a slower pace than usual.

"Are you okay?" Violet asks, genuine in her care for this woman.

"Not really, dear. Do you have a few minutes to talk?"

"Of course," Violet answers.

Marylou peruses the pastry case, points at a cookie, and then orders coffee. She usually comes to the shop in the morning and has tea.

The only customer in the shop is an older gentleman reading the *Wall Street Journal*, so Violet joins Marylou at her favorite table in front of the window. Marylou is regal in the way of Violet's grandmother. Like her grandmother, Violet has always known that she could count on Marylou if she ever needed her, and she wants to be the same kind of friend. She waits for Marylou to begin talking. Instead of words, Marylou sighs.

Violet touches her hand. "What is it?" Violet asks softly.

"My son is here, and I just needed to get out of the house for a bit."

Over the years, they have shared bits and pieces of their lives with each other. For instance, Violet knows that her son, Ralph, is in his seventies and is an only child. Before retiring, he was a law professor for many years. He never married, and Marylou has no grandchildren.

"He wants me to move into his house in Chicago." Marylou grimaces as though his house is in Outer Mongolia instead of the Windy City.

"Why?" Violet asks.

"He says I'm too old to take care of myself."

"You seem to take care of yourself quite fine to me," Violet says.

"I don't think I do such a bad job of it, either. I've kept myself alive this long, for heaven's sake."

"Exactly," Violet says.

Yet, at this moment, Marylou looks older than she

usually does, as though her son's beliefs have cost her some of her youthfulness.

"I mean, he makes a good argument," Marylou begins again. "After all, he is a law professor." She rolls her eyes and reminds Violet of her girls, who are experts at the gesture. "He says if I lived in Chicago, he could keep a better eye on me," she begins again. "He says I could have the entire downstairs of his house, and he would live upstairs. He even has plans for putting in a second kitchen so that I can keep my independence. But I think it's so I'll be out of his hair," she whispers.

Marylou sighs again.

"You don't seem happy with the possibility," Violet says, stating the obvious.

Tears gather in Marylou's eyes. "I've lived in Savannah my entire life, Violet, except for a couple of decades while I was dancing and also had a place in Manhattan. You know how much I love my house."

"I know you do," Violet says, giving her friend's hand a brief squeeze.

"Every day, I work in my flower garden. All my friends are here. I have the dearest friends." Marylou looks at Violet as though she considers Violet one of those friends.

Violet must admit, the thought of not having Marylou come in every morning feels like a loss more significant than she wants to deal with right now.

"I'm so torn," Marylou says. "I wish I had a crystal ball that would give me some direction."

"Would you like me to read your tea leaves?" Violet's spontaneous suggestion causes her to wish she could take it back. Old Sally gave her instructions, and Violet watched her give readings when Violet was a girl, but she hasn't done it much.

Her mind screams, *What are you thinking?* Marylou pauses as though receptive to the idea. "You can do that?" she asks.

"I think so," Violet says, sounding as hesitant as she feels. "My grandmother used to read tea leaves."

"Old Sally?"

Violet nods. Marylou sent flowers and a thoughtful card to the tea shop after Old Sally died.

"I regret that I never met your grandmother," Marylou says. "She sounds like such a wonderful woman."

"She was," Violet says, thinking how poignant a journey it is to move from *is* to *was*, present to past tense.

Marylou taps her cane on the floor as if making a decision. "I would be honored to have you read my tea leaves, Violet."

Violet offers a brief smile, her trepidation growing.

"Give me a couple of days to study up?"

"Of course," Marylou says. "Take longer if you need to. Ralph says I have until Christmas to make my decision, so that gives us a few months."

"Well, I don't need that long, but I would like to practice a little."

Marylou smiles for the first time since she entered the tea shop. Violet likes the thought of being helpful. And she doesn't want to let anyone down. Marylou leans in and places her hand on Violet's as though about to share a secret.

"You know, I think you should consider offering this service to others, too, Violet. It would fit right in with your tea shop."

Violet's eyes widen.

"What is it, dear?" Marylou asks as though picking up on her hesitation.

Violet debates how much to say, but Marylou is someone she can trust. "I'm concerned about how the neighborhood might react if they hear that I'm giving tea readings."

"You mean the rich white folks like me?" Marylou smiles.

"Well, I did learn how to read tea leaves from my Gullah grandmother," Violet says. "A woman who worked for the Temples. As did I. And if you hadn't stepped into the tea shop and encouraged people to come, I might already be closed down."

"Your success here is your own," Marylou says. "Besides, it's about time Savannah recognized the power of the Gullah ways. Don't you think?"

"I don't think it's up to me to decide," Violet says, though she appreciates Marylou's open-mindedness.

"I tell you what. If anyone has a problem with you reading a few tea leaves, I'll set them straight, okay? And you can help me stand up to Ralph."

They shake hands as though striking a deal.

After Marylou leaves, Violet imagines what it might look like to offer a few tea readings here at the shop. Whenever she washes the teacups, she already does impromptu readings based on what Old Sally told her about the symbols in the Gullah secrets book. The tea leaves reveal her customers' journeys, a new romance, or a recent illness. She never realized that this knowledge might help people move through something or help them make decisions about their futures.

Her mind starts racing ahead as customers trickle in and out. If she starts reading tea leaves, Ava will need to be available so that Violet can do the readings uninterrupted. On the days with good weather, she could read them in the courtyard. It wouldn't take long, perhaps twenty minutes, or the length of time it takes someone to drink a cup of tea, followed by Violet's input based on the leaves left in their cup.

In the meantime, her doubts rush in, and Violet convinces herself that it will never work. She doesn't want to be responsible for people making significant life decisions based on what Violet sees at the bottom of their teacups.

Yet despite her reservations, something prevents Violet from totally giving up on the idea of reading tea leaves. In this instance, Marylou has genuinely asked for Violet's help, and Violet doesn't see what harm it could do. Old Sally never hesitated to share her Gullah gifts with others. Not only with her family, but people on the island, too. Not to mention people in different parts of the country who came to her for her potions, root doctoring, and readings. As a child, Violet sometimes greeted friends and strangers alike at the door, invited them in, and then put on the teakettle.

For the first time in ages, Violet allows herself to feel hopeful. Old Sally used to tell her that when the ancestors have a message to send, they often pass it through other people. Perhaps Marylou is her messenger. If so, Violet has received the message. But can she act on what is being asked of her?

8

QUEENIE

"Iris left a diary?" Queenie's temper flares. The toaster dings while Queenie and Spud stand in the kitchen. Queenie butters her toast with a vengeance reserved for few bread products.

"I didn't mean to upset you right before I leave," Spud says.

"I'm not upset!" Queenie's voice rises as she sees the irony in her statement.

Spud's sharing slipped out innocently. While pouring Queenie's orange juice, Spud mentioned how distracted Rose has been after finding her mother's diary. Something Max told Spud while they were putting his suitcase in the back of Max's truck. But it was knowledge she could have spent the rest of her life not knowing.

"I'm not sure why you're getting so worked up about this, honeydew."

"Are you kidding? There's no telling what Iris wrote in that diary," Queenie says. "And any time a Temple writes a book, heads end up rolling."

Spud gives her a look that reminds Queenie how much he adores her—something she still has trouble believing. He apologizes. A car door slams.

"The others are waiting for me. Are you going to be okay, buttercup?"

You and those confounded names! she wants to say, but instead she gives him a quick kiss. "Stay safe, Mr. Grainger."

Queenie follows him out and waves as they drive off. Rose does the same from the cottage. They offer a silly wave to each other, too, and then laugh. However, there are serious things afoot. Queenie is not pleased that Iris had a diary, but she will shower and dress before talking to Rose.

By the time Queenie arrives at the cottage, her molehill of irritation has become a mountain. She isn't sure why she is so disturbed, except she hates it when Iris gets the last word.

She knocks, and Rose invites her in. With one look at Queenie, Rose asks her what's wrong.

"Why didn't you tell me Iris had a diary?"

"I only just found it," Rose says. "And I didn't want to upset you."

"Why does everyone think I'm upset?" Queenie asks, her voice rising again. But *upset* is what she is.

"Just when I think I've finally exorcised that woman from my life, here she is again and in print!" Queenie tacks on a whispered cuss word.

"I was shocked, too," Rose says. "It was the last thing I expected to find in that mess of old papers. I'm surprised she didn't destroy it."

"Is it only one?" Queenie asks.

"As far as I know."

Queenie takes a deep breath. "Well, what's in it?"

"Have a seat. I'll get it."

Rose leaves the room, and Queenie positions herself at the kitchen table in front of the window that faces what they all call the "big house." It is indeed big, considering how small Old Sally's house used to be. These days, the house Queenie grew up in only lives in her memories. It was half the size of Max and Rose's cottage.

When Rose returns, she is holding a small book that couldn't look more harmless. But if it belonged to Iris, there is reason to be cautious.

"I've only read the first couple of entries," Rose says, handing the book to Queenie.

Her shoulders stiffen just holding it, and she opens it as though it might contain a nest of water moccasins.

"Heavens to Betsy, I can't believe how nervous I am." Queenie wonders who in the world is *Betsy* and why this phrase even came to mind. Word origins have always fascinated her, as well as turns of phrase. She decides that Betsy is probably some white woman in Oshkosh hanging out her laundry, and here Queenie is conjuring her up worrying over another white woman.

Meanwhile, Queenie would recognize Iris's handwriting anywhere. Seeing it again transports her back to the Temple mansion in Savannah, where Queenie sat in the sunroom next to Iris, keeping her eyes lowered so as not to challenge her. One morning Iris was writing in a fancy book of some kind. Queenie now wonders if it was the diary.

Iris was still a young woman, all of forty, when Queenie started working there, and Queenie was twenty. Violet was only weeks old and staying at the beach with one of Old Sally's friends. On this particular morning, Mr. Oscar had threatened Queenie that she would lose her job if she ever divulged that he was Violet's father. With no other job possibilities, Queenie had stayed quiet. But when Iris had looked at her that morning, Queenie was convinced she had known, anyway.

"Should I read it?' Queenie asks Rose, looking at the book.

"It's up to you."

"Maybe I'll read just a page or two as you did." Queenie takes her red-framed reading glasses from her shirt pocket and focuses on the page. She reads the rant of what Queenie deems to be a spoiled rich girl who hates her life. After she finishes, she looks up at Rose.

"That's Iris at fourteen?" Queenie says.

Rose nods.

"Man, that girl is intense."

Rose laughs. "Well, at least she had a reason for being who she turned out to be."

"She had a reason and then some," Queenie says. "But it's still a little hard to feel sorry for a whiny white girl."

Queenie offers a quick apology, but Rose tells her there's no need.

"Did you know she was miserable when you were growing up?" Queenie asks.

"At some point, I figured out that she was impossible to please. I don't think I realized how bitter she was at that point, though."

"She was, indeed." Queenie thinks about Iris living her entire life in a house she hated. Both of them were prisoners in that old mansion.

"Are you okay?" Rose asks. "You look pale."

Queenie chuckles. "Not something I hear very often."

"You know what I mean," Rose says. "You look like you've seen a ghost."

"I was thinking about Iris and me being prisoners in that old house, so I guess you're right."

Rose puts a kettle on the stove to make tea and puts a plate of gingersnaps on the table.

"I'm sorry I didn't tell you about the diary sooner," Rose says. "To be honest, it has thrown me for a loop."

"I just hate being the last to know," Queenie says.

"You weren't the last, by any stretch," Rose says. "After Max, you're the first. How did you find out, anyway?"

"Max told Spud as they were loading up."

"Mystery solved," Rose says.

"Your mother was one tough cookie," Queenie says, taking a bite out of a gingersnap.

Rose agrees.

"I always wondered how she could have so much and be so mean. It never occurred to me that she might hate that drafty old mansion as much as I did." Queenie glances up at the light fixture, half expecting Iris to chime in. After she died, Iris sent electrical power surges through the entire mansion, causing lights to flicker and bulbs to pop.

"You know, I have moments where I'm glad that old mansion burned down," Rose says. "I know it was beautiful and historical, but that house had some bad energy."

"I still have dreams about it," Queenie says. "Especially the night of the fire."

"I do, too," Rose says.

Their eyes meet. Why have they not talked about this until now? In the distance, Angie follows Sally Rose to the swing set. Angie carries a cup of coffee. She is probably about to put Sally Rose down for a nap and wants to tire her out a little more. They watch for another minute in silence. Should she mention to Rose that Sally Rose heard Old Sally's voice earlier? But her mind shifts to another concern.

"Have you noticed a young couple hanging around the house down in the dunes?" she asks Rose.

Rose says she hasn't and asks why.

"It just felt weird how they were looking at the place," Queenie says.

"People often stop and look at the houses on their way to the beach," Rose says.

"I know," Queenie says. "I'm sure it's nothing, but I can't quite seem to let go of the nagging feeling that some-thing is off."

"You should probably trust that," Rose says.

"And do what?" Queenie asks. "Should I place them under citizen's arrest for looking weird or something?" Rose laughs again, and Queenie wonders why she often makes jokes about things that scare her instead of admit-ting she's scared.

Queenie looks at the diary again, taking note of the Asian design on the cover with flowers that look like azaleas, but she doesn't have any desire to read more. At least not now.

"Do you want to see the painting I'm working on for the tea shop?" Rose asks as though ready to change the subject, too. "It's almost finished."

"Absolutely," Queenie says, following Rose to her studio.

On the easel is a large painting of the tree in the

Gullah cemetery. Queenie recognizes it immediately and tells Rose how beautiful it is. Queenie doesn't have any talents such as painting or singing, and sometimes she wishes that she did. Queenie realizes that she hasn't heard Violet sing for an entire year. Before Old Sally died, Violet sang in the kitchen or while walking through the house. Joyful songs from the radio. Queenie misses them.

"Has Violet seen it yet?" Queenie imagines she'll love it.

"Not yet. I want it to be a surprise."

The last time Queenie went to the Gullah cemetery, she sat on that bench under that old tree and talked to her mama about how sad Violet was. Queenie even asked her to send Violet a message to let her know that she was still here. That was months ago, and as far as she knows, Violet has not received any messages. Although it seems Sally Rose might have.

"I worry about that bucket of tears Violet's been holding on to," Queenie says to Rose.

"Me, too," Rose says.

"I wish I knew what to do," Queenie says. "It's obvious she's suffering from the loss."

"I don't think Vi knows what to do, either," Rose says.

Queenie glances at the studio clock and tells Rose that she needs to get going to make her hair appointment on time. They confirm their plans of when and where to meet later in Savannah.

"Let me know if Iris writes anything about Spud in that diary of hers," Queenie says before leaving.

"Are you sure?" Rose asks.

Queenie isn't sure at all, and she wishes she had the fortitude to resist the past, but it seems she doesn't. Sometimes she's like a moth flying into a bonfire on the beach. Iris was her nemesis for over thirty-five years, and once upon a time, Iris intimately knew Queenie's one and only husband.

Intimately, she repeats to herself.

Thankfully, their relationship only lasted for a short time, a fact Queenie tells herself frequently. It also helps that Queenie has already been with Spud longer than Iris and Spud were together.

"When do you think you'll finish the diary?" Queenie asks as they stand in the kitchen again.

"I'm not sure. Why?"

"Maybe I'll read it when you're finished."

"Queenie, why put yourself through that?" Rose asks, as though knowing Queenie's moth-bonfire nature.

"Maybe reading it will be a catharsis and finally rid me of her," Queenie says, but even she is skeptical that this is true. Reading Iris's diary will probably bring Iris back to life more than ever.

9

ROSE

R ose has several errands to run before meeting Queenie and Violet at the restaurant. First, she must drop off a small painting to Kitty Tate's home, the current president of the Savannah Junior League. It is a donation for their next auction. Rose and Kitty were in the same grade at school when they were growing up. Their mothers both attended Daughters of the Confederacy meetings, and their parents mingled socially, though they were not close friends. Kitty was quite the snob back in those days, and Rose hopes that she has outgrown it, for Kitty's sake.

The painting Rose carries is a still life of one of the African violets in Violet's tea shop window. The framed eight-by-ten canvas features purple blooms among green leaves and light streaming through the window. Rose imagines it will raise money for the charity, and perhaps now they will leave her in peace.

After dropping off the painting, Rose will spend an hour sorting through the final old papers in the bank vault.

Rose is almost finished with a task that has taken up hours and hours of her life.

Now that she lives on Dolphin Island, Rose doesn't drive through downtown Savannah with any regularity these days. However, she is struck by how much the city is impervious to change. The squares are much the same as when she was a girl. They are beautiful in design—almost poetic—with enchanting live oaks and neatly groomed bushes. Massive homes hide behind brick or stone walls covered in English ivy or behind elaborate black iron fences with majestic gates offering glimpses of luxury cars.

Rose parallel parks on the street near Kitty Tate's house—streets that seem narrow after living out West—but Rose was always good about fitting her car into tight spots. This square is different from the one Rose grew up in but still familiar from when she was allowed to ride her bike in the city. High school friends lived in this square, and she visited on occasion, attending wild parties when wealthy parents were away.

The day is exceedingly warm and humid, though the scorching heat never bothered Rose when she was a girl. Sunshine twinkles through the mature trees and dots the sidewalk in front of her. All those years she lived in Wyoming, Rose missed shade, and here it is in abundance.

As a member of the Temple family, growing up in Savannah was about her family's status. This hierarchy was invisible yet seen by everyone. Her mother's diary is evidence of the system in place where grooming to meet expectations began at a young age. But Iris Temple was no martyr to her stature having ultimately embraced all expectations, and never let anyone forget her power.

Rose walks at a slower pace, taking in the scene around

her. A courtyard to her left has an ivy-covered brick wall with a black wrought-iron gate. An uneven brick sidewalk leads to a garden covered in thick moss. Camellias thrive in happy bunches along the brick walls. A fountain bubbles center stage. To anyone passing by, it might seem magical.

Yet Savannah never felt magical while growing up here. Perhaps all hometowns are taken for granted. But after living elsewhere for twenty-five years, she is starting to see it anew. Downtown Savannah is like a beautiful woman perfectly adorned. It is easy to fall in love with such beauty, even knowing that perfection comes at a steep cost.

The Tate house stands on the corner of a square. Rose steps through the redbrick entrance. A silver Lexus sits in the shade in the horseshoe driveway, brick steps lead up to the porch and front entrance.

Rose walks to the door. White rocking chairs line the porch alongside lush ferns in white wicker containers. It looks like something out of a garden magazine, the ultimate in elegance.

Suddenly Rose is a girl again, attending a birthday party at age nine, carrying a gift her mother bought to impress Kitty's parents. A party that seemed staged for when the photographer from the newspaper arrived. Rose didn't have fun. How could she? They were children wearing Easter dresses and pretending to be grown-ups.

Rose rings the bell, and a middle-aged black woman answers the door. Rose thinks of Violet and Old Sally before her. Rose smiles, wanting to convey that she isn't just any white woman. Rose is different. She lives with people of various shades of color who are like family. But even this seems too little too late, as the saying goes. Rose feels just as complicit as any white person who doesn't recognize the deck is stacked in their favor.

Rose asks for Kitty. The woman's demeanor is courteous, not genuine.

Rose sits on one of the rockers to wait as the past and present wage war inside her. A white woman on a white throne. Did her mother ever have an inkling of guilt over having Old Sally, Queenie, and Violet in her employ? Ancestors from families, generations before, owned by the Temples. Two of them had been bedded and produced offspring by their bosses—a tragic consequence of how things were.

Kitty joins Rose on the porch wearing a sleeveless dress and pearls. Rose telephoned earlier that she would be stopping by. Did she dress like this for Rose, or is this everyday attire?

Kitty swoops in for one of those quick hugs where you kiss the air near the person's cheek, and the courteous housekeeper arrives with iced teas that she places on a wicker table with a sparkling glass top. She puts a sugar bowl on the table along with a bowl of sliced lemon. Now that drinks are served, Rose regrets that she can't rush off.

They sit in the rockers and proceed to "catch up." White overhead fans move the hot air around as Kitty tells Rose how sorry she was when Rose's mother died. Yet Rose distinctly remembers how cheerful Kitty looked at the funeral reception at the house, along with her investment banker husband. It was as though with Rose's mother's death, their family's stock had risen, and they were now in possession of the burned broom of the Wicked Witch of the West. The mansion burning must have brought on initial shock followed by further elation.

When Rose hands her the painting, Kitty gives it a glance before handing it to the housekeeper, who has arrived with teaspoons for the iced tea, apologizing for the oversight.

Unlike Rose, Kitty has never left Savannah. She stepped in to fill the spot in the community that Kitty's mother once held. The elderly widow now lives in an expensive retirement community in Charleston and is supposedly having the "time of her life."

Kitty makes the usual noises about how Rose should come to the Daughters of the Confederacy meetings. Is the housekeeper listening and rolling her eyes at the cluelessness of her employer? What must it have been like for Queenie to go to those meetings with Rose's mother? She will have to ask her sometime.

Rose takes a sip of tea while Kitty drones on about the Junior League. She is struck by how complicated it is to make peace with the past. While Rose may not participate in this unconscious loyalty to the way things used to be, her family always has. She finishes her iced tea quickly and tells Kitty that she has a meeting at the bank.

As Rose is leaving, Kitty says, "Let's do lunch."

Rose smiles and nods, thinking this is not an invitation she will pursue. Kitty doesn't thank her for the painting, and Rose is grateful that they were never friends.

Minutes later, Rose arrives at the bank, the taste of sweet tea with lemon still in her mouth. She gives a quick wave to Red, who stands in his glass office on the main floor, his phone to his ear. Rose hurries upstairs to the bank vault. She isn't in the mood for his flirtatiousness today. Their last conversation was a replay of Red's glory days in high school, which wasn't a conversation at all, given he left no room for Rose to speak.

Another bank officer lets her into the vault. It exudes its familiar smell of old papers and Temple history. It feels weirdly comfortable to be here. Rose checks her watch, telling herself that she will devote an hour to going through the documents and organizing them. This task has fallen to Rose as the remaining member of the Temple family.

Ultimately, Rose had hoped this exercise would bring her closer to her family, reveal their characters, and make her feel more like she belonged. But instead, it has made her see how different she is from them. Except for her mother's diary and the secrets they collected on others, the Temples left no clues.

Everything left behind is transactional: money spent, things owned, documents verifying ownership. Rose hardly sees the point of keeping all this paper, except that it is history—Savannah history—and the history of the Temple family. A family who made their way to America to seek their fortune sometime shortly before the Revolutionary War.

Rose stands, suddenly having enough of the past, and slings her purse over her shoulder. She leaves the bank in need of the here-and-now and has one more thing to do before meeting Violet and Queenie for their girls' night out.

After leaving the bank, Rose starts her sweltering car, wishing she had left the windows cracked, though that probably wouldn't help much. At least Dolphin Island has the ocean breeze. She turns the car air conditioner on high while she drives to the Temple garden where the house once stood. It has become a lovely park.

Rose sits on a shady bench near where her bedroom used to be. Something about knowing that her mother always hated the house makes Rose want to pay homage to the site. She reaches in her purse and takes out her mother's diary. She is glad now that she grabbed it before leaving the cottage this afternoon. Rose opens the book, reading the next entry.

December 1936

Secrets! While Daddy was out, I went into his office to read more of the book of secrets he keeps. I don't see the point of it. Who cares if rich people lie, cheat, steal, and sleep with their mistresses and housekeepers? I have seen Daddy going into the kitchen to talk to Sally and locking the door behind him. I don't see him writing that in his scandal-filled book.

People think I'm this naive little rich girl, but I know way more than Mommy does. She turns a blind eye to practically everything Daddy does. I will never be that way. Never.

Rose stares at the page long after she stops reading. Her mother, a rebellious teenager, kept an eye on the adults around her to figure out the games they were playing. Yet everything her mother swore she would never do, she ended up doing. She turned a blind eye to Rose's father and Queenie. She placed the same expectations on Rose.

Past and present merge. It is 2004, but also 1936. Sally is in the Temple kitchen preparing the next meal, not even forty. Iris Temple is a teenager, swearing that she will never be like the people who raised her. History captures her, anyway. History captures Rose for a time, too, but she escaped.

In the garden, the hot breeze shifts and has a hint of coolness to it. Where Rose's family once lived feels oddly peaceful now, as though redemption is suddenly possible, and the sins of her family may be someday forgiven.

10

VIOLET

After speaking to Marylou, Violet takes the afternoon off. Ava is more than capable of handling things without her. Violet will meet Queenie and Rose later on River Street, but first, she will enjoy having the house to herself. The "boys" are on their way to Hilton Head, and Katie, Angie, and Sally Rose are away, too, meeting Angie's mom in Myrtle Beach for the weekend.

Violet isn't entirely without responsibility. She will take care of Katie's white terrier, Harpo, and Angie's cats, Zelda and Gertrude. Also on the agenda for this weekend is studying up on how to do tea readings for Marylou. But first, she will take a walk on the beach with Harpo, not only for exercise but stress relief. Her daily walks are what keeps her sane and functioning these days. That, and sweeping the sand off the wooden porch floors every evening like Old Sally used to do.

Several minutes later, Violet stands in front of the lighthouse while Harpo sniffs the tall grass nearby. A new lock is on the door, as well as a large Keep Out sign. The windows at the top of the lighthouse remained broken until recently. After the hurricane, it took months for the dunes to return, and the look of the coastline changed forever. Months passed before Violet could stand in front of this lighthouse without having flashbacks of the storm. But the flashbacks were nothing compared to the recurring dreams she had for over a year. Recurring dreams where the storm surge chases Violet up and up the metal stairs until she finally forces herself awake. But after Old Sally died, they finally stopped, and dreams of losing her grandmother replaced them.

Violet thanks the lighthouse once again for saving them before she and Harpo turn to go home.

Later, Violet sits on the front porch with a mug of ginger tea, Old Sally's favorite. She releases a sigh, grabbed by the breeze.

"Where are you?" Violet asks Old Sally. She wants to ask her about the tea readings and whether she thinks this is a good idea. Specifically, if this is something she thinks Violet can do effectively.

She has never felt so removed from the spirits of her ancestors. Even the ghosts who used to be part of everyday life while working at the Temple mansion went away with the fire. Her whole life shifted away from the invisible world, which was what had made her life rich.

The wind gusts, bringing to life the rocking chair next to her. Violet wonders briefly if Old Sally has decided to visit. She misses the solidness of her, the form. But the rocker stops when the wind passes.

Violet goes inside and returns with the Gullah Book of Secrets. When Hurricane Iris chased them up those lighthouse stairs, Violet had held the Gullah book close to her heart, a priceless treasure. Now, Violet keeps it in the bottom of a drawer with her sweaters, tucked away like something of seasonal use, if useful at all.

Old Sally told her that suffering means you have loved well and is necessary for being alive. But what if grief moves into your house and refuses to leave? What if grief paralyzes you?

The hardback notebook full of her ancestors' secrets sits unopened on her lap. A book filled with rituals, root doctoring, spells, and stories. In the months before Old Sally died, as she dictated to Violet, Violet's life bloomed with a higher purpose than making muffins and serving teas. She misses that now, almost as much as she misses her grandmother.

What was first an honor, to be the keeper of the Gullah secrets, now feels like an overwhelming task. It would be impossible to live up to this wisdom from her ancestors. What is she supposed to do with it?

With Tia and Leisha showing little interest in the Gullah traditions, Violet wonders if Sally Rose will carry them forward after Violet is gone. Although she isn't of Gullah ancestry, the connection between Old Sally and Sally Rose the first year of her life was extraordinary, and something Violet had never witnessed before. It was as if they had known each other before this lifetime. The others noticed it, too. Old Sally would hold the baby in her arms and talk to her in Gullah, and Sally Rose babbled back as though they were having a conversation.

Violet finishes her tea and stares at the formation of loose tea leaves at the bottom of the cup. She thinks again of Marylou, who needs help discerning what to do regarding her son's insistence that she leave Savannah.

When a friend is in trouble, Violet wants to help. But still, she questions why she offered to read tea leaves.

After opening the Gullah secrets book, Violet recalls the mornings she and her grandmother sat together on the porch and talked tea leaves while Violet wrote everything down. Old Sally predicted the storm that became a hurricane by reading her tea leaves. They showed chaos followed by a long path to recovery. But Old Sally had read them. Not Violet. She wishes now that she had shown more interest.

Looking down at her writing on the opposite page, Violet reads the words she wrote two years before: *When someone you love dies, grief comes like a hurricane and threatens to destroy you. But grief isn't bad. Grief means you've loved someone with your whole heart. Love and heartache go hand in hand. There is no other way.*

Tears come. Violet loved her grandmother with her whole heart. If Old Sally were here, she would capture Violet's tears in one of those tiny brown bottles with a dropper at the end that she always carried in her apron pocket. Tears make spells more potent, she often said.

Violet brushes them away, wary of their potency, understanding now that this is why she has avoided the book. It is full of her grandmother's words and stories. While they feel like the elixir for all that ails Violet, they are also unbearable. Yet, it is the only way she can move on. For the first time since Old Sally's funeral, Violet allows herself to cry. Not only for her loss but for how different her life is now. Void of purpose, like a ship lost at sea.

From a drawer of the wicker table on the porch, Violet pulls out several tissues and blows her nose loudly before tucking the used tissues in her pockets. She then laughs, thankful to be alone.

Violet studies the section on how to read tea leaves. Sometimes Violet forgets how much information is in this book. Old Sally gave her steps to read tea leaves to make it easier for her. She reads over them now.

- Become quiet and call on the ancestors to aid in the reading.
- Steep tea of choice for five minutes.
- Have the person receiving the tea reading drink the tea, leaving a small amount in the bottom of the cup that must not be emptied.
- With your left hand, take the teacup handle and invoke the ancestors.
- Swirl the leftover contents in a counterclockwise motion.
- Invert the teacup on the saucer.
- Leave the cup on the saucer for at least one minute so that all the liquid can drain out.
- Slowly, from the right, turn up the cup.
- Read the tea leaves and follow what your intuition tells you.
- Thank the ancestors for guiding the reading.

The pages following are full of common symbols and what they mean. Violet wonders if she will ever learn all the symbols. She studies them for several minutes before glancing at her watch. She has lost track of time and has less than an hour to get dressed and be in Savannah, so she takes the book and rushes inside.

Within minutes, Violet is out the door again, applying

lipstick and grabbing a light jacket in case the restaurant is cold. She locks the front door and notices two people in the dunes as she takes the walkway to her car. Her left shoulder pings in pain. A ping so quick she wonders if it is in a rush, too. Didn't Queenie mention something about seeing two people in the dunes?

They are so close to the house that Violet wants to shoo them away like the seagulls that sometimes swoop in begging for food. When they see Violet, they turn toward the beach, but something about the woman seems familiar. Her shoulder offers another ping. Violet's shoulder hasn't done this since Old Sally died.

Violet's lateness rushes her along. Her shoulder does this sometimes. It is the family sensitivity, and her body knows something that Violet doesn't know. This current wake-up call seems to be related to the people in the dunes. But she doesn't have time to explore it right now. Violet must get to Savannah.

11

QUEENIE

Queenie waits outside of the pub for Violet and Rose. If they don't go inside soon, they might have trouble finding a table. Sunlight sparkles off the river—a river dyed green every year during Savannah's St. Patrick's Day celebration. A celebration that Oscar, Iris's husband, loved. River Street draws multitudes of tourists, and this evening is no exception.

When Queenie first heard the history of this part of Savannah, she was shocked. In her thirties, at that point, she wondered how she had lived this long having never heard about the weeping time. She doubts few of these visitors know the history, either. Historically, River Street is where slaves came off ships from Africa and were auctioned in the nearby square. The redbrick buildings were where the cotton brokers bargained. After slavery was outlawed, a large boat carrying slaves docked, anyway. It rained for two solid days while they were secretly sold, and it was said that heaven wept. Now it is known as an area to get good seafood.

Rose walks toward her from a side street and waves. Queenie returns the wave. During those years that Rose lived in Cheyenne, they wrote letters every other week. Queenie misses writing letters sometimes. But now, all she has to do to catch up on Rose's news is to walk to the cottage.

Rose apologizes for being late.

"No problem," Queenie says. "Violet isn't here yet, either."

"She isn't?" Rose says. "Violet is never late."

"She's been a little spacey these days," Queenie says.

Queenie and Rose exchange a look that doesn't hide their concern.

"I know we've talked about this a million times," Queenie says, "but I wish I knew something to do to help her."

"Like what?" Rose asks. "You can't make the grief go away, no matter how hard you try."

"What if that isn't it? Tia and Leisha are leaving for college soon."

"Maybe it's a combination of those things," Rose says. "When Katie left for college, I cried every day for a week. It's a big deal not to have kids in the house anymore. I mean, they come home periodically, but it's never the same."

"Unless you move in together later and all live in a big house and a cottage." Queenie laughs.

"Exactly," Rose says.

A group of women gathers nearby. Is it another girls' night out? But Queenie quickly learns it is a book club. Several members are holding books and talking in animated tones about the main characters.

"Should we go inside?" Queenie asks Rose. "It's starting to get crowded."

"Probably," Rose says.

They squeeze into the bar, which is already noisy. Queenie approaches the hostess to ask if they have any seating in the courtyard. She tells Queenie that someone has just canceled their reservation. Queenie motions for Rose, and they follow the hostess into a quiet restaurant area. They settle at a table. Within seconds, a waitress comes to take their drink order.

Queenie requests a pineapple margarita, and Rose gets a ginger ale. She sometimes forgets that Rose doesn't drink. Queenie has never known the drinking side of Rose. It became a problem in Wyoming when she was dealing with being raised a Temple. She wanted to numb herself and told Queenie in a letter once that she could see that she was using wine to dull her pain. With the help of her therapist, Rose stopped cold turkey, as the saying goes, though Queenie has no idea what turkeys have to do with a glass of Chablis.

"How were your errands?" Queenie asks.

"Remember Kitty Tate?"

"Who could forget her?"

"Well, she hasn't changed," Rose says.

"I had a run-in with Iris's old crew recently, too."

"Who?"

"Two of her supposed friends came in the shop while Spud and I were helping out last Sunday. Nothing like having Savannah's elite bring you down a notch."

Rose grimaces. "I'm so sorry."

"I'm just glad I'm not doing that anymore," Queenie says. "I paid a high emotional toll."

"I'm sure you did," Rose says.

"I'm a little worried that Iris has decided to haunt me again. I had a bad dream last night."

"Mother was in your dream?"

Queenie nods. "It was her and those two friends of hers I told you about. In the dream, they had set up a booth in front of the Temple mansion and were telling lies about me for one dollar a pop."

"That sounds more like a nightmare," Rose says.

"Tell me about it," Queenie says.

They look at the menu for several minutes.

"I can't believe she left a diary," Rose says, putting down the list of specials. "It seems unlike her. But I'm not sure I even knew her."

"I don't think I truly knew Iris, either," Queenie says. "I mean, I knew her habits and moods, but as far as what went through her mind, I didn't have any idea. Have you read any more of the diary?"

"A little. It's kind of intense to hear Mother's voice so clearly as she writes. It feels a little bit like being haunted, too, or at least like a visitation."

"I'm not sure I want to read any more of it for that reason," Queenie says. "I mean, I'm curious, but curiosity killed the cat, you know."

"I'm a little afraid of what's in there, too," Rose says. "The diary spans decades. The last page is dated a week before her stroke."

"I always thought Iris was too mean to die," Queenie says, "but then she surprised me and went ahead and did it."

"It surprised me, too," Rose says.

The drinks delivered, Queenie takes the tiny yellow

umbrella from hers and playfully holds it over her head like it's raining.

Queenie always had a knack for making Rose laugh, even when Rose was a girl.

"I like being silly," Queenie says. "I'm lucky that Spud enjoys my silliness, too."

"Have you heard from him?"

"I called him from the beauty shop to make sure they had made it all right, and they had just returned from the grocery store to stock the condo."

They joke about what things besides pizza and beer they might have bought.

"But seriously, if Iris says anything in her diary about Spud, I want to know," Queenie says.

"Spud adores you," Rose says as if to reassure her.

"I know he does," she says. "But Iris adored Spud. That haunts me."

They look toward the door again and hope out loud that Violet is okay.

"So why did you see Kitty Tate?" Queenie asks.

"I dropped off a painting for one of their fundraising auctions."

"Lucky you," Queenie says, unable to hide her sarcasm. She feels a hot flash coming on and holds her frozen drink next to her neck.

"Whenever I brush up against Mother's old cronies, I get a glimpse of what my life might have been like if I hadn't left Savannah," Rose says.

"Talk about a nightmare." Queenie laughs. The drink is making it easier to find the humor in things.

"I never really fit in with the Savannah crowd," Rose says.

"You aren't missing anything," Queenie says. "They wear a lot of fragrances, and it drove Iris crazy. She thought they did it to spite her, and I think there may be some truth to that."

"Like Mother's funeral?"

"Exactly," Queenie says. "I still get a headache just thinking about it." What is also true is that Queenie needs to eat soon. The alcohol is going straight to her head. She wishes now that they had ordered an appetizer.

Queenie pats her broad stomach as it rumbles its hunger. Unlike Oprah, Queenie has never felt the need to lose weight. She likes being full-figured and enjoys food too much to be any other way. Rose looks like a skinny white girl. She's the same size she has been since college. And Violet has always been the beautiful one. So beautiful it is hard to believe they are mother and daughter. Not that Queenie is unattractive. She can tell that much from looking in the mirror. It helps that she is a lighter shade of brown than Old Sally, as is Violet, who is lighter still. As the generations have passed, their skin color has been like adding more and more cream to your coffee. She can thank the Temples for their unwelcome contribution.

Violet enters the courtyard and walks quickly to the table, full of apologies. They each stand to hug Violet, who then joins them at the table.

Queenie motions the waitress over to get Violet's drink order in hopes of bringing them one step closer to ordering their food. Violet asks for white wine, and Rose requests another ginger ale. Queenie decides to add one more umbrella to her collection.

"What were you doing on the front porch that caused you to lose track of time?" Rose asks.

"Studying," Violet says.

"I haven't studied since the '70s," Queenie says, thinking of her school days.

"Marylou needs my help," Violet begins. "Long story short, she wants me to read her tea leaves at the shop."

"I didn't know you read tea leaves," Queenie says.

"Well, I don't. Not much, anyway," Violet says. "But Old Sally gave me instructions on how to in the Gullah secrets book. That's what I was studying."

If reading tea leaves gets Violet out of this funk, Queenie is one hundred percent for it.

"Why do you seem so hesitant?" Rose asks Violet.

"Because I don't know what I'm doing."

"That never stopped anybody from doing anything," Queenie says, taking another sip of her drink.

Rose agrees. "Honestly, Vi, I think it's a great idea."

Violet smiles briefly before lowering her eyes. Queenie wonders if she is already having second thoughts.

"Mama would want you to use what she taught you," Queenie says.

"Would she?" Violet asks.

"Of course she would," Queenie says. Rose agrees.

"Is it hard to read tea leaves?" Queenie asks.

Over the years, her mama studied the bottom of every teacup she got her hands on, but she never shared with Queenie how she did it. She questions now why she wasn't more curious.

"It isn't hard, but you've got to be present and tuned into your intuition," Violet says.

"That should be easy for you," Rose says. "You're that way already."

Violet takes a sip of wine as though pondering the

possibilities. "I'll need to practice," she says. "Grow my confidence, if that's possible." She lowers her eyes again.

"We're happy to help," Queenie says, looking at Rose, who nods in agreement.

"Anything interesting in your mother's diary?" Violet asks as if wanting to change the subject.

"It's weird to read something my mother wrote almost seventy years ago," Rose begins. "I never knew she hated the mansion and couldn't wait to get out of there, and then never did. She was born and died in that house."

Queenie shudders. "I guess we'll never know for sure why your brother, Edward, was there the night of the fire. Maybe he hated that old mansion, too."

Rose nods, looking thoughtful.

"It was beautiful and drafty and haunted," Rose says.

"And trapped souls were in there," Violet says. "So it's probably a good thing it burned. Now all those spirits are finally free."

The waitress returns to take their order, pausing their conversation while Queenie salivates. Violet opens the menu, giving it a quick look before choosing something. Rose orders a salad, which to Queenie would never be enough food. Queenie orders the fish and chips and the server takes their menus. Violet mentions seeing strange people in the dunes.

"A man and a woman?" Queenie asks. "Like way too close to the house?"

Violet nods.

"I noticed them the other day," Queenie says. "It was like they were trying not to be recognized, with big hats and sunglasses."

"I don't like the way this sounds," Rose says.

"At first, I thought it might be reporters," Queenie says. "But no Temples are in the news at the moment."

"This is creepy," Rose says. "We should tell Max and Jack as soon as they get back so that they can keep an eye on things."

"My left shoulder gave a ping when I saw them," Violet says. "My shoulder hasn't chimed in since the storm."

"That's not good," Queenie says.

They agree that they should have a family meeting to discuss it as soon as everyone is back.

"I'm glad your shoulder let us know that we need to take it seriously," Queenie says to Violet, eyeing the untouched bread in a small basket on the table next to them. Perhaps she could snag a roll before anyone notices.

The restaurant has grown louder, and the book club appears to be having a grand time.

"While we're talking about mysterious things, I should also mention something about Sally Rose," Queenie says. "I think Old Sally is talking to her."

Even in the loud restaurant, Queenie hears Violet gasp.

"Did you hear Old Sally yourself?" Violet asks.

"It's more like I witnessed it," Queenie says. "Sally Rose got this faraway look like she was listening to something, and then said something about Old Sally talking to her. Or at least that's what I thought she said."

"She's only two. She barely speaks in full sentences," Violet says. "But she is precocious for her age."

"Old Sally and Sally Rose were awfully close before Mama died," Queenie says. "It almost makes sense."

"But remember the graveyard ritual?" Rose says. "Couldn't that be dangerous if Sally Rose is hearing Old Sally?"

"I wouldn't go that far," Violet says, "but it's something we should pay attention to."

Despite the umbrella drinks on an empty stomach, Queenie's thoughts are as clear as crystal on one thing: she refuses to let anything happen to that precious child.

"We'll talk to the men once they get back," Queenie says. "But for tonight, let's enjoy our time together."

They clink glasses as the food arrives, and Queenie offers a contented sigh.

12

ROSE

L ater that evening, Rose sits in her studio to read more of her mother's diary. Before opening the book, she takes note of how quiet it is not to have Max here. He isn't talkative, but he does have the television on every evening. They don't often spend a night apart, but she encouraged him to get away with Jack and Spud to Hilton Head. Getting him out of the house may help him not obsess over the long court case surrounding the sunken Temple ship and the exploits of Heather's lawyers. When the case was decided in Rose's favor earlier in the year, Heather's lawyers immediately appealed the decision, and they entered yet another phase of waiting for this ordeal to be over.

Heather, Rose's surprise niece, showed up the day of Queenie and Spud's wedding, the only uninvited guest. Until that day, Rose had no idea that her brother, Edward, had a child, nor did Regina, Edward's wife. Then Heather showed up again right before the hurricane. Rose questioned Heather's motives from the beginning.

Sometimes Rose gets tired of dealing with the Temple legacy. Her mother's diary is something she didn't anticipate, as well. But at least it isn't an obligation as much as it is a curiosity.

Rose opens the diary to her mother's handwriting, a red tassel marking the page. This entry is in blue fountain pen ink. It has faded more than the black, but it is still legible.

July 4, 1937

Being an only child is so dull. If I have children, I will have at least two: a boy and a girl. And I promise to marry someone "beneath me," since Mommy is so afraid I'll do just that. Why should I listen to her lectures about good breeding all the time? You would think I was a thoroughbred mare.

She didn't even raise me. Sally did. It is summer, so her daughter, Ivy, comes to the house almost every day. Mommy and Daddy allow it, which surprises me. Who is running this house, the arrogant servants?

There is a big party here later. I am to be on my best behavior. Not that anyone will notice, anyway. I should show them who is really in charge!

Rose pauses to take it in. She smiles at the absurd comment, as well as the notion that her mother planned to marry beneath her to get back at Rose's grandmother.

Rose reads another entry. This one is short.

September 1937

A new boy, Oscar, enrolled at my private school. He smiled at me today in the hallway. His family

makes suits. Tailors. Riffraff, as Mommy would say.
But I like him. He doesn't even seem to care that I am
a Temple.

It is the first mention of Rose's father. Rose didn't
realize they went to school together. In her memory, she
can hear her mother saying the word *riffraff*, in that
haughty way she did when Rose was growing up. It never
occurred to Rose that this was her grandmother's judg-
ment before it was her mother's—a word used in her
family whenever someone didn't measure up, and a word
her mother hated but ended up repeating. A hand-me-
down.

Rose's Grandmother Temple died when Rose was a
girl. Her bedroom was always dark and stale, and her
windows stayed closed. The heavy drapes allowed only a
sliver of light into the room. After she died, Rose's mother
got rid of her things, and Rose's father moved into that
room.

At least Father opened the drapes.

Sometimes Rose would sit on his bed and tell him
about her school day while he mixed a drink from the
small bar in the corner of the room. He had portable bars
in his office and his bedroom. She can still remember the
smell of bourbon mixing with the cologne he always wore
—a musky sweetness.

Rose's other grandparents, the *riffraff* side, were never
invited to the mansion—at least from what Rose remembers. She was discouraged from seeing them and only
visited a handful of times with her father on afternoons
when Rose's mother was out of town. Their house was
modest, not at all grand. His mother always tried to get

Rose to eat, accusing Rose of picking at her food like a bird. Mounds of potatoes were served at every meal.

On those trips, she heard her father speak with a thick Gaelic accent. A language he only spoke with his parents.

Poor Father, Rose thinks. A pawn in a revenge scheme. No matter how hard he tried, he could never measure up. Is that why he drank? Or perhaps it was one of many reasons.

Rose's mother refused to take his surname of Bell and refused to let Rose carry his name, too. Rose was to be a Temple, and Rose's mother arranged for that to happen. When the time came, Rose didn't take Max's name, either. Max didn't understand at first, but then he let it go. The name Temple was the equivalent of royalty in Savannah.

Something you hold on to, her mother told her more than once.

Somewhere along the way, Queenie changed her name to Temple, too. Queenie's father was the grandfather Rose doesn't remember, although his portrait loomed over the staircase when Rose was a girl, always watching her.

Rose closes the diary and walks out onto her small porch. Waves crash in the distance. The big house is dark. Queenie and Violet have probably already gone to bed, but Rose is wide awake.

She returns to the diary. It is like reading a mystery novel where the main character has been dead for four years. Turning the page, it is years later. Rose's mother is now in her early twenties and engaged to Rose's father.

March 1941

Mommy is on the warpath. She refuses to go to the rehearsal dinner that Oscar's family arranged, calling them stupid dirty Irish. My parents are snobbish and arrogant, and they threatened Oscar to comply or lose my inheritance. They have agreed to give us five thousand dollars a month for an allowance, but we must live in this dark old mansion with them. Daddy will give Oscar a job. We had planned to move to New England this summer to start my last two years at Smith next fall. But my parents refuse to fund it, saying college is no longer warranted. It doesn't matter what I want.

Rose takes a deep breath as things start to make more sense. All the fights she and her mother had about Rose going to Smith were just as much about her mother's losses as her control issues. An ultimatum was given. No Smith, no money for anywhere else, and Rose must finish school before she married. Her mother's attorney even drew up a legal contract to the agreement. Rose not only wanted to get out of the house but also out from under her mother's oppression.

To her surprise, Rose thrived at Smith. For once, she felt like she halfway belonged somewhere. It was in their art department that she first fell in love with painting. It was also one of the few times her mother showed an interest in Rose's life. She called every Sunday afternoon, wanting details of classes, parties, and campus life. Her sophomore year, she even came to Northampton for a student art show in which Rose had two pieces. Not that she complimented her on them or encouraged her. Her mother still thought it was a ridiculous career choice. But being on campus was the happiest Rose had ever seen her.

But then Rose's father died during Rose's junior year. An unforeseen heart attack. After that, the momentary closeness between Rose and her mother was over. Perhaps they parted so that they could grieve. Perhaps they parted to survive. Either way, they never found their way back to one another, even though Rose ultimately returned to Smith and finished her degree.

Wasn't it William Faulkner—another Southerner like her father who drank himself to death—who said that the past is never past? Thanks to a single diary entry, Rose now understands her mother's insistence about Smith.

A light knock on the kitchen door pulls Rose from the past. She walks through the kitchen and turns on the outside light to see Violet standing at the door, dressed in jeans and a T-shirt.

Rose opens the door. "What's wrong?"

"My shoulder," she says, her eyes revealing her pain.

"Do we need to get you to the emergency room?"

Violet nods, yes. "I'm sorry," she says.

"Don't you dare apologize," Rose says. "I'm glad you came." Sliding into her sandals by the door, she grabs her purse, putting her mother's diary into the pocket to read if it is a long wait.

Violet holds her left arm as she gets into Rose's car.

"I had a dream about the lighthouse, and all of a sudden my shoulder started throbbing so bad it woke me up."

"Should we tell Queenie we're going?" Rose asks, looking over at the house.

"I don't want to wake her up," Violet says.

Once they are on the road, Rose asks Violet the details of what happened.

"I had a cup of chamomile tea before bed, and the tea

leaves said that something bad is going to happen." Violet's voice is calm, though convincing.

"How should we prepare?" Rose asks.

"I wish I knew," Violet says.

When Rose lived in Wyoming, she kept a constant eye on the weather. Storms came up quickly with sometimes devastating results. Snowstorms would strand people in cars in June. Tornados sent people into storm shelters throughout the summer. You could leave for Denver on a sunny warm day in the early fall and have the highway be closed by a blizzard within an hour. Rose deals with stress by focusing on preparation.

Rose glances at Violet. Even as a girl, Violet had a shoulder that knew things before everybody else did. Now it seems the tea leaves are reinforcing that gift.

In the ER, a dozen people wait in the brightly lit room. Rose imagines that the emergency room is the last place either of them wanted to be at midnight on a Friday night. As they sit in the waiting room, Violet leans her head on Rose's shoulder. She apologizes again for the inconvenience.

"Why do women apologize so much?" Rose asks. "It drives me crazy sometimes. Especially when I hear myself doing it."

"Habit?" Violet says.

"You're probably right."

"I miss Old Sally," Violet says, her voice sounding small in the big waiting room.

"I know you do," Rose says, her words softer. "I do, too." She isn't used to seeing Violet this vulnerable. "I do, too."

"Do you think she's angry at me?" Violet asks, sitting up.

Rose turns to look at her. "Why would you say that?"

"Because she won't talk to me, and I'm starting to forget what her voice sounded like." Violet wipes away a tear.

"I think she would be in touch if she could," Rose says. "She would never do anything to hurt you. You know that, right?"

Violet nods, another tear falling.

Rose reaches into her purse for a tissue and hands it to Violet. Seeing her mother's diary in her bag, Rose realizes she hasn't missed hearing her mother's voice at all, and it is startling to read her writing. It is curiosity, not longing, that steers her interest in the book. Her mother was a mystery to Rose and is perhaps the most significant influence on who Rose became. Even today, she struggles to trust and believe in herself. She can't imagine what it is like for Violet to lose Old Sally, who was such a positive force in her life.

"I feel so far away from the Gullah ways," Violet begins again. "Maybe Old Sally has been here all along, and I am the one who got distant."

"Why would you get distant?" Rose asks.

Violet shrugs and then winces. "Without Old Sally here, the Gullah ways feel empty," she says. "Things don't make sense anymore."

Rose doesn't begin to know what the answer is. "Maybe it's like a puzzle, and you're just one piece away from seeing the big picture."

"I wish," Violet says.

"Or maybe it's about surrender, Vi. You know those

stories you hear about a couple finally adopting a baby because they couldn't have their own, and then they get pregnant because the pressure to procreate drops? Maybe it's something like that. Maybe you need to surrender and let her go."

"Maybe." Violet gets quiet for a time while the ER becomes more active. Violet is moved into another room to wait to see the doctor and asks Rose to join her. The wallpaper looks like bamboo. Rose feels like she has entered a jungle. A jungle with an overabundance of tongue depressors.

"You may be right about surrendering," Violet says finally. "I'm tired of feeling so lost."

Rose apologizes for not knowing more answers.

"Do you honestly think that Sally Rose can hear her?"

"Who knows," Rose says, downplaying her concern.

"That first year, they had such a strong connection," Violet says. "That's why Old Sally was so intent on me passing Sally Rose over her grave."

"I remember," Rose says. "Do you think your shoulder has anything to do with that?"

As if on cue, Violet leans over with another wave of pain.

"I'll take that as a 'yes,'" Rose says as they exchange worried looks.

By the time Violet sees a physician and is released, it is 3 a.m. They have found nothing wrong with Rose's friend despite Violet being in agony. The doctor even mentions that it might be psychological, which causes Rose to clench her jaw. She can't imagine anything less helpful.

On the way home, Rose thinks of her mother's diary. The importance of reading it is more apparent than ever.

Maybe Rose needs to surrender, too, and let go of all the Temple expectations of preserving their legacy and status.

Meanwhile, Violet's left shoulder has sent up a warning flare. A storm is on the horizon, and they must prepare for whatever is coming.

13

VIOLET

Home again, Violet closes her eyes and tries to sleep. Yet, her mind refuses to relax, and the thoughts keep coming despite the pain medication the doctor gave her. They took an X-ray, too, but Gullah intuition doesn't appear on X-rays. From experience, Violet knows that the best way to make it go away is to read the signs.

The family sensitivity has rarely proved this sensitive. It's been years since her pain was bad enough to go to the emergency room. Something is up. Her shoulder has been very reliable at warning her of something coming. To her surprise, the tea leaves chimed in with her shoulder as if the two intuitions had joined forces.

If only Old Sally were here, and Violet could ask her what this all means. A new sadness threatens to wash over her. *Surrender*, she tells herself. And with these early moments of letting go, a nudge from somewhere deep inside reminds her of Old Sally's protection spells. Her eyes open. Within seconds Violet makes her way into the kitchen holding the Gullah Book of Secrets. From the kitchen window, she sees the light still on in Rose's studio. She can't imagine what it's like for Rose to have found Miss Temple's diary. Yet, in a way, the Gullah Book of Secrets is Old Sally's diary, as well as a way of staying in contact.

For the first time in a year, Violet feels a purpose in her actions. She stands on a step stool from the pantry to reach the back of a tall cabinet. On the shelf is an old flour canister, the letters faded. Inside are things Old Sally left for Violet that she might need for spell-making, neatly stored in plastic ziplocked bags inside the canister. They include petrified chicken claws, fingernails, hair clippings of various lengths, different roots, and graveyard dirt.

Violet turns on another light and positions the book on the countertop near the stove to read it. She turns to a basic protection spell that will cover everyone in the house. With only Queenie upstairs, Violet doesn't have to worry about accidentally waking anyone. As for Queenie, she sleeps like a hibernating mother bear. Spud is the light sleeper, but he is away for the weekend. In the last year, he and Violet had several conversations during their sleeplessness. Violet would go into the kitchen to make herself a cup of chamomile tea only to find Spud coming downstairs in his housecoat to heat some warm milk.

Best to get on with the task at hand.

Violet has always been a hard worker. She survived Miss Temple's wrath for years by simply completing the tasks set before her. Keeping silver and antiques polished. Appliances cleaned and maintained. Food ordered. Refrigerators filled. Meals made. Expectations managed. It is stunning how quickly a life can gallop by simply getting things done.

However, this task seems more important than all the others. Violet arranges the ingredients for the protection spell, opening the different bags, and then reading the instructions Old Sally left. She mixes them as though mixing up one of her food recipes and then heats it on the stove. A familiar unpleasant odor fills the room that reminds her of the odd smells coming from Old Sally's kitchen when Violet was a girl.

Despite the massive renovations and expansions, her grandmother's kitchen is basically in the same place. She imagines her standing at the old-timey stove, telling Violet a story about her mother or grandmother mixing up the same potion while standing on the same land. Old Sally often spoke of her ancestors while in the kitchen.

At this moment, it feels as though history stands with Violet. Generations on top of generations. As the ones in charge, the women protected it all. Old Sally always thought that women were the stronger ones who protected hearth and home. They were the storytellers and the keepers of magic. Stirring the ingredients, Violet honors her early ancestors figuring out these different potions and spells. She must trust the process. Not question it. Magic does not hold up well when analyzed.

The concoction thickens under the low heat, and Violet gives it a final stir before turning the stove off. This potion is the first Violet has mixed since Old Sally died. The last protection spell Old Sally made in this kitchen was a few days before the hurricane.

Meanwhile, somewhere in the house, a clock is ticking. Violet can't decide if it is in the past or present, or perhaps even the future. Will Tia, Leisha, or Sally Rose stand in this kitchen someday making the same spell, another layer added to the story, just as Violet's grandmother did and her grandmother before her? At this moment, they feel inseparable, three possibilities all happening at once.

Violet stirs the mixture one more time, pronouncing it done. At sunrise, she will spread the potion around the doorways outside and all the windows she can reach. Once Jack returns, she will ask him to do the ones she can't. Until then, Violet turns out the light in the kitchen and another one over the stove and sits on the sofa facing Old Sally's portrait in the living room.

A light attached to the top of the frame gives Old Sally a luminous quality. It is the only light in the dark house. It is strange to look at her grandmother this way, her image captured on a canvas. It is her and yet not her, too. It reminds Violet of all the portraits in the Temple mansion. Most of those men wearing the cloaks of wealth yet appearing hollow and empty. At least Rose has captured Old Sally's essence. Kindness is in her eyes, as well as wisdom. She wears a simple indigo blue dress and holds a piece of fabric with an *A* embroidered in memory of her infant daughter Annabelle. Rose's attention to detail adds a realness to the image.

Violet touches her chest, feeling a heaviness. She has never missed anyone this much. Not even the mother she thought she had lost growing up.

Sobs catch her unaware, released from a secret storehouse Violet didn't realize she had. They dwarf her earlier tears. She surrenders, as Rose suggested, her exhaustion aiding the release. Words lodge in her throat, threatening to choke her if left unspoken.

"I've missed you so much," she whispers between the weeping.

As she has come to expect, only the silence answers her, causing her sorrow to deepen. But then she turns her head toward the horizon, the direction all her ancestors face in the Gullah cemetery, as a thin line of yellowy-orange cracks open the dark sky.

14

QUEENIE

Queenie sips on her second cup of coffee while she waits in the kitchen to speak to Violet. It is already eleven o'clock. Violet is usually up and moving around long before now. She presses her fingers into her temples to calm her dull headache. Perhaps she had a bit too much fun on their girls' night out. Queenie has a hard time resisting those cute umbrella drinks.

Meanwhile, a bitter smell permeates the kitchen. Queenie recognizes it as one of her mama's protection spells. Violet must have made it last night, although Queenie has never known her to conjure up things like Old Sally used to, only yummy stuff for the tea shop or for here at home. Is this because of the strangers in the dunes they talked about at the restaurant?

Spud called at seven this morning. She hates to admit how much she misses him after only one night away. Considering how inexperienced she is at love, it seems pretty miraculous how well things are going, despite them not being teenagers anymore in the lovemaking department. The overall goodness of her marriage sometimes makes Queenie afraid of jinxing it.

When Queenie goes downstairs to make coffee, Tia and Leisha are already up early to go out with their friends. They have barely been home this summer. When Queenie was their age, going to college wasn't an option. She had already given birth to Violet, albeit secretly, and was working for Iris.

Queenie realizes how much her life has changed from a mere four years ago when the new century began. At that point, she was still living at the mansion and putting up with Iris's constant commentary on what was wrong with every aspect of Savannah and its people, including what was wrong with Queenie. Queenie hadn't dated in decades, and it was still a secret that Violet was her daughter. Now Iris is dead, the mansion is gone, her secret is out, and Queenie is married and lives at the beach in a house full of people who have become an extended family. As the girls would say, it blows her mind.

Violet enters the kitchen looking as though she hasn't slept.

"Are you okay?" Queenie says. "Rose told me about your little adventure last night."

"Rose was here?" Violet touches her shoulder as though remembering.

"Just briefly. She wanted to remind me to let you read my tea leaves today."

"Ah," Violet says as though tea leaves are the least of her concerns.

Violet pours herself a glass of orange juice before joining Queenie at the table.

"It smells like my childhood in here," Queenie says. "You been conjuring up some Gullah magic?"

"One of Old Sally's standard protection spells. I put it around the doors and windows at sunrise this morning." Violet yawns and glances at Old Sally's portrait in the living room and then reaches for a tissue. "Something about doing one of her spells made me miss her even more."

The beginnings of tears form in Violet's eyes.

"You want a hug, sweetie?" Queenie asks.

Violet nods, and they embrace.

"I just kept hoping that she would come to me as she promised," Violet says. "But whenever I ask for her, nothing happens. Only silence."

"We believe in all sorts of magical things when we've lost someone," Queenie says. "We believe that people will just walk in the door someday, even if they've been dead for years." She glances at the front door thinking of Iris. Do ghosts receive change-of-address forms?

"Tell me about your shoulder," Queenie says. "Is it better today?"

"It is, but it's still a mystery what it might be trying to tell me."

"Does it have a timeline?" Queenie asks. "Does it predict things in the immediate future?"

Violet pauses as though taking a quick inventory of the past. "It's different every time. Sometimes nothing happens for days or weeks. Sometimes it's immediate."

Queenie doesn't reveal her concern. "You were smart to make up that protection spell," she says instead.

The phone rings and startles them both. Queenie answers. It is a wrong number, but something about the voice sounds familiar. Her head hurts too much to figure it out. It isn't even noon, and she's ready for a nap, but she wants to let Violet practice reading her tea leaves. She takes down a canister of loose tea from the top shelf.

"It would be good to practice," Queenie says, not entirely convinced that a hungover person and a tired person should practice anything.

With some convincing, Violet goes to her bedroom to get the book containing Old Sally's secrets, and Queenie puts the teakettle on. While waiting for the water to boil, they talk about Tia and Leisha and their busy summer.

They decide to conduct the tea reading on the front porch. It is a cloudy day, humid and warm, with no hint of blue sky behind the thick clouds. The weather sets an ominous tone for a tea reading. They turn the rockers to face each other. Violet places the book on a small table between them.

"So, where do we start?" Queenie holds the teacup with the brewing tea.

"Well, the first thing you need to do is drink your tea," Violet says.

Queenie laughs. "For some reason, it never occurred to me that reading tea leaves might require drinking the tea."

Queenie has been drinking coffee all morning and feels bloated but finishes her tea, as requested, leaving a teaspoon of liquid in the bottom. Queenie then places the cup on the table in front of her.

"What's next?" she asks.

Violet studies the book between them and then instructs Queenie how to invert the teacup on the saucer and then turn it three times. Then she is taught to tap the bottom of the cup three times before handing the cup back to Violet. With this process complete, Violet looks inside the cup.

"This will be a very informal reading since it's my first time other than for myself," Violet says.

"Fine by me," Queenie says, wishing she had taken an aspirin.

"To start, please calm your mind," Violet says.

Queenie chuckles. "Honey, my mind hasn't been calm for fifty years!"

"Please try," Violet says. "Maybe close your eyes."

Queenie does as directed and the two of them sit with closed eyes. The sound of the waves and coastal birds fill the silence.

"Do you have a question you'd like to ask the tea leaves?" Violet asks.

"A question?" Queenie opens one eye.

"Yes," Violet says, her eyes closed.

Questions complicate things. "I thought a reading just gave you an overall impression on how things were going. Like fortune-telling."

"I can do that, too," Violet says, "but people often have a specific question."

"Okay." Queenie closes her eyes again and pauses to give this some thought. "Do I need to say the question out loud?"

"No, you can keep it private. Whatever you want to do." To Queenie, this seems easy and hard at the same time.

They sit without speaking while Queenie ponders a question.

"Got one?" Violet asks.

Queenie says she does. She wants to know what's inside Iris's stupid diary.

Violet opens her eyes, takes Queenie's cup, and stares into it as if it's written in another language. But then she appears to relax.

"Okay, the tea leaves have scattered around the edges and bottom of the cup," Violet begins, looking back at Old Sally's book. "Most of it is in the bottom. That's supposed to be about the past. The future is closer to the rim."

Maybe that's good, Queenie thinks. Maybe there is nothing in Iris's diary that has anything to do with her. She relaxes into the rocker, wondering why in the world she was getting so worked up over a silly diary. But then it occurs to her that the past can be recent, like yesterday or this morning. Queenie just wishes her headache would go away.

Violet turns the cup around a few times as though a message is coming into view, but then her expression changes.

"What is it?" Queenie asks, feeling her blood pressure tick up a notch.

Violet doesn't answer but narrows her eyes and looks at the book again.

Queenie squirms in her seat, something she hasn't done since grade school. She can't decide if she's nervous or she needs to empty her bladder.

"What is it?" Queenie asks again. Is it supposed to take this long to read a few tea leaves?

"From what I can tell from Old Sally's writings, something is about to be revealed that will make things go topsy-turvy. At least for a while."

"Topsy-turvy?" Queenie doesn't like the sound of this.

Violet pauses a bit too long.

"What are you afraid to tell me?"

"There's a bird in the bottom," Violet begins again, widening her eyes.

"Birds are bad?" Queenie asks.

She looks up at Queenie. "No, birds are meant to be good luck. It's good that it isn't a dragon. At least I don't think it's a dragon. Dragons signify large and sudden changes, which no one likes, right?"

Is this a rhetorical question? At this point, Violet seems to be talking more to herself than Queenie. It occurs to her that maybe reading tea leaves isn't Violet's forte. Perhaps she should stick to baking pastries and serving beverages. But that may be her nagging headache talking.

"What else do you see?" Queenie asks, almost afraid to know.

Every time Violet pauses, Queenie feels her heart race a little faster like it wants to leave the scene of a crime that hasn't happened yet.

"Something is in process, Queenie. I'm not sure what it is yet, but I think we need to be cautious and, at the same time, not panic."

Not panic?

Violet's shoulder only hurts with a potential threat, and Queenie's tea leaves hint at something that might turn her life upside down. Whatever it is, it isn't good.

Violet puts down Queenie's cup. "Well, that was a disaster."

"What makes you say that?" Yet Queenie knows why she might.

"I have no idea what I'm doing, Queenie, and if Old Sally were here, she would probably take this book away from me to keep me from doing any harm."

"Don't be silly," Queenie says, thinking Violet's loss of confidence may be more damaging than any of the other possibilities. "You've got to start somewhere. Nobody is automatically a master at something. It takes practice."

Violet thanks Queenie for her faith in her and closes the book.

Meanwhile, the clouds have thickened and grown darker. The ocean can transform into a dark force when a storm comes ashore, and suddenly Queenie wishes Spud were here.

They are about to go back inside when a car drives up. They hear voices in the driveway. Around the sidewalk runs Sally Rose. Queenie's uneasiness from the reading releases with an exhale. She looks over at Violet, who is smiling, too. Despite the dark clouds, the world seems brighter again.

To Queenie's delight, Sally Rose giggles her joy upon seeing her.

Sally Rose climbs the steps, using both arms and legs to conquer the summit. Then Katie and Angie come into view. Their hands are full of totes and travel bags. They look exhausted and relieved at the same time.

When Sally Rose arrives at the top step, Queenie opens her arms, and the child playfully folds into them as though Queenie is a life-sized teddy bear. Being full-figured allows for soft, cuddly embraces.

"Hi, Key." Sally Rose pats both of Queenie's cheeks with her soft hands.

"Did you have fun?" Queenie asks.

Sally Rose gives a playful nod.

At that moment, ominous tea leaves predicting a topsy-turvy world feel far away.

"You're home a day early," Violet says to Katie and Angie.

Angie goes inside while Katie stops on the porch. Angie is not in the best mood.

"Did something happen?" Queenie asks.

"Long story." Katie drops the large tote bag to the floor by her leg. "The short version is her mom is difficult, at best. She criticized Angie about everything—how she hung a beach towel on the balcony, how she tied Sally Rose's shoes. She even criticized the children's books that Angie brought along to read to Sally Rose."

"That would be hard for anyone," Queenie says.

Violet agrees. "Let us know if we can do anything to help."

Katie thanks her. Sometimes Katie reminds Queenie of Rose. Calm. Even-tempered. Angie, in contrast, is more high-strung. But to her credit, if a bad mood strikes, she has the good sense to do what she has to do to keep the peace.

"It must have been hard for you to watch," Queenie says.

"It was," Katie says. "At one point when Angie and her mom were arguing, I left and took Sally Rose for a long walk on the beach. Then when I came back, Angie said she was ready to go."

"Well, I'm glad you're home." Queenie kisses the blond curls on top of Sally Rose's head as she leans in to rest her head on Queenie's shoulder. She smells of suntan lotion and baby shampoo.

Katie gives her daughter an adoring look. "She'll be ready for a nap soon."

Their living arrangement has allowed Queenie to enjoy

Sally Rose without the fuss. Two moms are always nearby to handle the mothering, and Queenie gets to be a fairy godmother of sorts. A role she is happy to play.

Before going into the house, Katie promises to return shortly for Sally Rose.

Queenie nods. "We'll just rock a bit, okay, sugarplum?" For a moment, she sounds like Spud, with his food-related endearments.

Queenie thinks of Angie and her mother. She feels lucky that she got along with hers. Relationships are never easy. Secrets aside, Queenie and Violet have made great strides as mother and daughter. But Queenie envies what Katie and Rose have. A history that lasts a lifetime, with years of photographs together. Of course, not all mother/daughter histories are rosy or end well. Queenie can hardly imagine what it was like for Rose to be Iris's child. Iris—as an employer and half sister—was bad enough. But being raised by someone who was already turning bitter at fourteen would not be easy, as Iris's diary testifies, and her father wasn't much better.

As Queenie rocks Sally Rose, it seems days ago that Violet read Queenie's tea leaves. It is hard to imagine something terrible happening. However, they have been through storms before, and they have done hard things together. Even things that may threaten to turn her life upside down. Again.

15

ROSE

In her studio, Rose steps back to assess her latest painting. It has been nice not to have Max around for a couple of days. Not that he is a demanding person. He cleans up after himself and has a thoughtfulness that few cowboys have, but she automatically changes when around him. She becomes a caretaker, whether he needs one or not. It is a mystery to Rose how this happens. It is as if he beckons her simply by breathing. With him away, she flourishes. She fights the same instinct with Katie. A certain amount of energy goes out to the people Rose loves. It doesn't matter if Katie needs Rose's attention or not. Sometimes Rose wishes there was a switch to turn it off.

Meanwhile, every time Rose is in her studio, her attention turns to her mother's diary. It pulls at her like a magnet. When her attempts at focusing fail, she tells herself that she will read one entry and get back to work.

Rose washes the paint from her hands and goes to her chair. She opens the diary, flipping through the pages to take in its scope. Her mother doesn't write with any regularity. Sometimes years pass between entries. Rose imagines her mother's life was full of the day-to-day life of being a Temple—yearly trips to Europe, monthly board meetings, events, and parties given by the other elite members of Savannah culture, many at the Temple mansion. Parties that took days to prepare, with Old Sally doing all the work.

Her mother's writing seemed to have been done at random times. Yet, it is randomness laced with secrecy. The latest entry is no exception.

December 1950

I finally made Mommy and Daddy proud. I gave birth to a boy to carry on the Temple name. He is called Edward, like my father, grandfather, and great-grandfather before him. Oscar passed out cigars in front of the mansion until Mommy stopped it, concerned about what people would think.

Riffraff, she said in the hallway, loud enough for me to hear.

Now she has a grandson who is half riffraff!

Unfortunately, Edward is an unhappy baby. Only Sally can get him to stop crying. I have a nanny in the evenings after Sally goes home, and Oscar helps when he can. The baby is on formula, which cuts down on the need to have me around. But he is such a sullen little thing. This isn't at all what I thought it would be like being a mother.

Rose closes the diary as this revelation opens another door to the past. Memories of Edward, even as a baby, are almost always unpleasant. As he grew up, Edward became a bully. He bullied Rose. To think of him as a sullen baby expands her view of him. Perhaps Rose wasn't the only one to suffer their mother's indifference. Yet Rose always thought of Edward as the favored child. Temple sons were foundational, something to build on. Temple daughters were window-dressing. Rose's mother was the exception. She graduated from window-dressing and worked to expand the Temple family's power.

Enough, she tells herself, and Rose returns to her canvas. Grays and greens fill her painter's palette. Periodically, her mind wanders to the diary entry. Rose's mother did what was expected of her by giving birth to a male Temple heir. Rose would come along six years later, long enough for her to wonder if she was unplanned. Her mother never liked surprises.

The morning passes, and Rose makes herself a large salad for lunch. As she eats, the magnet pulls at her again. She retrieves the diary from her studio and brings it to the kitchen table. In the next entry, five years have passed.

March 1955, Charleston

I am visiting Margo, one of my old finishing school friends. She married a Ravenel and is bored silly. She invites me to see her when things get unbearable. I don't trust her as far as I could throw her, but she sure knows how to entertain. Last night we went to a jazz club off Broad Street and listened to music until midnight. A quartet was playing—piano, bass, saxophone, and drums. They were from Savannah, although I had never heard of them before. During the first set, the saxophone player caught my eye. We played a game of flirtation the entire evening. The wine helped make it more interesting.

Margo introduced us when they took a break. His name is Henry Grainger. (Why am I always attracted to people beneath me?) But he is handsome, has a friendly smile, and wears bow ties. A look that somehow works for him. Not to mention he is immensely talented on the saxophone. Margo picked up on the mutual attraction and suggested I come up again the next weekend that they play. I shrugged it away. But maybe I will?

Rose's eyes widen. She rereads it. Henry Grainger is Spud before Spud was Spud! But this doesn't match up with the story Rose heard. They supposedly met in 1978, when Spud's jazz band played at the reception at the mansion when Rose married Max. But according to her mother's diary, she met him in 1955.

It was Queenie who told Rose the 1978 version of events, and Violet who told Queenie. How could they be off by over twenty years, and how might this newfound information affect things? Has Spud lied to Queenie all these years?

It seems the Temple legacy is full of secrets contained in books, the latest being her mother's diary. A book that might prove more relevant than the two useless Temple Books of Secrets relegated to the bank vault again.

Unable to stop herself, Rose turns the page to read more. The next entry is from a few months later.

November 1955

Henry and I just returned from Hilton Head. We stayed at our favorite hideaway. If anyone finds out about my secret, my parents will cut me off financially. They have threatened to do as much for minor transgressions, and this is not at all minor.

Never in my life did I think that I could love someone so completely. It doesn't help that Oscar has started drinking and grows irritating by the day. I don't doubt he has someone on the side, too. It is a loveless marriage. I was stupid to think this would work. And as a Catholic, divorce is out of the question. But a woman needs to feel alive, doesn't she? She needs passion in her life.

Rose stands, putting a hand over her mouth. As far as Rose could tell, the only thing her mother was passionate about was elevating the Temple family name. It is hard to believe that she might fall in love with another man. But not just any man. Henry Grainger, a.k.a. Spud. A person Rose has gotten to know much better over the last few years. A nice man. A decent man. A man who is now married to Queenie. A woman who hates being lied to and is highly susceptible to big feelings and significant reactions. Now, Rose must hide the diary from Queenie for her protection. She hasn't even shared it with Violet, who is currently distracted by her grief.

Convinced she can go no further, Rose puts the diary back in her studio. On the way, she steps over Ethel and Lucy. Two border collies now retired from their ranch jobs. Rose cleans her paintbrushes and palette and puts her painting apron on the hook on the back of the door. When Max calls her tonight, Rose will share the latest revelations about her mother. Revelations that haven't sunk in quite yet, though they are beginning to.

When Rose goes to the big house, she learns that Katie and Angie have returned early and Sally Rose is taking a nap. Everyone has gathered in the kitchen. It reminds her of growing up in the Temple mansion. Everyone gathered in the kitchen there, too. Old Sally would be there, as well as Queenie and sometimes Violet. While the mansion felt like a wasteland, the kitchen was an oasis. This new place echoes the old. But perhaps it isn't about places at all, but about the people filling these places.

Queenie greets Rose at the kitchen door, and Rose lowers her eyes. Already she is keeping something from her. She thinks again of the revelation. According to the diary, Spud and Rose's mother were together much longer than anyone suspected. Rose is confident that Spud had reasons for not telling Queenie the truth, but Rose is also confident that Queenie will not understand them.

Katie gives Rose a look that says she will explain later why they are home early. Rose nods and greets Angie. Meanwhile, Violet looks distant as usual, as well as distracted.

"What's on your mind?" Rose asks her.

"Tea leaves," Violet says. "Before Katie and Angie came home, Queenie and I practiced."

"How did it go?" Rose asks.

"I was a fish out of water," Violet says.

"But is it a possibility?"

Violet shrugs and then winces. Her sensitive shoulder isn't convinced.

"You need to get back on the horse," Rose says, wondering why they have resorted to clichés.

"You think so?" Violet asks.

Rose nods.

Violet's girls come home, along with a friend named Lydia. They join the festive group in the kitchen. How will Violet react to them leaving for college in a few weeks? It will change the dynamics in the house to have them gone. Just like not having the men here has changed the dynamic of their current gathering. The guys will be back soon enough, but sometimes it is nice to experience a room full of women, young and old. The chatter is lively. Earthy. Soulful. If only Rose could capture this energy on canvas. It isn't a landscape or a still life. It is *real* life.

A party unfolds. Violet puts out fruit and cheeses on the kitchen table, along with crackers and a large bowl of grapes. Rose grabs napkins and plates. Water is coming to a boil in the kettle, and Violet places different teas on the counter. She winks at Rose and then gets everyone's attention. The room quiets.

"Earlier, Queenie was nice enough to let me practice reading her tea leaves, and it was pretty disastrous."

Queenie laughs and says, "Amen, sister."

"But Rose was just saying that I need to get back on the horse. So, I was wondering if I could practice on you."

They are all in. Conversations and laughter ripple across the room. The phone rings. Rose answers. When she asks who is there, no one answers. Then they hang up.

It is hard for Rose to imagine her mother in a roomful of women like this. Her mother didn't have close friends or any friends for that matter. Women were competition, people to control.

For the next half an hour, they are drinking tea, flipping cups on saucers, while Violet comes around carrying the Gullah secrets book to practice reading whatever message the tea leaves leave behind. Rose didn't realize there were so many movements to the process.

Violet turns to Angie's cup and looks inside.

"You have some grieving to do soon," Violet says to Angie.

Angie offers a tired chuckle. "I can believe that."

Katie puts an arm around her as if to offer her support.

From the looks of her, Angie's grieving has already begun.

It is Queenie's turn next; she appears apprehensive. "This is my second tea reading. No more topsy-turvies, please."

"No more topsy-turvies," Violet repeats.

Violet narrows her eyes as though this helps her to see more clearly. "It says here that you will be taking a long journey in the future."

Queenie exhales as though relieved. "Mr. Grainger has always loved trips," Queenie says playfully.

Katie's tea leaves reveal her losing something of great value that she will find again, but after a significant search. She tells Angie to help her keep an eye on her car keys.

When it is Rose's turn, Violet lifts Rose's teacup and repeats the ritual. Her smile fades as quickly as it comes. The leaves have revealed something unexpected. Violet looks at Queenie and then back at Rose.

"I apologize," Violet says, her voice soft. "I don't think this was a good idea."

Violet turns toward the door and walks out of the house, stopping only briefly to put on her sandals. Everyone is silent as Violet leaves, as well as Tia, Leisha, and Lydia.

"What was that about?" Katie asks.

"I'm not sure," Rose says.

Angie bites her lip, something she seems to do when stressed.

"She saw something scary in the tea leaves," Queenie says. "She saw something in mine earlier, too."

"Did you see her grab her shoulder?" Rose asks Queenie.

Queenie nods, and they exchange a look.

"What can we do to help?" Angie asks.

"Violet has already put a protection spell on the house," Queenie says. "Rose, your tea leaves must have confirmed it."

"Maybe it's nothing," Katie says, glancing at her mom.

"Or maybe it's something that we need to prepare for," Rose says.

"Violet isn't the type to make things up," Queenie says.

"Where do you think she's going?" Katie asks.

"Probably the lighthouse," Rose says.

"Should we go after her?" Queenie asks.

"Best to just let her walk it off and think. She'll be back," Rose says.

One by one, they go their separate ways. But instead of going back to the cottage, Rose walks to the beach to catch up with Violet. Her mother's diary seems to be hinting at something big, too. But Rose will keep quiet. One premonition at a time is enough.

16

VIOLET

Violet walks up the beach, remembering the night Hurricane Iris came ashore. Their makeshift family —tethered together with a long rope—slowly made their way to the lighthouse while the wind and rain beat against them. How did they ever make it? Yet, no one faltered that night. They did it together. Whatever is coming feels equally as threatening, and Violet wants to believe that they will get through that together, too.

She rubs her shoulder, but the surrender she seeks feels impossible. Violet believed that her grandmother would somehow stay connected, just as Old Sally's ancestors stayed connected and sent messages to Old Sally with some frequency. What is Violet doing wrong?

Breathing the salty fresh air, Violet recalls the gathering in the kitchen. She wanted reading the tea leaves to be a fun thing. But Rose's reading pointed to danger and an event that would prove traumatic, as did Queenie's earlier reading. Like her shoulder, the tea leaves don't lie. They point to something meaningful.

Violet speeds up her walk, thinking of how Old Sally walked this stretch of beach every day for years. She knows now that her grandmother had memories at the lighthouse that drew her there—memories that included the tragic death of the man she loved and their baby. Violet's memories draw her here, too. Memories of the storm. Memories of her grandmother. Memories are all she has now.

In the lighthouse during Hurricane Iris, Old Sally hummed "Amazing Grace." If ever there was a need for grace, it was that night. The others joined in. Violet hums the tune now to calm herself. Her shoulder is predicting something, and the tea leaves are echoing that warning.

In the last year of Old Sally's life, Violet took slow walks on the beach with her. Old Sally's promise to stay in touch feels blocked by a combination lock. A lock where Violet has forgotten the last number. Her thoughts spin the dial looking for the combination that will unlock her ability to talk to Old Sally again. Meanwhile, Violet is tired of thinking so much, tired of feeling powerless. And what do the tea leaves have to do with anything?

At the lighthouse, Violet remembers when the storm surge hit and chased them up the inner staircase. It is the stuff of nightmares. Even recalling it causes her heartbeat to quicken. She reminds herself that she is safe, at least for now. Hurricane Iris taught her that nature always wins and that being human is fatal.

Violet touches the metal door with the new Do Not Enter sign as a touchstone to remind her that she made it out of there alive.

When Violet turns to go back, Rose waits in the dunes at the bottom of the concrete steps. They exchange waves.

She joins Rose on the beach, and they turn toward the house.

"You okay?" Rose asks.

"A lot's going on," Violet says. "For you, too?"

Rose nods. For a long stretch of beach, they walk in silence.

"We've walked along this beach together practically our entire lives," Violet says, "except for when you lived out West."

"We have," Rose says. "Our Sea Gypsy days are happy memories for me."

"For me as well," Violet says.

As girls and best friends, they used to hold hands as they walked. Now Violet would be too afraid of what people might think. When did she get so careful?

"Remember racing to the lighthouse when we were girls?" Rose says. "I wish I had that much energy now."

"Me, too." Violet hears the faint sound of her girlhood braids clicking together as she runs. Back then, Old Sally wove colored beads into Violet's hair, making it musical. Magical, too, as far as Violet was concerned.

They walk in silence again as the waves push onto the shore. Violet leans over to pick up a sun-bleached sand dollar and hands it to Rose.

"I love these," Rose says. They walk with ease as they match strides in the silence. It is Rose who speaks first.

"You seemed so stressed by whatever the tea leaves revealed in my cup. Is that something you want to talk about?"

"Getting predictions is so much scarier without Old Sally here," Violet says. "I relied on her to explain them to me."

"Oh my, I never thought of that," Rose says.

"She was good about reassuring me that I wasn't crazy." Violet laughs a short laugh.

"Well, you aren't crazy," Rose says. "You're expanding your awareness with the tea leaves and learning how to maneuver this new terrain."

"It is new terrain, isn't it?" Violet finds this perspective helpful, like there might be hope for her after all.

"It is," Rose says.

"I just wish I could shake the dread I feel," Violet says. "If I had a hint of what was coming, I could prepare. Is it something to do with the shop? The girls? Jack? The number of things that could go wrong is too many to count."

"I wish I could help," Rose says.

"You've already helped," Violet begins. "Plus, you've got a lot going on, too. Tell me about your mother's diary."

Rose pauses, forming words that might explain the bigness of Rose's discoveries.

"Let's just say that I went to therapy for years thinking I knew my mother and all her many sins. But it turns out I didn't know her at all."

Violet nods. She worked for Miss Temple for decades and felt the same. "Any revelations?"

"Well, if Queenie reads it, it could be bad," she says.

"Like how bad?"

Rose hesitates again.

"Let's wait until it feels like the right time," Violet says.

Rose thanks her for understanding.

Violet has trouble imagining what Miss Temple might confess in a diary. She isn't the type to have a secret life. But is anyone as they seem?

When they reach the house and walk up into the dunes, Violet feels more determined to understand the formation of tea leaves and their meanings. Her grandmother believed the folk magic had value, and Violet wants to believe that, too. Besides, it seems they need all the help they can get. Another storm is brewing.

17

QUEENIE

A picnic on the back patio is prepared to celebrate everyone being home. Max and Jack have burgers cooking on the grill, and Queenie and Spud have provided potato salad and baked beans. Having Spud home again has them acting like newlyweds, exchanging playful banter about nothing and everything.

Thankfully, with Jack home again, Violet appears noticeably relaxed. She is busy putting food on the table. Tia and Leisha put out plates and utensils while two of their friends watch. They are just back from a swim in the ocean, and after using the outside shower, they now sit chatting near the kitchen door.

Nearby, Spud begins to push Sally Rose on the swing, her giggles rising and falling with the motion. Spud is such a natural with kids that it seems unfortunate that he never had children of his own, or grandchildren. Although he never mentions it, Queenie has surmised this is a great sadness for him. She thinks briefly about all those wasted years he longed for Iris and didn't marry someone else. But perhaps his loss is her gain. Otherwise, he might never have been available when it was Queenie's turn for happiness.

However, if they had married three decades earlier, Queenie would have treasured having a child with Spud. She believes they would have been loving parents. A sadness descends that feels bittersweet. Queenie can't imagine her life without this sweet man, yet it could have easily been the case.

Spud and Queenie became a couple after Violet inherited the mansion. Queenie was giving a hand with the spring cleaning and taking down all those heavy draperies when Spud showed up to help. While he had been to the house dozens of times, and Queenie had watched his interactions with Iris at the Piggly Wiggly every week for years, this was the first time Queenie had spent any time with him. As they cleaned windows together, she discovered Spud was much more than he appeared. Not only did he laugh at her jokes, but he wanted to know all about her.

Someone wanting to know you is the most beautiful thing of all.

Katie and Angie sit on the patio talking with Rose. Queenie walks over just as they are discussing preschools. Is it time to decide that already? Sally Rose is only two. Queenie never attended a preschool in her entire life, and it didn't hurt her any. At least she doesn't think it did. But today's parenting seems much more complicated than when she was growing up.

Queenie walks toward the swing set, and Sally Rose calls out to her as if she hasn't seen Queenie for months.

"Push me," Sally Rose insists.

Spud smiles before stepping aside, giving Queenie a

quick kiss on the lips. She anticipates a *sweet mystery of life* moment later tonight.

The scene seems idyllic, but Queenie hasn't been able to ignore the tea leaves and their prediction. For the next several minutes, they take turns pushing Sally Rose, and life seems perfect. Queenie lives in a beautiful house by the sea with the man she loves. And a bunch of other people. But most of the time, that's fine, too.

When Max announces that the burgers are ready, Queenie delivers Sally Rose to Katie and Angie, who already has her high chair at the picnic table. They gather, eat and talk. While it was nice to have a little space over the weekend, it is also lovely to have everyone back home.

Yet she can tell something is bothering Violet, and Queenie makes a point to sit next to her at the picnic table.

"Everything all right?" Queenie asks. Violet nods, but Queenie knows when Violet isn't telling the truth. She is not someone who hides things well.

"You seem to be catching on quickly with the tea leaves," Queenie says. "You'll be an expert in no time."

Violet thanks her but doesn't look so sure.

Queenie leans in, prompting Violet to do the same. "Everything's going to be fine," Queenie says, her voice lowered.

"I wish I believed that," Violet says.

Queenie decides to let it go, but it is hard to watch someone you love struggle.

~

LATER THAT EVENING, while Spud is in the bathroom readying for bed, Queenie props herself up with two pillows wearing one of her queen-size negligees, red with black trim. Queenie throws back her shoulders to show off her full figure as Spud comes out of the bathroom.

"Va-voom!" he says, pretending to be frisky. But Queenie can tell that this is one of those nights when he is more tired than romantic.

"Would you like to save this for in the morning?" Queenie asks.

"Could we?" Spud looks relieved. "The band played until one o'clock last night. I forget I'm an old geezer until the next day."

"Well, you're *my* old geezer, and I know how it is, so let's get some sleep."

Queenie changes into her regular nightgown, soft and comfy, neither red nor black, but a pale blue. Spud has never asked her to wear anything sexy. He says he likes her just the way she is, but Queenie has trouble believing that any man might love her just as she is.

Lights off, they face each other in the dark so that they can talk.

"What was up with Violet tonight?" Spud asks.

"She's thinking about doing tea readings at the shop, and I think she's terrified," Queenie says, opting for the simplest explanation.

"That's big," Spud says. "She's never done anything like that."

"While you were gone, she practiced on me."

"How was it?"

"She read the tea leaves just fine, but evidently our lives are about to be turned upside down."

"Uh-oh," Spud says.

"I know," Queenie says.

"But it's good she's finally thinking about her heritage, isn't it?"

"If only it were that simple," Queenie says. "If she had Mama here, I bet she wouldn't worry."

"A little courage might help, too," Spud says.

Queenie agrees. "For years, Violet took to all this Gullah folk magic like a duck to water. If anyone can carry on Mama's work, it would be her."

Spud asks next about Rose and how she is dealing with Iris's diary. If he is worried at all that he might be in there, he doesn't show it.

"I think sometimes Rose wishes she'd never been born a Temple," Queenie says.

"It does seem to have its negative aspects," Spud says. "Max was telling us about that court case. What a mess."

"Heather is a piece of work, that's for sure," Queenie says.

Spud asks again about the diary. Maybe he is more curious than he is letting on.

"Rose showed me one of Iris's entries when we were out the other night. It seems Iris started it when she was fourteen, and her last entry was a few weeks before she died. So, she only wrote in it occasionally."

"Iris was more of a letter writer," Spud says as if he has been on the receiving end of one.

Queenie tries not to think about how much it bugs her that Spud knows about Iris's letter-writing habits. What else does he know? If Queenie were him, she would be first in line to see what Iris might have written about her. Of course, it was only for a short amount of time that they were together. But still. Diaries exist for romances.

Queenie asks herself how she might help Violet be

braver about reading tea leaves and claiming Gullah folk magic. At least Marylou is encouraging her. Sometimes it helps to have someone older who believes in you.

In the meantime, Queenie tunes into the faint sound of waves, her constant lullaby as a child growing up. She likes thinking that Sally Rose has this same lullaby. She is a lucky child. But then the tea leaf prediction nags at her again.

We best be buckling our seat belts, she says to herself before drifting off to sleep.

18

ROSE

That evening, when Rose and Max are alone in the kitchen, Max tells her about their time on Hilton Head. How Spud impressed everyone with his playing and how much the other players respect him. At some point over the weekend, Jack confessed how worried he was about Violet. He even suggested to Violet a few months ago that she see a counselor or attend a grief support group. Rose tells him about their girls' night out and Violet's emergency room visit later that evening. Max doesn't remember that Violet's shoulder predicts things and, to Rose's knowledge, only bad things, but Rose doesn't feel the need to remind him. At least not yet. To her surprise, Rose doesn't mention the latest revelations in her mother's diary.

They quickly fall into their old routines, and Max falls asleep in front of the television, Lucy and Ethel at his feet. Rose returns to her studio. Not to make art, but to have a private place to read more about her mother's life. She turns on the light next to her chair and settles in. It feels right to read these entries in secret. Did her mother ever imagine that Rose might read them someday? At times, it seems that her mother is speaking directly to her.

Rose opens the book to where she left the thin, red ribbon to mark the page and puts on her reading glasses.

January 1956

I am in Charleston again, staying with Margo. I don't tell her the real reason I am there. The test from the doctor's office in Charleston came back positive. I wasn't about to get the test done in Savannah and run the risk of my secret getting out the first day.

Now, what do I do? Do I tell Henry? Do I pretend the baby is Oscar's?

Unfortunately, Oscar probably isn't pickled enough to forget that we haven't made love in months. Deception is required. My husband is getting lucky tonight, but I need to catch him before he blacks out.

"What?" Rose gasps, staring at the words. Lucy comes in to check on her and nuzzles Rose's knees. The muffled sound of the television plays in the next room. At some point, Max will wake up and go to bed. He won't question if she isn't there yet. Rose often reads in her studio late into the night.

Rose rereads the passage. It is January 1956, and her mother has gone to a doctor's office to get a pregnancy test. The test proves positive. It is not her husband's child. Rose will be born later that year. Henry Grainger is her father. Henry Grainger, nicknamed Spud. A saxophone player with a penchant for wearing bow ties. Rose sits very still, her heart beating as if she is a rabbit with a fox nearby.

How is this possible?

Rose doesn't typically keep a bottle of wine in the house, but she set one aside after Heather gave it to her and Max as a gift after the hurricane and before the court case started. They joked that Heather must have poisoned it. Heather. Like Rose's mother, Heather seemed incapable of connecting in any kind of genuine way. Rose thinks of the seemingly unending lawsuit tangled up in the court system for who knows how much longer. Thank goodness Max has been handling the details. Otherwise, Rose may have already been drinking again.

When Rose hid the bottle, tucking it away under the dishtowels in a kitchen drawer, she knew this wasn't a good thing for an alcoholic to do. She was also aware that it was a strange gift for Heather to give them, given Rose remembers telling her niece at Queenie and Spud's wedding that she didn't drink. Her nondrinking status has never been a secret. However, her nonsecret threatens to become a full-fledged one now if she acts on what she feels like doing. All it would take is one drink to undo two decades of sobriety. Rose stands in the shadows of her kitchen, contemplating her next move. What does one do when they find out that the person they thought was their father isn't? If this were happening in the movies, the protagonist would reach for a drink—a stiff one. But wine will do.

Unfortunately for Rose, the bottle requires a corkscrew, which she threw away years ago to avoid the temptation. A walk to the big house is needed. Her shock dulls with her new mission. She takes her key to the back door and walks across the dark patio. Solar lights illuminate the walkway.

Once inside, she finds Katie in the kitchen putting water in Sally Rose's sippy cup.

Knowing everyone else is asleep, they greet each other in subdued tones.

"What are you doing here so late?" Katie asks.

Rose hesitates. Two seconds. Maybe three.

"Did you forget?" Katie smiles as if Rose's growing forgetfulness is endearing, not an early sign of dementia.

"Matches," Rose says, reaching into the drawer that contains the matches and also a corkscrew.

"You don't have matches at your place?" Katie doesn't look away.

Rose feels caught and also irritated. *Can't an alcoholic get a little peace for a change?*

All Rose needs is for Katie to use her empathic powers to read through to her real intention. "I couldn't find any. I'm a bit restless, so I thought I would take a bath and light some candles." Rose is surprised at how easy it is to lie.

Fortunately, Katie buys it, and they exchange a quick hug before Rose walks out the back door with the matches and without the corkscrew.

Instead of returning to the cottage, Rose stands in the house's shadows, waiting for Katie to turn out the kitchen light and return upstairs. Checking her watch, Rose makes herself wait five minutes, thinking how devious she can be when wanting a drink. Addicts are like this. Rose is no different. Like a burglar with a key, she makes quiet and careful moves. Returning to the empty kitchen, she returns the matches to the drawer and retrieves the corkscrew.

In her cottage kitchen again, Rose stands in partial darkness, trying not to make any noise. She unwraps the foil on the wine bottle and inserts the corkscrew. Her mouth waters, and she can already taste the red wine.

Behind her, Max flips on the overhead light.

Rose jumps, stopping midscrew, and turns around. "You scared me," she says to Max.

"What's going on, Rosie?" Max's voice is calm, like his job is to talk someone off the edge of a cliff.

"You wouldn't believe me if I told you," Rose says.

Max steps into her field of vision. Lucy licks Rose's hand. Ethel must still be sleeping.

"Try me." Max eyes the bottle of wine, and then Rose. If he is unprepared for this moment, he doesn't reveal it.

The wine bottle, impaled with the corkscrew, sits on the countertop. Rose turns to face her husband.

"To be honest, I was about to pour myself a glass of wine," she says.

Max narrows his eyes, but there is caring there. "What's the occasion?"

Rose sighs. Not only is she caught in the spotlight of her addiction, but she also suddenly realizes how tired she is—tired of carrying her history. A history that has never made sense to her until now.

Rose loved her father. She never questioned his love for her, and she was devastated when he died. Yet, the two of them never shared much in common. When he died, this lack of connection was part of the devastation. Rose felt like she didn't even know him. Nor did he know her. And his death closed that door forever.

"Rosie?" Max's voice remains calm, but there is intention there, too. An intention that he get her to wake up to the choice she is about to make.

Tears gather in her eyes as she steps into his embrace

and begins to cry. He holds her as she cries into his terry-cloth robe. A robe, oddly enough, that seems designed for tears. She loves how solid Max is and how he isn't pushing her for answers but just letting her be a mess for a while. Rose grabs a tissue from a nearby drawer and asks Max to sit with her at the kitchen table. It takes three tissues to ready herself for what she needs to say.

"As you know, I've been reading my mother's diary." Rose pauses as though impending news this big requires a pause. "When she got pregnant with me, it wasn't my father's baby, but someone else she saw at the time."

Max looks at her as though Rose has revealed that she is pregnant herself, a biological impossibility at this point. "Your father wasn't your father?"

"No, he wasn't," Rose says.

Rose hates seeing the worry on his face, but she is worried, too.

"Is it somebody you know?" Max asks as though waiting for an unexpected shoe to drop.

"Yes," Rose says. "It's Henry Grainger."

"Wait. Isn't that…?"

Max laughs like it is April 1st, and Rose has tricked him into being an April fool.

"It's true," Rose says. "Spud met Mother at a jazz club in Charleston in the late '50s. They used to meet in Hilton Head to be together."

Max nods as though this is a feasible scenario. Why else might Rose's mother bequeath Spud three condominiums in Hilton Head?

Rose goes into her studio to get her mother's diary and lets him read the last two entries. Rose watches his eyes move as he reads, taking in every word.

"Wow," he says, looking up at Rose. "That must have blown you out of the water."

"It has," Rose says. "And the first thing I thought to do was to have a glass of wine. I almost had one, too."

"I can see that," Max says. "Do you still want one?"

"You have no idea how much." Rose laughs a short laugh, though addiction isn't the least bit funny.

"Where'd you get the wine?" he asks.

"Heather gave it to us a couple of years ago, remember? I think she used it as an excuse to drop by once. We made a joke about her poisoning us."

Max nods. "Must have been before she decided to sue."

"It was."

"Shall I get rid of it?" Max acts as if the wine is a loaded gun, and Rose is suicidal, which may not be far from the truth.

Rose says she will get rid of it, and Max doesn't fully relax until Rose pours the entire bottle down the sink. She smells the fermented grapes and misses the taste, as well as the feeling of escaping her life. Yet, in reality, she doesn't want to run anymore.

"Do you think Spud has any idea?" Max asks.

"I don't think so," Rose says. "He isn't the type to hide things."

"No, he's not," Max says. "He's a stand-up guy."

"Yes, he is," Rose says. "I guess if you're going to have a surprise father, he's a good one to have."

Max agrees.

"If it's any consolation, I probably would have wanted a drink, too." Max washes the wine bottle out in the sink before walking it outside to the recycling bin. Lucy and Ethel follow and do their business.

In bed, Rose doubts she will sleep. Like Max, Rose has always had a great deal of respect for Spud. But to find out that he is her father is what Max would call a game changer.

Rose lays awake full of questions and rethinking everything. It was Violet who told Rose about Spud's affair with her mother when he was so torn up at her funeral. She had been shocked then, too. Spud and her mother seemed too different to be compatible. Was it a simple case of opposites attracting?

At 4 a.m., Rose gets up to go to her studio. The diary waits next to her chair. Rose opens it to read another entry from a month later.

February 1956

I almost told Henry tonight, but something stopped me. If I tell him, he will never let it go. He will have to tell people the truth, and he will insist on being in the baby's life. That's how he is. It will torture him every day of his life going forward. I know he wants children. But I have already told him that children are something I could never give him. The only way I could do that would be to leave my family altogether.

I am not someone who can give up everything for love. I know that now. I have convinced myself that love isn't everything. Love doesn't buy houses, pay expenses, or build entitlement—unless one marries well like Margo. But is Margo happy? I venture not.

I will never tell Henry that the baby is his. It will be

easier that way. He will assume the baby is Oscar's, that Mommy and Daddy suggested we have another child. He knows how susceptible I am to their wishes. Next time we are together, I will lie to him, and he will never know.

Rose closes the book. Thanks to her mother, Rose's entire life has been a lie. But from here on out, Rose vows to live in the truth.

19

VIOLET

Violet's shoulder has only had a few twinges since her emergency room visit, but she knows that whatever has it worked up has not been resolved. It is a mystery, with few clues to point her toward the answer. Her shoulder doesn't give false alarms. Nor does it imagine things. It reveals things.

With Queenie and Spud helping at the tea shop, Rose offers to go with Violet to Old Sally's grave, as she did on the anniversary. Except for their time together in the emergency room, they have barely had time to talk these last few weeks. Life does that to friends sometimes. Pulls them in different directions until they find themselves together again with almost too much to say. Violet can't begin to tell Rose how the possibility of reading tea leaves has thrown her, and yet she has been studying their meanings every evening.

Rose is quiet on the drive over to the southern tip of the island, where there are no houses, only a palmetto forest and a smattering of oaks.

"Are you okay? It's not like you to be this quiet," Violet says. "I'm usually the quiet one these days."

Rose looks at Violet, almost startled.

"Something has distracted you. Is it the diary?" Violet asks.

Rose pushes a piece of her hair behind her ear. A gesture Rose has made since she was a girl.

"Can we talk about it when we get there?" Rose asks.

"Of course," Violet says.

Minutes later, they sit on the bench in the Gullah cemetery, under the live oak that watches over things. Violet sighs as she sits. She finds this place more comfortable than being with people right now.

Rose pulls out a book that must be Miss Temple's diary from her baggy purse. As a girl, Violet got a diary for Christmas one year from Queenie. It was a small, thick book with a tiny gold key attached to open the lock. Violet wrote about the boys she liked at school and the books she read. She even drew in it sometimes. But Miss Temple's diary is different. It looks expensive and made for someone important.

Meanwhile, Rose hasn't looked up from the book.

"I read something last night, Vi. That was such a total surprise that I think I'm still in shock."

"Really?"

Rose nods and opens the diary, and instructs Violet to read the entry.

Violet does as requested, her mouth opening in surprise as she reads about Spud and Miss Temple. Spud told Violet himself about how their affair had begun after Rose's wedding. Yet the diary reveals an earlier version of events and a pregnant Miss Temple with Spud's child.

She places the book on the bench between them and then looks at Rose.

"No wonder you've been so quiet," Violet says. "This is unbelievable."

"Isn't it?" Tears form in Rose's eyes, and Violet takes her hand.

"Why didn't she tell me?" Rose says.

"I have no idea." Violet thinks of Queenie lying to her for all those years, and how similar the situation is. Violet was furious at her for keeping her motherhood from her. Violet felt not only lied to but cheated of the truth. But slowly, Violet began to see how fearful Queenie had been. Even the smartest, most loving people make stupid choices when fear gets involved. As for Miss Temple, maybe she was fearful, too.

"What will you do now?" Violet asks, squeezing Rose's hand before releasing it.

"I'm not sure," Rose says. "Mother never told him. He has no idea."

Violet recalls the shock of finding out at Miss Temple's will reading that Queenie was her mother. The news made her faint. She thought that only happened in movies. It was only later that Violet found out how Mr. Oscar had sworn Queenie to secrecy, threatening her livelihood if she told, as well as Old Sally's.

"Do you think I should tell him?" Rose asks.

"How could you not?" Violet can't imagine Spud's reaction to the revelation that he now has a daughter he never knew he had. But she is sure of one thing. It is time for the truth to be known.

Violet looks over at Rose, who stares at the ocean. For the first time, Violet notices the similarities between Rose and Spud. They are both calm and gentle. Creative. Both artists. Spud as a musician, and Rose as a painter. They are also similar in height. She remembers now that Mr. Oscar was tall and lean, as was his son, Edward. Rose didn't look anything like Miss Temple, whose features were much more severe. Yet, Violet never thought about it before until now.

"You must be rethinking your whole life," Violet says, which is something Violet did, too, when the truth came to light.

"I am," Rose says. "It's like when somebody dies, and you keep reminding yourself that they're gone. I keep telling myself over and over that Spud is my father."

"I did that, too, when I found out that Queenie was my mother. It took days just to get used to the idea, and then weeks for it to settle in."

"I forgot all about that," Rose says. "You know what this is like."

"I do," Violet says.

Rose pauses as if deciding whether to say more. "I almost had a drink last night. After two decades of sobriety." Rose's words are soft like she is in a confessional. "I mean, if Max hadn't come into the kitchen, I probably would have. I just wanted to feel numb."

"I'm glad you didn't do it," Violet says.

"Me, too," Rose says.

While they were best friends as girls and perhaps best friends now, there was a considerable gap in their lives where they weren't in touch. They were raising families, and Violet was working for Miss Temple. Violet would hear things from Queenie's letters from Rose, but she never knew until recently that Rose went to AA.

"How do you think Spud will take it when I tell him?" Rose asks.

"I think he'll be thrilled but also upset," Violet says. "Miss Temple betrayed him, too, and about something incredibly significant. You two have lost nearly half a century of being together and knowing the truth."

"And how do we make peace with that?" Rose asks.

"One day at a time," Violet says, a cliché Rose uses often. "The good news is that you did find out. What if you hadn't found the diary? What if Miss Temple had never written it down?"

Rose agrees. "It's a miracle I found out at all," she says. "I could have spent the rest of my life thinking that Spud was just that nice man that Queenie married."

For several seconds they sit quietly while waves of heat dance along the horizon.

"When do you think I should tell him?" Rose looks at Violet.

"It's up to you, of course," Violet says, "but maybe not until you're over the shock a little so that you can be there for him."

Rose nods in agreement.

Violet has always thought of Spud as a father figure, and now Rose is fortunate enough to have him be the real thing. With the knowledge that Mr. Oscar was her father, Violet and Rose thought that they were half sisters. But this is no longer the case.

"I guess this means I'll have to tell Queenie, too," Rose says.

Violet's eyes widen. "Perhaps not any time soon."

They share a brief laugh. Violet doesn't envy Rose breaking the news to Queenie, but she imagines that as soon as Spud knows, Queenie will have to be informed, too. Then they will all have to prepare for the fallout.

Violet glances at the diary between them. "I wonder what else she has to say."

"Right now, I don't want to know." Rose places the diary back in her purse.

"Do you think Old Sally knew that Mr. Oscar wasn't your real father?" Violet asks.

"I always assume Old Sally knew everything," Rose says. "But that doesn't mean she ever spoke it."

"She never told me about Queenie being my mother," Violet says. "She kept that secret for nearly forty years."

Rose's eyes widen. "I guess even the wisest of women have their faults."

"Or their fears," Violet says, wondering what secrets Old Sally may have taken to her grave. But she is tired of secrets. Not only Temple secrets, but also Gullah ones. She wishes she could lighten up. Life has been so serious lately.

"Life isn't the least bit simple, is it?" Rose asks.

"That's for sure," Violet says. "Your mother was having a secret affair, and a child, with a saxophonist. And my mother was having a secret affair with *your* father," Violet says. "Unbelievable, right?"

"And confusing," Rose says.

As they are leaving, it feels to Violet as though something has shifted. For the first time in a year, being at the cemetery hasn't felt devastating. Because of Rose's news, she hasn't even thought of her grandmother that much this time. Miss Temple always did have a peculiar talent for getting in the last word on every subject. Meanwhile, the mystery of what her shoulder is trying to tell her is no closer to being solved.

20

QUEENIE

Is it her imagination, or are Rose and Violet being secretive lately?

Queenie dabs at her hair, newly styled at the Gladys Knight and the Tints hair salon. Whenever Queenie is at the salon, she thinks of Iris and the meanness she put up with all those years. Not to mention how dangerous Iris was behind the wheel of that giant Lincoln Continental. Queenie could smell the remnants of KFC in that car whenever Iris picked her up at the beauty parlor. It always baffled her how someone could talk endlessly about her delicate stomach and then eat a greasy bucket of chicken in one sitting. Something wasn't right with that woman.

Queenie wishes she could forget the memories involving Spud and Iris. Every week for decades, Iris would stand in front of the meat counter holding court while flirting with him. Well, you couldn't call what Iris did flirting, exactly. It was more like she was showing up to receive an award. The award being Spud's attention.

Queenie's face warms as she remembers Spud's ability

to charm Iris, all the while petting his mustache. He used to straighten his bow tie when he was nervous. Now he tugs at the bottom of his Hawaiian shirts. Does he do that charm thing with Queenie?

More and more, Iris has been showing up in Queenie's life again. First, in the form of those old, wealthy white ladies, who were supposedly Iris's friends, and who confronted Queenie at Violet's Tea Shop and insulted her, an experience that bothered her for days. Of course, after they left, Queenie thought of a dozen witty comebacks that she could have used.

Then to make matters worse, Rose announced that she had found Iris's diary in the bank vault. Something about that discovery raised the hair on the back of Queenie's neck. Rose talked about the diary when she first found it, and she even showed Queenie a passage. Lately, however, Rose hasn't mentioned that stupid diary at all. Maybe that's why Rose and Violet are acting so strange. Rose must have come across something that she doesn't want Queenie to know about and has told Violet about it.

If Queenie hadn't been a companion to Iris for all those years, she imagines she could have made a good detective. She has read enough mysteries to be an expert at solving crimes. Not that this is a crime, exactly. But it is a mystery.

When Queenie gets back to the house, she will ask Rose about it. They have never kept secrets from one another, and she doesn't want to start now. Besides, she knows the destructive power of keeping things from people and how much damage secrets can do when they come to light. And they *always* come to light. Besides, now that she is in her sixties, Queenie has sworn off being deceitful.

Before leaving the Piggly Wiggly, Queenie grabs a few groceries, including a bag of Oreos, from the cookie aisle. Tonight, she and Spud are watching *Fried Green Tomatoes* on the VCR in their bedroom. Before she has time to stop herself, Queenie finds herself wondering if Spud and Iris ever shared a bag of Oreos in bed. Her face turns hot.

Spud loves her. Rose and Violet adore her, too. Them acting strange is not because they don't love her. If anything, they are probably trying to protect her from something. But from what?

Twenty minutes later, Queenie arrives home on Dolphin Island. She puts away the groceries and then goes to the back cottage to find Rose. Max answers the door. He tells her that Rose has taken a walk but should be back any minute.

"Do you mind if I wait for her?" Queenie asks.

"Of course not," Max says, "make yourself at home."

He tells Queenie that he is about to walk Lucy and Ethel and grabs their leashes at the door, leaving Queenie sitting at the kitchen table to wait for Rose. The kitchen clock ticks loudly in the silence, and Queenie fidgets in the chair, not knowing what to do with herself. She has never been good with downtime. Queenie wanders into Rose's studio. The outlines of another giant tree are on the canvas on the easel.

Queenie doesn't have the patience to be an artist, although she loves seeing an artist's studio. It is a place where the magic happens. Paints and an assortment of brushes sit on a long table next to Rose's oversized easel. As Queenie scans the room, she notices the diary on the table next to the side chair in the corner. It feels as tempting as the bag full of Oreos she just put away.

Queenie walks over and takes the diary in hand. She hesitates. It's not like she would be reading Rose's diary. It's Iris's, and Queenie did put up with Iris for thirty-five years. Queenie sits in the chair, weighing the pros and cons. Pro: it will solve the mystery of whether Violet and Rose are keeping something from her. Con: it does seem a bit dishonest. Indeed, it isn't Rose's diary, but it is in her possession. Pro: it will stop Iris from haunting her again, as long as there is not something alarming in them. Con—*I can't think of any more cons.* Queenie looks over at the door like a thief worried about getting caught.

But then she opens the book. She reads the first few entries Rose told her about and then the one Rose showed her. Reading Iris's words is like having her rise from the dead and be young again. In this entry, it is 1955. She is a woman in love with a man who, over forty years later, would become Queenie's husband. A hot flash hits Queenie just as she starts to read the next entry, and she resists throwing the book against the wall. Queenie closes it but then opens it again. She keeps dipping into the diary and indulging her curiosity until she sees these words:

October 1956
    Welcome, Rose Temple, to the world. Her smile is Henry's. And her eyes are more gray than blue, like Henry's, too.

"Sweet Jesus," Queenie whispers. A tear drops onto the page.

The tea leaves were right. It suddenly feels like the ground is no longer under Queenie's feet, and she isn't sure how to get it back.

Why would Spud lie to her about when the affair with Iris started? Queenie has never known Spud to outright lie to her. Never. Lying is something Iris would do to cover her tracks. But why would Spud agree to it? And why would he continue the lie after Iris died? But didn't Queenie continue her lie after Oscar died? Queenie stifles a scream.

Rose must have read this and been—what—devastated? She hasn't said anything to Spud, or Queenie would know about it. But Rose must have told Violet.

Queenie closes the diary, puts the book back the way she found it, and walks to the big house. If Spud knows, she'll be able to tell. His world will be topsy-turvy, too. Queenie goes to her bedroom, where Spud sleeps in the chair as he does every afternoon about this time. Queenie closes the door again, knowing that he is blissfully unaware of how his life is about to change. Queenie walks back downstairs and instinctively grabs her car keys and purse. She needs to go somewhere to be alone and think this through, but she isn't sure where.

Queenie gets in the car and starts to drive. All she wants is to get as far away as possible from this news and Savannah and Dolphin Island. She drives off the island and merges onto the interstate going north.

21

ROSE

"What did Queenie want?" Max unleashes the dogs and lets them run into the cottage.

"What do you mean?" Rose asks. "Queenie was here?"

"I left her here in the kitchen waiting for you about thirty minutes ago."

"You did? Did she say what it was about?"

"Nope. But she seemed kind of different. Antsy."

He kisses Rose on the cheek and announces that he will be in the toolshed. He has projects to work on.

Rose tells him to have fun. Then she picks up the telephone and calls Queenie's number that rings in her bedroom. When Spud picks up, Rose hangs up the phone, surprising herself.

Well, that was brilliant, she tells herself.

Hearing Spud's voice throws her. This man isn't just Spud now, but her biological father. Will she ever get used to that fact? Yet, it still feels too soon to tell him. She would be a blubbering mess. She needs courage, calmness.

Okay, focus, she tells herself.

Queenie is her first order of business. Rose thinks through different scenarios that might have brought Queenie out to see her at the cottage. A fight with Spud is unlikely. They still act like newlyweds. Boredom, perhaps— she may just need to talk. But Spud is home. She usually goes to him.

Rose walks into her studio and glances at the diary on the side table, now slightly askew.

Oh my God. Queenie knows.

Rose tries to convince herself that maybe Lucy or Ethel knocked over the diary while looking for a tennis ball under the chair. But no, something in her knows that Queenie knows. The mystery is how Queenie reacted to the news that Iris and Spud had a child together, namely Rose.

She looks out into the driveway. Queenie's car is gone. When she walks to the big house, she finds Spud making chicken salad in the kitchen. Her breath catches. It is the first time she has seen him since discovering that he is her father. Spud smiles when he sees her, acting as though nothing has changed between them. He asks about her day.

In answer to his question, Rose says, "Fine." Although *fine* is the last thing she is. However, she isn't horrible, either. *Stunned* is a more accurate descriptor. Surprised.

For the first time, Rose wonders if he ever thinks of her mother when he sees her. She is a Temple, after all, and it turns out they had a significant relationship. Rose is the daughter of the woman who broke his heart once, maybe twice.

"Have you seen Queenie?" Rose asks.

"Not lately," he says, cutting up a stalk of celery.

"Which is kind of odd, given her car is gone, and she didn't tell me she had plans this afternoon."

"She didn't leave a note?" Rose asks.

"She didn't." Spud puts the chopped celery in a bowl. "I imagine she just ran out for something and will be back any minute."

"I'm sure," Rose says, not so sure of anything these days.

At least she knows now that Queenie didn't tell Spud what she found out if indeed she did find out. He acts as normal as he always does. Not an ounce of awkwardness. It is Rose who feels awkward. Cringingly awkward.

"I forget that you know how to cook," Rose says, quickly deciding how lame her statement is.

"I was a bachelor for years," he says, looking up at her. "But I'm happy not to be a bachelor anymore." He smiles at her again.

Is he always this pleasant?

Rose pauses, unsure of what else to say. This man is her biological father. She can't stop telling herself that. With that in mind, Rose wants more than small talk. She wants to know everything about him.

"Have you lived in this area your entire life?" Rose asks.

The look he gives her is of curiosity. This isn't a question she has ever asked him.

"Yes," he says, "but I've traveled a lot."

Spud's Southern accent has softened over the years. "Do you still have family here?" The real question being: *Do I have family here?* Rose now has a whole set of relatives she never knew existed.

"Some second and third cousins," he says. "But my brother lives in Virginia, and my sister is in Tulsa."

"That's right. I met them at the wedding." *Not knowing they were my aunt and an uncle,* she tells herself. "I can't remember. Do they have children?"

Spud covers the chicken salad and puts it in the refrigerator.

"No, they don't, unfortunately," Spud says. "I would have loved to have a few nieces and nephews running around. But my sister never married, and my brother is divorced and never had children. Once the three of us go, our whole side of the Grainger family will die out."

He seems genuinely sad about this fact, but Rose isn't ready to correct him.

"You're talkative today," he says.

Rose hesitates. "I guess I realized that I didn't know anything about your family."

"Well, it's nice of you to ask." He smiles again. "How's the painting going?"

"Good," Rose says, although her painting plans are now on hold. "Whenever Queenie gets back, could you tell her I'm looking for her?"

"Of course," Spud says.

When Rose steps outside, she exhales, not realizing she has been practically holding her breath. She thinks of the man she always thought of as her father. At times it seemed the only thing they shared was a desire to steer clear of Rose's mother. A feat they did expertly together, going to summer matinees or driving to the coast for an hour or two. She liked their drives the best.

Back in her studio, Rose sits in front of her work-in-progress with no interest in progressing it. She needs to talk to Queenie and see what she knows. And if by some miracle Queenie doesn't know, it may be time for Rose to tell her. As it is, this secret is already busting at the seams to get out.

Rose picks up her mother's diary to see what Queenie might have noticed.

October 1956

Welcome, Rose Temple, to the world. Six pounds, eight ounces. Compared to Edward, she is an easy baby. She doesn't look like Oscar or me, but no one seems to question the lack of resemblance. She is beautiful. Her smile is Henry's. And her eyes are more gray than blue, like Henry's, too.

Oscar is thrilled. He seems to have taken to Rose more easily than Edward, who is not thrilled with his new sister, as if he knows there is an interloper in the house. Someone who isn't who they appear to be. When we returned home from the hospital, Edward, six years of age, screamed for us to return her. Not only did this tantrum threaten to damage our eardrums, but it made Rose cry. Oscar leaned Edward over his knee and spanked him. Something he had never done before. But at least it stopped the screaming.

The last time I saw Henry, he wasn't thrilled with the news of this baby that he believes to be Oscar's, and he said he needed some time to think. My pregnancy dashed his hopes that we might someday be together. More than once, I've told him his dreams are not realistic.

I imagine he saw the announcement of Rose's birth in the Savannah newspaper last Sunday.

No wonder Edward hated me, Rose tells herself. *They bring me home from the hospital, and he gets the first spanking of his life?*

Every one of her mother's diary entries contains a revelation. Rose goes into the bathroom and looks at herself in the mirror. She smiles to see if it is like Spud's smile. To think that her mother studied Rose as an infant, trying to see the resemblance of the man she loved.

Love aside, Rose feels a surge of anger and returns to her studio. Her mother made a crucial decision to lie and not tell Rose the truth. For almost fifty years, Rose has been unknowingly living a falsehood. Now that the secret is out, what happens next?

October 1957

Yesterday was Rose's first birthday, and Sally baked a cake. We put a single candle on it and helped her blow it out. Sally and I exchanged a brief look, and it occurred to me that she probably knows that Rose isn't Oscar's child. She has a witchy quality about her that I've never liked.

In the kitchen afterward, I mentioned how much her loyalty means to me. All she said was, "Yes, ma'am," and got busy cleaning again.

Rose adores Sally. Almost too much. If I didn't need her to hold everything together, I might fire her.

Tomorrow, I am to meet Henry in Hilton Head. I have told the family that I'm going to Margo's in Charleston and have told Margo to cover my story if need be. Margo was thrilled to have my confidence, but I think it might cost me. We shall see.

Henry has refused to see me for over a year now. I wrote him a letter to get him to agree to meet me. I told him how much I missed him and that we needed to talk. I knew he wouldn't be able to resist if I got in touch with him. I forget how young he is sometimes. Fifteen years my junior. I was practically robbing the cradle when we met. He was all of twenty.

I want him back. I want to tell him how much Rose reminds me of him. I want to tell him my secret.

Did she tell Spud her secret? Rose tries to imagine Spud at twenty. A young man in love with an older woman. A wealthy older woman. What did he see in her? Nor can she imagine her mother enthralled with watching Rose as a baby. What changed? By the time Rose started elementary school, her mother had made constant corrections of her. She was to stand straighter. Walk slower. Don't run in the house. Stay quiet. Put on a dress for dinner. Rose was a Temple. Being a Temple required perfection. Rose also has a hard time imagining her mother crying over someone or even feeling rejected. The woman Rose knew was a fortress. Impenetrable. Unfeeling. And whether she told Spud her secret, the answer will have to wait. Rose is already overwhelmed. She wonders if things like this happened in other mansions in Savannah or just her own.

Rose goes to the kitchen window to see if Queenie's car is back. Spud is probably getting concerned unless Queenie has called him by now. In the meantime, Rose is tired of thinking about the revelations of the last few days. Her mother is not the person she believed her to be. Nor is Rose.

22

VIOLET

Violet answers the phone at the tea shop. It's Queenie. "Tell Spud this isn't about him," Queenie begins. "I just need some time away. Until I can get my head straight."

"Where are you?" Violet asks.

"I'm calling from a restaurant in Charleston."

"Charleston? But why?" Ava looks over at Violet as though she can tell something's up. Violet's eyes widen to confirm her suspicions.

"I don't want to talk about it right now," Queenie says. "I just need some time. Please tell Spud what I told you."

Violet agrees that she will, and before she can say anything else, Queenie hangs up.

"Everything okay?" Ava asks.

"I'm not sure," Violet says. "Something's going on with Queenie."

Ava's eyes soften. "I like Queenie. I hope she's okay."

Violet thanks her and asks Ava to cover the front while she goes back to call Rose. Rose picks up on the first ring.

"Queenie just called from Charleston. She says she needs some time away to think."

"I was afraid something like that might happen."

"What do you mean?" Violet asks.

"She must have read the diary, Vi. She was waiting for me here at the cottage, and it was sitting on a table in my studio."

Violet pauses. "Earlier today, she accused me of acting strange. She said both of us were—you and me. So, she must have known we were keeping something from her."

"This can't be good," Rose says.

Violet agrees.

"Does she know anyone in Charleston?"

"Not that I know of."

They both are quiet, but Violet's brain won't shut up. She glances out into the tea shop, seeing that Ava could use some help.

"What should we do?" Rose says finally, sounding as clueless as Violet feels.

"I guess the first thing is to tell Spud," Violet says. "He's probably worried. I'll run home after the lunch crowd clears out." She pauses. "I shouldn't have read her tea leaves," Violet adds.

"What makes you say that?"

"They predicted her world was about to turn upside down," Violet says. "And there was something about her taking a long trip. Maybe that planted a seed."

"Maybe the tea leaves were right," Rose says. "Both those things have happened."

Violet hadn't thought of that possibility. Ava comes into the back to grab some fresh scones, and Violet apologizes for taking so long, but Ava tells her not to worry.

"Have you ever known her to do this before?" Rose asks.

"Never," Violet says. "Have you?"

"Never."

"Well, I guess we just need to let her do what she needs to do," Violet says, noting a bit of worry in her voice. "I mean, she's in her sixties not a sixteen-year-old. She'll call us if she needs us, right?"

"She will," Rose says. "But I imagine she's devastated."

"Those Temples can create a ruckus even from beyond the grave," Violet says, before remembering that Rose is a Temple, too. She apologizes.

"No, you're right," Rose says.

"How are you dealing with Spud being your dad?" Violet asks.

"I asked him about where he grew up and about his family this morning," Rose says. "Talk about awkward."

"But Spud's one of the most easygoing guys on the planet," Violet says. "He probably didn't think anything of it. Are you any closer to telling him about what you learned in the diary?"

"I am," Rose says. "But now it makes more sense to focus on Queenie. How do you think he'll react?" she adds.

"He'll be worried," Violet says. "But I can't imagine Queenie staying away for that long."

However, Violet guesses that Queenie has never received news like this. Miss Temple's relationship with Spud has bugged Queenie ever since they got together. And if she found out that Spud and Miss Temple were together much longer than she thought and had a child together? Violet is worried, too.

They agree to talk later and let each other know if they

hear from Queenie. In the meantime, Violet thinks of Old Sally and suddenly knows what her grandmother would tell Rose and Violet to do: ask the ancestors for help.

23

QUEENIE

A s she used to do on her way out of Savannah, Queenie does some primal scream therapy in the car as she crosses the bridge from Charleston into Mount Pleasant, heading north on Highway 17. It gives her only momentary relief. She can't stop thinking about Iris and Spud having a child together. Queenie's only consolation is that Spud never knew.

Queenie remembers how heartbroken Rose was when Oscar died. She was away at college but came home immediately and didn't go back to school right away. What must it be like to find out that Oscar wasn't even her biological father? Queenie taps the steering wheel, thinking about what a mess we humans make with our secrets and lies.

Queenie doubts Oscar knew that Rose wasn't his child. He adored Rose as much as anyone could while pickled in expensive bourbon. Unlike Iris, however, Oscar was able to be kind. And even though Queenie felt taken advantage of by Oscar in many ways, he also looked out for her. He gave her money for Violet's upkeep, which Queenie would pass on to Old Sally. It wasn't much. But in his way, he owned up to his part. If only he hadn't insisted that Queenie never tell anyone about Violet. He threatened her with banishment and possible ruin if she did. Her story—and Violet's—may have played out differently. Regrets are horrible things any way you look at them.

Now, when Queenie least expected it, another secret has bubbled up from the past. She wonders when in the world this cauldron between the two families will finally be empty. Queenie strengthens her grip on the steering wheel and lets out another scream.

Iris must be laughing in her grave. It would be just like her half sister to rub it in. It would give Iris great pleasure if Queenie believed Iris was Spud's first and last love. Queenie's face warms.

Sitting at a red light in Mount Pleasant, Queenie lets out another full-throated scream. She glances over at a young mother in a minivan who smiles and gives Queenie a thumbs-up. Two children sit in the back seat, aghast.

It isn't like Queenie to get in her car, head up the highway, and just keep driving. When living with Iris, she used to fantasize about doing this very thing. In her fantasy, back when Queenie was working for Iris, Queenie always imagined taking Iris's giant Lincoln Town Car to New York City, or maybe even to Canada. Queenie had all manner of exit plans while she was Iris's assistant and before Violet came to work there. But once Violet was there, Queenie's wanderlust subsided, and she then had an excuse to spend more time with her daughter. A secret daughter at that time. And now Spud has a secret daughter, too.

Queenie twists her wedding ring and imagines Spud is

worried. But that doesn't stop her from being angry at him, too. What in heaven's name would cause a man to fall in love with such a vile creature as Iris Temple? While Queenie is confident that Spud loves her, this news changes everything.

At this moment, Queenie isn't so sure she trusts love anymore. She has always held back in the love department, and she isn't sure why. Even with Sally Rose, the most lovable creature on earth, Queenie is hesitant to open her whole heart.

With Spud, there are times when loving him feels almost dangerous. What if she loses him? What if he rejects her? And why does it bother her so much that Iris had him first?

Queenie wishes Old Sally were here. Her mama's presence always made her feel better. But Old Sally's death has changed everything, too. Queenie hates to desert Violet when she seems so out of sorts, but Queenie is out of sorts, too. Someone needs to tell her what a person does when they find out their enemy has had a child with her own husband. To be fair, this happened before he was Queenie's husband, but it still matters.

While Queenie can be funny and charming at times, she still can't imagine Spud—or anyone, really—genuinely wanting to take her on full-time. Queenie isn't sure why she has this pervasive lack of confidence. It doesn't help that she is brown-skinned in a white world. Or that Iris told her every day for thirty-five years the many ways in which Queenie was inadequate.

Iris. Queenie wishes she could forget that woman ever existed. But it seems her half sister is just as active in death as she was while she was alive. Always meddling. Always playing *one up* when Queenie was *one down*.

Meanwhile, Queenie drives. It's all she knows to do in this instance. She remembers a trip she took with Iris to Charleston to visit Iris's friend Margo. Iris insisted on driving, of course, leaving Queenie in the passenger seat, gritting her teeth, and holding on to the door handle until her brown knuckles turned white. They pulled up in front of one of the most impressive houses on the Battery, and Margo and Iris disappeared into another part of the house, leaving Queenie sitting in the living room all by herself. Finally, Queenie realized they had no intention of return-ing, so Queenie walked down to Market Street and watched the basket weavers—prominent black women masterful at their craft. Queenie bought a small basket for Violet that sits in their kitchen window at home.

Queenie had also walked through all sorts of shops in the market area where the people shopping all were white. While she browsed, vendors watched Queenie as though she might slip something into her pocket without paying. She was also struck by how populated the city was with the descendants of former slaves who seemingly don't hold a grudge. Queenie didn't feel that generous.

Queenie returned to Margo's house, exhausted and hungry. The middle-aged housekeeper—Molly—told her Iris and Margo had left for a dinner reservation. Her expression said: *that's what you get for trying to hang out with white folks.* But then Molly softened, perhaps realizing that Queenie had already had a rough day. She asked if Queenie might like to have some of the pot roast she made the night before. When Queenie agreed, they had a friendly conversation in the kitchen. Although, the entire time, Queenie felt tested to see if she was arrogant. Molly asked whether Queenie was a live-in servant and ate in the kitchen or the dining room with Iris. She even asked the amount of money Queenie made, but Queenie thought it was none of her business and told her so.

Why is she thinking of something that happened twenty years ago? Perhaps she is being tested again. No matter how much happiness Queenie grasps, Iris—and others like her—seem to want Queenie to stay in her place. And what does this have to do with Spud? Probably nothing. But that doesn't stop Queenie from thinking about it. She is overthinking everything right now.

As evening approaches, Queenie realizes how tired she is and pulls up in front of a motel. Once she gets in her room, she contemplates calling home, but she isn't ready yet. Instead, she watches *Jeopardy!* and a silly movie on HBO and then turns out the light to go to sleep.

Later that night, she dreams that Iris and Spud are married and are living together in the Temple mansion with a dozen children of varying ages. All look like Spud, and wear Hawaiian shirts in kid sizes, with matching bow ties. Queenie wakes in a cold sweat. It is still dark out, and she goes to the window and pulls back the heavy curtains to look out over the lit parking lot.

From her bedroom window on Dolphin Island, Queenie can view the vast Atlantic Ocean. Sometimes she takes it for granted. Emptiness fills her stomach, and she realizes how much she misses Spud. It is the first time something has happened in their relationship that Queenie doesn't see a way through to the other side.

Fitfully, Queenie sleeps another hour or two before getting dressed and going downstairs for the continental breakfast. She microwaves a generic cheese Danish that tastes a bit like cardboard with icing. Nothing like Violet's homemade pastries. Next, she fixes a Styrofoam cup of English breakfast tea to go. Violet would never buy Styrofoam or serve bakery goods made in a factory. While Queenie's departure may not be the best timing for Violet, who now struggles with whether or not to read tea leaves, she has to admit that the tea reading Violet gave her about her life turning topsy-turvy was spot-on. Violet may end up being as good at reading tea leaves as she is at making pastries.

Meanwhile, Queenie checks out of the motel, fills her tank with gasoline, and hits the road again. To her increasing surprise, she has run away from home, and all she wants to do is drive.

24

ROSE

E veryone gathers in the kitchen of the big house for an impromptu family meeting. Rose stands next to Violet, who didn't go to the tea shop this morning. Katie, Angie, and Sally Rose are in the living room on the couch. Max and Jack sit at the kitchen table, quiet. Spud stands at the end of the table with dark circles under his eyes like he hasn't slept. Rose can't blame Queenie for hitting the pause button and taking off in her car, but it is out of character, and Spud is the one who is suffering.

Whenever Rose looks at Spud now, she sees her biological father. This news is still surprising but is not as shocking as before. Perhaps she should tell him that Queenie left because she found out this secret. Maybe it would help him understand and not worry. As soon as she has a chance, Rose will ask Violet what she thinks. So far, Violet is the only person to know besides Max and Queenie, who is suddenly on the run.

Meanwhile, Sally Rose is asking for "Key." Rose hasn't told Katie and Angie the details, either. All they know is that Queenie left. Katie has never had a grandfather. Both Max's dad and Rose's father had died before she was born, and Rose has no idea how Katie will take the news that she suddenly has one. Not to mention that Sally Rose now has a great-grandfather. Everything is evolving quickly, like an unveiling of some kind.

Rose knows that Katie likes Spud. He adores Sally Rose, and he and Queenie are always making everyone laugh.

But right now, Spud isn't laughing. He looks suddenly older, as though he is aging right in front of her.

"Should we call the highway patrol and the hospitals?" he asks.

"I don't think that's necessary," Violet says. "I think maybe Queenie just needs a little time."

"But why?" Spud looks genuinely perplexed. "She was fine yesterday morning. We were planning a picnic on the pier today. I made chicken salad. She was going to pick up croissants at the tea shop."

Rose and Violet exchange looks. They have no idea how long Queenie will stay away, and this is torturing him.

"How about we go fishing this morning?" Max says to Spud. "Take your mind off things."

"I don't think I should leave the house," Spud says. "What if she calls?"

If Queenie knew how her absence was affecting Spud, she would come home. But she doesn't know. Rose can only imagine how upset she must be that Rose's mother and Spud had a child together.

Me.

The others talk among themselves, tossing suggestions

around, and Rose asks Violet to step into the den for a moment of privacy.

"I should tell him, right?" Rose can't stand seeing Spud suffer.

"Are you ready to do that?"

"What choice do I have?" Rose says. "He needs to understand why Queenie has taken off."

"The news will throw him." Violet looks worried.

"But it's better than him thinking that Queenie has left him, right?"

"It's impossible to know."

They pause, waiting for ideas to come.

"Maybe you could read my tea leaves, and we could ask them what to do," Rose says.

"Tea leaves? Are you sure that would be helpful?" Violet looks like this is the last thing she wants to do.

"Well, your first reading was very accurate," Rose says.

When they return to the kitchen, the others are dispersing. The consensus is to let Queenie have more time to get in touch, although worried looks abound.

Spud is the last one left in the kitchen. "I'm going to research the internet to see what to do when someone goes missing," he says.

"I thought you were going fishing with Max and Jack," Violet says.

"I couldn't possibly," he says. "Not with my sugarplum out there somewhere."

Violet hugs him, making him promise to tell her if he needs her.

Spud says he will and goes upstairs.

Meanwhile, Rose doesn't believe Queenie is missing at all. She just needs time to think and put this news in a proper place in her mind before she can move past the shock of it. Rose can relate.

"Okay, let's do this," Violet says, putting on the teakettle.

Rose thanks her. After she drinks her tea, Rose turns the cup over on the saucer as Violet instructs her. Then Violet opens the Gullah Book of Secrets to the pages that describe the formations and how to read the tea leaves.

"Before we do anything, we need to ask the ancestors for help," Violet says.

"Tea leaves involve the ancestors?"

"Always," Violet says. "We need their blessing *and* wisdom."

Rose wishes Old Sally were here and feels a momentary sadness.

"What if it says something bad?" Rose asks.

"Then we'll deal with it," Violet says.

Having experienced tea leaves only one other time, Rose remains skeptical. But she can be shortsighted when trying new things, even if they are an ancient practice, and her gut tells her it's worth a try.

Violet stares into the cup and consults her book again.

"It's showing blue skies and openness in the present," Violet says. "The future is a question mark. Nothing definite there. And the past is showing a bridge of some kind."

"Does that mean I should tell him or not?"

Violet pauses, furrowing her brow. "I'm not sure. But at least it doesn't show anything disastrous happening. At least not today."

"I guess nothing disastrous sounds promising." Rose looks at the leaves in the cup and sees nothing but a bunch of tea leaves sticking to the sides. But she trusts Violet's intuition, even if Violet doesn't.

"So, how exactly do I tell him?" Rose's confidence is waning.

"Ultimately, this is something that you need to decide. But the tea leaves are saying everything will be okay."

Rose thanks her again, and Violet wishes her luck. When Rose returns to the cottage to get her mother's diary, Max is in the kitchen, making himself a ham sandwich for lunch. She tells him of her plan to tell Spud.

He pauses as he puts on the mayo. "Are you sure you're up for this?" he asks.

"I've had time to get used to the idea," Rose says. "Now I'm worried he won't believe me."

"You mean you're afraid he won't want you as a daughter?" Max asks.

"I know it's silly," Rose says.

Max assures her that Spud will be thrilled. Rose hopes he is right.

In her studio, Rose rereads the diary entries that changed everything a couple of days before. Second thoughts come. Maybe she should wait and read the entire diary to see what else her mother might say about the situation. But Spud needs relief now, and that is what Rose hopes to give him.

But first, there are the logistics. How do you tell an unsuspecting father that you are his long-lost daughter? Spud will probably be as surprised by this news as she was. It takes an hour to work up the courage, but Rose walks over to the big house and knocks on Queenie and Spud's bedroom door. When he calls to her to come in, Rose finds him sitting at their computer in the far corner of the room, wearing his reading glasses and gazing at the screen.

"Can I talk to you?" Rose's voice quavers with the prospect of telling him this news. "It's important," she adds.

Spud looks up from the computer screen, peering at her from over his glasses. "Have you heard from Queenie?" He looks even more tired than he did earlier.

"No," Rose says. "But I think I can help you understand why she left."

Spud stands immediately, and Rose suggests they talk on the front porch. Spud agrees as Rose leads the way. In the living room, she glances at the portrait she painted of Old Sally. Rose could use her counsel right now.

Outside, clouds are rolling in, and the wind has picked up. Afternoon thunderstorms are frequent this time of year, and it looks like one is blowing in. Whenever Rose comes out on the porch, she always looks at the empty rocker where Old Sally sat, almost expecting her to be there.

Rose sits in one of the other rockers and pulls one over for Spud. She places the diary on the table between them and takes a deep breath to exhale her nervousness.

"How can I help you, Rose?" Kindness is in his eyes, along with fatigue.

"I need to fill in a few puzzle pieces regarding Queenie."

"That would be nice," he says.

Rose looks over at Old Sally's rocker again to ask for courage. "A few weeks ago, I found a diary in the Temple bank vault," Rose says. "It was my mother's."

"Yes, Max mentioned that before we went to Hilton Head."

"He did?"

"Yes," Spud says. He motions to the book in front of them. "Is that it?"

"It is," Rose says, suddenly forgetting the words she practiced.

"What does this have to do with Queenie?" Spud asks.

Though Spud may have been in love with Rose's mother many years ago, it is evident to Rose that whatever feelings he had, Queenie has long ago replaced them.

"A few days ago, I told Queenie about the diary, and I shared a couple of entries with her," Rose says.

"I can't imagine that went over very well. Queenie hates Iris." Spud uses the present tense as if Rose's mother isn't entirely in the past.

"Before Queenie left, she was in the cottage alone, and I think she may have read the next few entries."

Spud turns his head as though trying to solve a riddle.

"And what was in those entries?" He looks genuinely curious.

Rose glances at Old Sally's rocker again.

"Please, just say it." Spud's shoulders relax as though surrendering to whatever is coming.

"It seems—"

Rose's heartbeat flutters like a bird she held as a girl on a summer day like today. It had accidentally flown into Old Sally's big picture window and lay on the sand below.

Everything will be okay, Rose told the bird, cradling it in her palms. Eventually, the bird was able to recover from its shock and fly away. But Rose has never forgotten its rapid heartbeat in her hands. She tells herself the same message.

Even if Spud rejects her, Rose will be okay. Her heart will mend.

"My mother didn't tell you the truth about her second pregnancy," Rose begins, her words softer than she intends. "It was your child she birthed. Not my father's."

Spud doesn't speak. His eyes move as though he is calculating dates. His reaction is a nonreaction. Like the bird, Spud has flown into a window of the past and is now stunned.

"I couldn't believe it, either," Rose begins after a long silence. "I can show you in the diary. She has several entries about deceiving you because she doesn't think you could have ever kept it a secret. And other entries where she talks about how much I look like you at certain times."

"Yes, please, I'd like to see them." His mouth opens as though he might say more if he hadn't forgotten how to form words.

Rose opens her mother's diary to the page where she goes to Charleston to take the pregnancy test and hands it to him. He reads and rereads the pages. When he finally looks up, his eyes are rimmed in red.

"I'm not sure what to say." Spud looks out at the horizon as though posing more significant questions to the universe. Then he hands back the diary. "And you think Queenie read about this?"

Rose nods. "She's probably upset that you and my mother had a child together."

"Oh, heavens, yes," Spud says, sounding for a moment like Queenie.

In the next second, Spud takes Rose's hand, his palm warm in hers. There is acceptance. Tears come to her eyes and quickly roll down her cheeks. They sit in comfortable silence for several minutes as the waves keep time to how their lives have changed. Their initial awkwardness fades, along with Rose's tears.

When Spud speaks again, his words are full of emotion. "It has been the great sorrow in my life that I didn't have children. Or I thought that I didn't."

They squeeze hands as though affirming the grief of lost time. Another long silence follows. When Spud speaks again, his words are softer than she expects. "I am thrilled beyond words to learn that you are my daughter, Rose."

With this, she begins to cry in earnest. Spud hands her a blue bandanna handkerchief from his pants pocket. She blows her nose and wipes her eyes, laughing at herself for this uncharacteristic sudden downpour of emotion. Spud reassures her that she has every right.

"I don't blame Queenie for taking off," Spud begins again. "I have things to atone for. I lied to Queenie about the length of time I was with Iris. I lied to Violet, too. Iris was good at covering her tracks and didn't want anyone to know about the early days. I'm sure you know how persuasive your mother could be when she wanted something. But that doesn't let me off the hook at all. I shouldn't have lied."

"Mother could be quite manipulative," Rose says.

The exchange a look of agreement.

"That's why Queenie is so upset. I didn't tell her the truth. But I swear to you, Rose, I had no idea. No idea."

Rose tells him she believes him, which is true.

"It's a total betrayal that she didn't tell me." His jaw gets firm. Rose imagines he will get angry next, as she did. Rose predicts that finally knowing the truth will bring many emotions for both of them, including anger.

"I thought I should tell you," Rose says.

"Yes, it makes sense now," Spud says. "She needs time away to make peace with it. And as soon as she returns or gets in touch, I have an apology to make. I hope she can forgive me for lying to her."

"I think she can," Rose says. "But it may take time."

Spud stands. "I'm so glad you told me, Rose. It must have been hard for you."

"It was," Rose says.

"If you don't mind, I think I'll take a walk on the beach and let it all settle in," Spud says. "But first." He opens his arms, and they embrace. It is their first hug where both of them know Spud is her birth father.

"We have so much to talk about, Rose," he says.

She agrees.

He smiles at her before walking toward the beach, and it feels like the beginning of something important.

Once Spud leaves, Rose takes her mother's diary from the small table between the rocking chairs to return it to her studio. Perhaps she found the diary because her mother finally wanted to set things right. Rose wants to believe that redemption is possible. Even for her mother.

25

VIOLET

"How did it go?" Violet steps onto the porch as soon as she sees Spud walk through the dunes.

"He was shocked, of course. But he also seemed moved," Rose says.

"You're so lucky," Violet says. "I wish he were my father, too."

"Our family lineage has always been interesting, although confusing," Rose says.

It is no longer the case that Rose and Violet share the same father, but that doesn't make them feel any less like sisters. They walk back inside and sit at the kitchen table. It is tranquil—one of those rare moments when nobody is around.

"How do we get Queenie back?" Violet has already lost one family member and can't bear to lose another.

"She's got a lot to think about," Rose says. "Spud regrets lying to her about how long he and Mother were together. He will ask her forgiveness as soon as she gets back."

"He lied to me, too, if they were together for years before they reunited after your wedding," Violet says. What she doesn't say is that he owes her an apology, too.

Rose asks about tea leaves, but Violet doesn't want to talk about that now. She hates how scared she is without Old Sally here to encourage her.

"It's always surprised me how insecure Queenie can be when it came to Spud and Miss Temple's relationship," Violet says, choosing to speak of Queenie's insecurities instead of her own. "Does she not realize how much he loves her?"

"Working for Mother all those years must have taken a toll," Rose says.

Violet agrees that Miss Temple could be a bully sometimes, and especially to Queenie.

"My mother insisted on having the upper hand in every situation," Rose says. "Which is odd because it turns out that she was living a life that wasn't her first choice."

"Not everything that glitters is gold," Violet says. "Even the wealthy and powerful have their demons and angels."

"You sound like Old Sally," Rose says.

Violet lowers her eyes, her face warming. Old Sally would not hesitate to read a few tea leaves to help her friends or even strangers. She would do anything to help someone. Yet Violet can't seem to get there. It seems impossible to fill the void her grandmother left behind, and something in Violet doesn't even see the point. She will never be her grandmother. All she has is a sensitive shoulder and a book of Gullah folk magic that she rarely uses.

"I guess Queenie will come back when she's good and ready," Rose says.

"I'll tell her that Spud knows the next time she calls," Violet says. "That might speed things along."

"No pun intended?" Rose smiles.

"No pun intended," Violet says. "You look tired," she adds.

"To be honest, I feel like I just climbed Mount Everest. Who knew that telling someone that they are your real father could be so exhausting?"

They laugh, and Violet appreciates the lightness. Life has become so heavy in the last year.

Before Rose returns to the cottage, Violet promises to let Rose know when Queenie calls again.

In the meantime, Violet goes to find Jack in his home office, sitting at his desk. He is working on Spud's accounting from the jazz club. He asks if Violet has heard from Queenie.

"Not yet." Violet leans over and kisses his cheek.

"You feeling better? You haven't been sleeping that great." Jack swivels toward her in his office chair.

"I'll get there," Violet says with a sigh, thinking, *Will I?* "Where are the girls?" she asks.

"Bowling alley." He rolls his eyes.

"They're gone constantly these days," Violet says.

"I think they're practicing for the Big Goodbye," Jack says.

The look they exchange is of parents who have spent two decades raising kids and all the worries that come with it. Launching them into the world in a few weeks will open a different set of concerns, but perhaps blessings, too.

Violet reminds herself to lean toward the blessings.

"I hope Queenie hasn't made a Big Goodbye," Violet says.

Jack's confusion prompts Violet to tell him about the latest diary revelations. He leans back in his chair, his eyes widening. "Wow. Spud must be blown away."

"Rose, too," Violet says. "If Queenie calls, tell her to call me at the shop, okay?"

"Definitely." Then Jack says, "Wow," again before swiveling around to his desk.

While driving to the tea shop, Violet can't stop thinking about how out of character it is for Queenie to run away. But if Violet knows anything for sure, it's that when secrets come to light, people do unexpected things. It was Queenie, after all, who kept the truth from Violet. Now Queenie is experiencing something similar.

Meanwhile, Violet stands on the threshold of something and doesn't know whether to walk through or turn away. Her grandmother is gone, her mother is missing, and her shoulder predicts something terrible is coming. Where are her ancestors when she needs them?

26

QUEENIE

Q ueenie stops at a grocery store in Virginia Beach to buy herself a Styrofoam cooler to put in some drinks and snacks. According to Oprah, junk food is how we deaden our anger and sadness. If this is true, Queenie must have a lot of it, along with disappointment. Disappointment in Iris that she lied to everyone involved. Disappointment in Spud, who lied to Queenie about the details of his affair with Iris. Disappointment in herself that these things even matter.

Iris and Spud were together longer than Queenie thought. He should have told her before their wedding. Maybe by that time, he had forgotten all about it. The news wouldn't have gone over well with Queenie and probably would have stopped the wedding no matter the timing.

Other than driving and thinking, Queenie has no plan. After filling her cooler in the trunk, she sees a phone booth in the Food Lion parking lot and thinks about calling home. About six months ago, Spud offered to get her one of those newfangled car phones, but she rarely drove anywhere, except occasionally to Savannah and back, and most of the time, they took Spud's newer car. Now she sees the convenience of carrying a phone in the car. She will have to remember this if she ever runs away from home again.

Queenie imagines Spud is worried about her. However, she still can't seem to bring herself to call him. Maybe she wants him to suffer more.

Queenie sniffs back tears and attempts to crunch her disappointment away with the help of a handful of chips. Unfortunately, they are simply making her feel sadder.

Before hitting the open road again, Queenie has second thoughts at the traffic light and makes a U-turn. She doubles back to the phone booth and parks. A cemetery of cigarette butts litters the ground in front of it. She tiptoes over them, trying not to get any on her shoes.

After looking at her watch, Queenie realizes that Violet is getting ready to close the tea shop. She inserts several quarters and dials the number. Ava answers and then hands the phone to Violet.

"I'm so glad you called." Violet sounds relieved, as though she wasn't so sure she would hear from her again. "I know you're so upset."

"Rose told you?"

"Yes. She's concerned about you. We all are."

"I'm fine," Queenie says, though *fine* is reaching. "I'm still pissed as hell, though. And tired," she adds. It is not like her to be this honest, but her backside is hurting from all the driving, and she is hungry for real food.

"Come home, Mama," Violet says as if knowing that

the *mama* will get Queenie's attention. Even after all these years, Violet still calls her "Queenie" most of the time.

"How's Spud?" Queenie asks.

"Worried to death."

"Good," she says, even though holding something against Spud that happened over forty years ago doesn't seem entirely fair.

"Rose and Spud talked today," Violet begins. "Spud had no idea."

Queenie scoffs. "Iris was an expert at keeping secrets," she says, reaching for a Kit Kat bar. "As far as I knew, they were just together for a brief time after Rose's wedding. Now it turns out that they had a child together twenty years earlier?"

Queenie hears Violet's sigh through the telephone line. Her mother's breakdown is probably the last thing she wants to be dealing with right now, considering everything else going on.

"Why Spud was keeping that secret even after she was dead is what I want to know," Queenie says, unable to let it go.

"He regrets it now," Violet says. "He wants you to come home so he can apologize and explain."

"What possible explanation could he have for lying to me?"

"At least hear him out," Violet says, sounding tired.

Queenie wonders how life got so complicated and exhausting.

Bells jingle in the background. "I'll let you go. You have a customer."

"Ava will take care of them. Tell me how you are."

Queenie pauses and looks down at the cigarette butts

feeling like Iris snuffed her out with her fancy old-lady shoes. "It feels like Iris won again. All my life, she's been winning."

"But Spud loves you, not her."

"Does he?"

"You know he does."

An automated voice tells Queenie to add more quarters, and they pause as she does.

"I'll come home eventually," Queenie says. "I'm just not ready to come back yet."

"Where are you?" Violet asks.

Queenie hesitates and then wonders why the secrecy. It's not like she robbed a bank or anything. "I'm in Virginia Beach."

"That's over seven hours away," Violet says.

"Tell me about it," Queenie says. "My butt's been numb since Pawleys Island."

Violet suggests that Queenie slow down and spend the night in Virginia Beach.

Queenie must admit she likes the idea of getting horizontal for a while. Her back is giving her fits. She has no idea where she is headed, anyway. She will have to turn around when she reaches Canada because she doesn't have a passport. Or maybe she doesn't need one. She doesn't even know. Queenie is already the farthest north she has ever been.

"Please consider it," Violet says.

"How's Rose?" Queenie asks, thinking how odd it must be to find out Oscar wasn't her father, after all.

"She's adjusting," Violet says. "I mean, Miss Temple did a number on her, too."

"Iris did a number on all of us." Queenie feels her

anger growing again and pops the top on a soda amid growing telephone static.

"Promise me you'll spend the night?" Violet says.

It occurs to Queenie that she already knows her options. She can keep driving until she runs out of land, or she can go home. At the moment, going home sounds pretty good. If for no other reason than to have her bathroom back instead of using McDonald's restrooms. More importantly, Queenie misses her makeshift tribe. Family and friends who range in age from toddlers to baby boomers. It doesn't help that she hasn't had a good snuggle with Sally Rose in over twenty-four hours, not to mention her husband.

Violet reminds Queenie again of how much Spud loves her and how worried he is about her.

"I'm just so tired of Iris being a part of our story," Queenie says.

"What can I do to help?" Violet asks.

The sincerity in her daughter's voice causes a lump of emotion in Queenie's throat. But that doesn't bring her any closer to knowing what to do.

"What would Oprah do?" Violet asks.

Queenie can almost hear her smiling through the phone and wonders why she didn't ask herself this question. She pauses, already knowing the answer. Oprah would take the time to get clear on what she needed. Then she would go and have a conversation with Stedman or, in Queenie's case, Spud. Relationships are complicated, and there are bound to be bumps in the interstate.

"I'll spend the night here in Virginia Beach and head back in the morning," Queenie says finally.

"Really? Can I tell Spud?" Violet says.

Queenie says she can.

"He will be so relieved," she says. "We all will. We love you, Queenie. Home is not the same without you."

"I've missed you, too." Queenie's shoulders relax. After they say their goodbyes, Queenie realizes that running away doesn't solve anything. A fact she knew all along. After she gets some rest, she will turn the car around and head south. Iris be damned. Everyone she loves is waiting for her on Dolphin Island. Queenie is going home.

27

ROSE

Violet calls Rose with the news that Queenie will be returning tomorrow. They share their relief. Afterward, Rose sits in her studio with a cup of herbal tea to read. She has reserved the afternoon and evening for finishing up her mother's diary entries. She wants it over. If there is anything else Queenie needs to know about, Rose will show it to her.

Meanwhile, Spud has been in his bedroom all afternoon. Perhaps he needs some time to think about Rose being his daughter and the news that Queenie is coming home.

Before opening the diary, Rose takes a deep breath to prepare herself for what might come, but then jumps when she sees Max standing in the doorway.

"You startled me," Rose says, stating the obvious.

He apologizes. "You seemed mesmerized."

"I was." She doesn't tell him of her mission to finish the diary. He announces he's going to bed. She tells him she's not tired yet.

"Big day?" Max looks at her as if to determine if he should hide the car keys. Will she go in search of another bottle of wine?

"It was," she says in a reassuring tone. Over dinner, Rose told him about her talk with Spud.

"I'm glad Queenie's coming back." Max wears flip-flops now instead of slippers. Black ones. She always knows where he is in the cottage because of the flopping sound of his shoes. She is surprised he was able to startle her earlier. He walks over to hug her.

"Don't stay up too late," he says before turning to walk away.

"I won't," she says, knowing she probably will.

Her tea already cold, Rose returns to the diary. As soon as she starts to read, her mother's voice comes alive again.

November 1965

Years have passed since I've written in this silly book. I hardly see the point of it. My life is not the least bit interesting. Even my travel these days involves something to do with the family. A networking thing. Or a donation where a roomful of people pretend to care about me.

Mommy and Daddy passed away within a year or so of each other. Since then, I haven't had a chance to catch my breath. Managing the Temple estate and philanthropic endeavors is a full-time job. Not to mention all those secrets. It would be helpful if Oscar were of use. But Oscar has a life of his own at this point. He goes out when he feels like it, has friends I have never met, and stays in his office drinking until all hours. We haven't slept together for years. Meanwhile, I have started going to the Piggly Wiggly on Fridays to see my favorite butcher.

Rose grew up knowing that her parents were not close. From a young age, she surmised her father was miserable. Now she realizes that her mother was the same. A tragic story for many afraid to question the status quo.

The cottage quiet, Rose goes into the kitchen to rewarm her herbal tea. She looks out the window to see a half-moon. The natural world seems to know what it's doing, much more than humans. When she returns to her studio, she begins again.

July 1970

I went into the kitchen just now to adjust the menu for this evening, and there was Sally and Rose laughing so hard they couldn't catch their breath. I asked what was so funny, and they stopped instantly. I can't remember the last time I laughed.

At that moment, Rose looked so much like Henry, with her big smile, that I tried not to gasp. To make matters worse, Sally gave me a look, with that Gullah way of hers, that said: I know your secrets.

Rose seems more at home with the servants than she does with me. Maybe that's the riffraff part of her. (I sound more and more like Mommy!)

At least Mommy and Daddy now rest in the Temple mausoleum and are impervious of gossip. If word got out about who Rose's father is, the scandal would wreck the family.

Edward is off to military school in the fall. I can't say I will miss him.

Rose wonders if Edward read their mother's diary. He spent time going through the safety deposit box and the books of secrets. Did he read Mother's disdain for him and decide to release those secrets to the newspaper for spite? Could this have been his motivation for also burning down the Temple mansion? Rose thought Edward was the favored child all these years, which doesn't appear to be true.

Rose glances at the small clock sitting on the shelf of her bookcase. It is approaching midnight, but she can't seem to stop reading. Thumbing through the second half of the book, Rose notices the entries get shorter and shorter. It shifts to become more of a business diary for listing events she has attended and menus for events held at the mansion—dry details instead of juicy admissions.

She turns the page. More years have passed.

December 1978

I hired Henry's quartet to play at Rose's wedding. It was so wonderful to hear him play again. Even Rose seemed to enjoy it. I have fallen out of favor with her over the years. She resists every instruction on how to be a Temple. Like me, she has rebelled from expectations, refusing to marry into the right family. Instead, she chooses a cowboy! Western riffraff!

When I paid Henry for the wedding, I asked him if we could see each other again, if only for dinner. He agreed, and I wondered at the time if he felt sorry for me. We are to meet next weekend in Hilton Head, at the place we used to meet. What he doesn't know is that I own the site now. I bought the property years ago purely for nostalgic reasons. If only I could go back and do my life over again.

Rose wakes in the chair at 2 a.m., the diary still in her hand. Her mother wanted a do-over?

`Rose imagines that as the Temple name became more prominent in Savannah, her mother lost more and more of herself. Rose turns to the book's final entry. It is dated shortly before her mother had the stroke that led to her death.

March 2000

Who is releasing those stupid secrets in the newspapers? My attorney says nothing can be done. I feel physically ill from all that is happening. I just rattle around this big old house every day; it should have burned down when Sherman's army came through on his way to the sea. If I'd had the nerve, I would have burned this place to the ground myself after Mommy and Daddy died. I also should have married Henry when I had the chance. It seems my entire existence has been about keeping all the ghosts happy while I grow more miserable every day. I've decided to make things right in my will. That will give me the last word. Maybe this will finally lay all those ghosts to rest.

Rose closes the diary and hugs it close to her chest. Minutes later, Rose slides into bed next to Max. She exhales the tension she has been holding while reading her mother's diary. To her surprise, there was also a life-changing revelation hidden within the pages. Not only is Spud her biological father, but her mother was someone who gave up on love and a life she could call her own. Her mother's entire purpose was being who her parents wanted her to be. She was the prisoner of a name—a prisoner of affluence and what was expected of her. Rose left Savannah so that the same thing didn't happen to her, and now she has returned to live a life her mother wished she could have had. Not as just an artist, but someone free to find her purpose.

As a result, no one ever knew the *real* Iris Temple, especially Rose, her only daughter. But in the end, even she wanted to make things right. A final act of redemption.

28

VIOLET

Last night, Violet dreamed of Old Sally. In the dream, Violet was searching for her and finally found her grandmother on the edge of a faraway cliff overlooking the ocean. Her back was to Violet. Repeatedly, Violet called her name, but Old Sally wouldn't turn around. Violet became so frantic in her calling in the dream that it forced her awake.

Later, at the tea shop, Violet can't shake the image from her mind. What will it take for Old Sally to turn and look at her again? Violet feels deserted by her Gullah ancestors and void of Gullah folk magic even on her best days. It is an emptiness she wouldn't wish on anyone. But at least Queenie is driving back to Dolphin Island today, which is one less thing to cause her to worry.

The bells jingle, and Marylou enters. She was already here earlier this morning, but her countenance has changed.

"I need to get that reading today," she says to Violet

with a tap of her silver cane. Her dancer's body is perfectly poised. "I need some clarity."

"I thought we had plenty of time," Violet says, feeling suddenly anxious.

"My son showed up after lunch unexpectedly. He's adamant that I move to Chicago."

Violet wants to help Marylou, but she isn't ready for this. She thinks of the dream again. Why wouldn't her grandmother turn and face her? What does Violet need to do to get her attention?

"We'll need to use a loose-leaf tea." Violet's shoulder responds, which feels more like a nudge than a pain.

Marylou smiles. While Violet readies the tea, Ava agrees to take over the front counter. It is after three o'clock, and business has slowed. Violet suggests they sit at a table in the courtyard and promises to join her when the tea is ready.

Violet walks Marylou through each step of the process, which is getting easier to remember and starting to make sense. By the time Violet looks into Marylou's cup, the tea leaves have already formed their message. Momentarily muddled, Violet questions whether she can do this. More than anything, she doesn't want to let Marylou down.

"Claim it," Marylou whispers as though sensing Violet's hesitation.

The words have a startling effect. Violet looks at her.

"I used to teach young dancers at Julliard," she begins, "and I could always tell which ones hadn't fully claimed their gifts. They always hesitated somewhere during the routine. They didn't trust themselves."

"And you think that's what I'm doing?" Violet asks.

"If the ballet slipper fits," Marylou says with a wink.

They exchange a smile. Violet's grandmother believed that messengers were everywhere if only we trained ourselves to notice. Perhaps Marylou is delivering something Violet needs to hear.

"Shall we do this?" Marylou asks.

Violet nods. "Did you want to ask a specific question?"

Marylou pauses only briefly. "I want to know what's on the horizon for me."

Looking into the teacup, Violet asks her Gullah ancestors to join her in the reading, including Old Sally. At first, the tea leaves' formations look like a puzzle just out of the box where it is impossible to discern which pieces are sky and sea. A wave of panic rises and falls as her mind grapples with the chaos. Then Violet realizes that it isn't her mind that needs to be engaged but her heart.

Claim it, she tells herself, closing her eyes to center herself.

When she opens her eyes again, the patterns of the leaves begin to make sense to her and become transparent.

"You are in a perfect place to begin something new," Violet says, translating to Marylou what the leaves are telling her. "Everything is lining up."

Marylou leans toward the cup that Violet is holding, her eyes steady. If she is alarmed by this initial reading, her face doesn't show it. If anything, she seems intrigued.

"Timing is important," Violet continues. "But also passion. Energy."

Marylou nods as though letting her words sink in. "Can I ask questions?" Marylou asks.

"Of course," Violet says.

"Is this new venture here in Savannah or Chicago?"

Violet peers into the cup. She wants Marylou to stay

here, but she also wants what is best for Marylou. She works to remove herself from the reading, asking her ancestors and the tea leaves to take over and clarify.

"They are telling me here," Violet says.

"What will stand in my way?" Marylou asks.

Violet isn't entirely sure what she means, but that doesn't seem to matter. The tea leaves are speaking, not her.

"What stands in your way is second-guessing yourself," Violet answers. "Waiting too long to act."

Marylou's eyes widen, and she sits back in the wrought-iron chair. Violet relaxes, too. The reading feels over. Violet places the cup back on the saucer and takes a deep breath. When she looks at Marylou, her shoulders have relaxed.

Marylou smiles again. "You don't know this about me, but those are exactly my challenges when it comes to just about every decision in my life."

"Well, the tea leaves seem to be encouraging you to act," she says. "To not put something off."

Marylou thanks her and then laughs as though experiencing a momentary joy. "See, you're a natural."

Violet is still not convinced, but she likes that Marylou thinks so.

"You've inspired me," Marylou begins. "I now know that this isn't the time to move to Chicago, and my son will just have to cope with that. I've known for years that I've got more I want to do here in Savannah."

Violet can't remember the last time she inspired someone.

"I have another question," Marylou says, sitting forward again. "Would you consider having some different kinds of readings here? In addition to your tea readings."

In addition to her tea readings? Violet suddenly feels as though she is in the deep end of the pool with questionable swimming skills.

"Poetry readings," Marylou continues, "small dance recitals, music, art showings, and possibly some author readings. I've had this idea for years, and your tea shop would be the perfect place for it."

"We close at five o'clock," Violet says. "Aren't poetry readings usually in the evenings?"

"They are," Marylou says. "You would have to stay open later, one day a week."

Violet isn't the type to jump into ventures quickly. It took her twenty-five years to start her tea shop. But perhaps it is the time for her to claim more and not second-guess herself, too. Violet invites Marylou to tell her more about what she is thinking. They speak of how many people might attend and the hours they would need to stay open.

Violet likes the idea of her tea shop being not only a tea shop but a place for the community to gather, and she has a brief awareness that Old Sally might, too. From the beginning, Marylou has encouraged the tea leaf readings. But she needs to think this through.

After thanking Violet again, Marylou leaves, her countenance changed from before the tea reading. Violet and Ava clean tables, vacuum, count money, and get ready to close. Violet can't stop thinking about Marylou's suggestion.

While her early tea readings with Rose and Queenie were awkward, Marylou's was different. Violet could feel a remarkable shift. A shift away from her insecurities and into a deep desire to help the other person.

While Violet was growing up, a steady stream of people visited their small house by the sea. They were Old Sally's customers, at least two or three a week, from all over the country. They would sit and talk with Old Sally on the porch and then carry out small jars of elixirs for whatever ailed them.

Before she left, Marylou offered to pay her for the reading, but Violet refused. Money never changed hands when Old Sally offered her Gullah services. Yet people often left things for her at the house: a dozen fresh eggs, fresh fish, a bucket of blueberries, handfuls of flowers, or whatever they had to give. Old Sally always made them a cup of tea, too, and read what the tea leaves had to say about the directions of their lives. As far as Violet knows, Old Sally never questioned herself about whether she should be doing Gullah magic or not. She was a Gullah healer. A medicine woman. Perhaps Violet is, too. Maybe she is being asked to accept this legacy as her own.

29

QUEENIE

As she merges onto the road that leads to Dolphin Island, Queenie lets out a huge sigh. She has missed her home. She has also missed her husband. Thankfully, as the miles added up, her anger and upset has lessened. But they still need to talk.

Queenie finds Spud sitting in a chair on the back porch waiting for her when she pulls into the driveway. He wears his usual straw hat and one of his Hawaiian shirts that replaced his bow ties when he retired. He stands when he sees her and walks to the car before she has a chance to get out. Queenie's bottom lip quivers, but she tells herself not to weep.

Spud opens the door for her, and she steps past him, avoiding a hug. She isn't ready for that yet, though her body wants nothing more. After they got together, the feeling of Spud's body against hers made her instantly relax. It wasn't about weakness but rightness. Queenie and Spud are meant to be together. She is sure about that. But even paradise sometimes requires a pause.

Spud's expression is full of relief and love, and he looks like he might cry, too.

"It's good to be home, but we need to have a conversation." Queenie puts her arm out like a school-crossing guard to make sure Spud keeps his distance. But he isn't the type to storm barricades.

"Where would you like to talk?" he asks softly.

Queenie pauses. "Could we take a walk on the beach? I've been driving for three days, and I need to stretch my legs."

Spud agrees and motions for her to go first as they take the walkway toward the dunes. When they get to the beach, Queenie turns toward the cemetery instead of the lighthouse. Was it only two years ago that Hurricane Iris sent them running for their lives?

Iris. Always Iris. Queenie has been battling that woman for forty years. What will it take to make peace with her finally?

Their walk isn't like the power walks people take along the shoreline. With Queenie and Spud, it is more of a Southern mosey. They are tortoises, not hares. Queenie has always been slow and steady, life being a marathon, not a sprint. Also, she is a late bloomer in many ways. Not only did love bloom later in life, but also contentment. Unfortunately, she doesn't feel either of those at the moment. But the motion and sound of the waves are already soothing her. It is good to be home.

"I'll let you start," she says.

Spud clears his throat and hesitates before speaking as though not wanting to mess this up.

"I was wrong not to tell you the full extent of my relationship with Iris," he begins. "She made me promise, but sometimes promises have to be broken to serve a greater truth. I wasn't thinking, and I am so sorry that I kept the truth from you and hurt you." A young couple passes holding hands, and Queenie wonders how her life might have been different if they had met when they were younger. "Iris made me swear that I wouldn't tell anyone about us," he continues. "She even threatened to make sure my quartet never got another job in Savannah. Iris could be quite manipulative when she wanted to be."

Queenie crosses her arms. *Is he just now figuring this out?*

"When you and I started dating, you were already so jealous of her I didn't dare tell you anything more than I did," Spud begins again. "I didn't want to hurt you then, and I don't want to hurt you now. I'm sorry, sugar." The look in his eyes is one of genuine remorse and causes Queenie to unfold her arms. He is right about her being jealous of Iris. They had the same father and yet had different lives. The "white" experience fell to Iris, with Queenie living in her shadow as a servant. It was Cinderella without the prince and the slipper.

Queenie stops walking and turns toward him. "Tell me the true story of your relationship with Iris. I want to know what happened."

Spud grimaces. "But I just said I don't want to hurt you."

"Sometimes the truth hurts, but it can't be any worse than letting my imagination fill in the missing pieces." Queenie hopes this is true.

Spud leads them through the dunes to a shady spot among the pines. They sit on a log, and Spud turns to her.

"Iris was the first person I ever loved," he begins. "I'd never met anyone so sophisticated, and I was so surprised when she paid attention to me." He pauses, looking out toward the sea. "She reminded me of a beautiful bird in a gilded cage," he continues. "I felt sorry for her, and I think I must have wanted to rescue her from a life she hated."

Spud looks over at Queenie as though checking to see if she wants him to continue. She tells him to keep going.

"Iris was in charge of everything," he begins again. "What we did. Where we went, what we ate, when we had sex. Everything. I didn't realize until later how I was playing a part in a drama that was her creation. And I am sad to say that not once did I complain. But I was in love with her—head over heels. At least I thought I was for a long time. But then I met you, Queenie, and I realized love was something different than what I thought."

Spud takes her hand.

"It wasn't until I met you that I knew how fake everything was with Iris because you are the real deal." He squeezes her hand, and his thin white hair blows in the ocean breeze revealing the contours of his head.

"You had no idea that Rose was your child?" Queenie asks.

"No idea," he says. "If I had known, I would have done everything in my power to be near the child. I think Iris knew that, and so she lied to me. I will never forgive her for that."

Another couple, a man and woman, stroll by the shore. The man is younger and has a beard and reminds Queenie of the couple she saw in the dunes. Whatever happened to them? Before she explores that thought, she must put her marriage back together.

"I didn't know what to do after I read Iris's diary, so I hopped in the car and started driving," Queenie says. "I was distraught. I made it to Virginia Beach before Violet talked me into coming home and talking to you."

"I'm so glad she did," Spud says.

"But what do we do now?" Queenie asks.

"Can you forgive me?" Spud asks. "I promise to never lie to you again. Not even a lie of omission."

Queenie has never seen him with so much sincerity, except for perhaps their wedding day.

"I will forgive you," Queenie says. "And I will work on my issues with Iris. What I realized while I was driving is that she wasn't any better than me, even though her life certainly seemed better."

"You're twice the person she ever was, buttercup. I wish you could see yourself the way I see you."

"I wish I could, too." Queenie sighs.

With that, Spud pulls Queenie to her feet. They face each other as if repeating their marriage vows.

"Trust me when I say that you are amazing, Queenie Temple. You are kind and funny and sincere, and the person I waited my entire life to marry. Unlike Iris, you are authentic. And if you will allow me to say it, it is my great honor to be married to you."

Queenie's face warms, and she hugs him, their bodies fitting together in that squishy, incredible way that they always do. She suggests they turn around and go home to explore the *sweet mysteries of life* again. Spud agrees.

Offshore swim a school of dolphins. Queenie thinks of Violet reading her tea leaves a few days ago and how the reading had been uncomfortable but also accurate. Her life did turn upside down, and then there was a trip. But then she returned, and the world righted itself again. A dolphin leaps out of the water in the distance as if to celebrate their reunion.

30

ROSE

R ose sits on the shady back porch of the big house drinking her morning coffee. It promises to be another hot, sticky day. Sally Rose plays in the sandbox next to the swing set. Her moms, Katie and Angie, have a session with their couples therapist in Savannah this morning. From what Rose can gather, Angie is still struggling to get over their recent fiasco with Angie's mother, who, from what Katie has told her, sounds a lot like Rose's mother.

Rose believes in therapy. She went to a Cheyenne therapist for two years to heal old wounds and understand her family dynamics. So, she is happy to keep Sally Rose while Angie and Katie get the support they need. They will also grab lunch while downtown, which will extend her time with her only grandchild.

"Can I join you?" Spud walks out the kitchen door of the main house.

For the first time in days, he looks rested. Queenie returned home yesterday. She imagines they have made amends.

"Of course," Rose says. It is still odd to acknowledge that Spud Grainger is her father, yet she is getting used to the idea. It helps that she already likes him quite a bit.

He pulls up a wooden rocker next to hers. In Rose's view, a beach house can never have too many weathered rocking chairs, and they have an ample number of ones on the front and back porches of the big house. Their cottage has a smaller front porch that is more for passing through than sitting.

"How are you and Queenie doing?" Rose asks him.

"I think we're getting back to normal," Spud says.

"I'm glad," Rose says.

Seconds pass as they watch Sally Rose. Young children give Rose hope. They are innocent, fresh, and uninitiated into the ways of the world. After 9/11, Rose didn't feel hopeful for months. Now, three years later, she is only beginning to trust the world again.

Spud hands Rose a pink envelope with her name written on it.

"What's this?"

"A little something very late in coming," he says.

Rose opens the flap of the envelope. Inside, the card says Happy Birthday, Daughter in yellow print, with a beautiful photograph of hummingbirds sipping nectar from the purple blooms of butterfly bushes.

Inside Spud has written:

This card is for all the birthdays I've missed. I look forward to all the coming years we will celebrate together.

Love, Spud

Rose thanks him and takes his hand while tears form. They hold hands for a few awkward seconds before Rose breaks contact and puts the card back into the envelope. She loved the father who raised her, and what is also true is that she has Spud's DNA inside her. This thought confuses her, as well as threatens to bring a gush of tears.

"Have you told Katie?" he asks.

"I was waiting to talk to you," Rose says. "Are you ready for everyone to know?

"Of course," Spud says, approaching exuberance. "I'm delighted that you are my daughter."

"Then I'll tell her later today," Rose says, doing her best not to gush tears. "She'll be thrilled. She's never had a grandfather. Both Max's father and mine died before she was born. And she has always liked you."

Spud smiles and shakes his head as though disbelieving of his good fortune.

Rose can't imagine what it has been like for Spud to find out he has a secret family hidden in plain view and living on the same property. Rose has the same disbelief. All this time, she has been interacting with her biological father, not even knowing it.

Sally Rose plays in the sandbox. "And to think this gorgeous child is my great-granddaughter," Spud says.

Taking a clean bandanna from his pocket, Spud wipes away fresh tears. "I've discovered that it's much easier for me to cry when I'm happy than when I'm sad," he adds.

"Me, too," Rose says. His birthday card to her was such a poignant gesture. She wonders if he fretted over the right card and if it was hard for him to give it to her.

Spud excuses himself to get Queenie. Perhaps he is as

overwhelmed by all that's happened as Rose is, with all this reshuffling of roles.

She walks over to push Sally Rose on the swing. With the swinging, her mind wanders to when Katie was the same age as Sally Rose. The only trees on their ranch in Wyoming were a line of cottonwoods down by the stream. A wooden swing hung from one of the trees. Rose's first significant gallery sales were of paintings she made of those cottonwoods. It seems only natural that she would now move on to live oaks.

Sometimes, when Rose missed Savannah, she would take Katie and a picnic and spread a blanket out under the shade of those resilient trees that had figured out how to survive in the rugged high plains. Rose survived there, too, though it took some adjusting. Now, more than ever, Rose realizes that Cheyenne is the opposite of Savannah. Barren instead of lush. Dry instead of moist. High altitude instead of sea level. However, ancient seas used to be along the high plains, too, and the land possessed a different kind of beauty. After she and Max moved back to Savannah, the only thing Rose misses about their ranch is those cottonwoods.

Spud returns with Queenie on his arm, the corners of his eyes crinkling when he smiles. If there is any leftover drama from her mother's diaries and between Queenie and Spud, Rose can't detect it.

Rose and Queenie embrace. It still seems odd sometimes to see Queenie in person after living for so many years apart. Without Queenie's letters, living in Wyoming would have been much more difficult. Queenie kept her connected to her childhood home, telling Rose highlights of what was happening in the mansion and Savannah.

Rose still has moments when she can't believe she is back in the area and other moments where it feels like she never left.

Seeing Queenie and Spud together, Rose can't imagine her mother standing in Queenie's place. Her mother wouldn't have known what to do with this much love. A thought Rose finds sad. Her mother was married to the Temple legacy, with little room for the people in her life.

Spud asks Rose if she would like to join them for lunch at the little seafood restaurant on the island and she declines, not wanting to infringe on their reunion. Spud and Queenie leave in Spud's car, with Sally Rose waving from the swing set. They are the only ones left at the house. Sally Rose insists on more swinging as the phone rings in her kitchen. Rose debates whether to answer it. To unbuckle Sally Rose from the swing seat will take longer than she has, but at least she will be safe from climbing down or falling.

"Nana will be right back," Rose says to the smiling child as she runs from the swing set to the kitchen door.

Rose picks it up on the fifth ring, right before it would have gone to the answering machine. It is Max.

"You won't believe this," he says, his voice lifting. "Heather dropped the appeal."

"Why would she do that?" Given how unrelenting Heather has been to get her share of the Temple spoils, this makes no sense.

"I don't know," Max says, "but isn't it great?"

Rose agrees it is, but something smells as fishy as the pier at low tide.

"Let's talk about it when you get home," Rose says.

"Sally Rose is strapped in the swing, and I need to check on her."

She hangs up and goes outside. Why would Heather pursue this expensive court case, as well as an appeal, for over two years and then drop it? Has she run out of money? Or did her attorney finally convince her that it was a lost cause? Heather's sense of entitlement to the manifest in a Temple ship that sank 150 years ago has always baffled them. It felt like something in an Indiana Jones movie where the thief is convinced the treasure rightfully belongs to them. Her mother's attorney referred a firm to them which had dealt with a similar case. Max had taken charge of their end. But Heather's motives have been a topic of conversation for months.

Now, Rose must figure out her own. It seems too soon to pursue the Civil War ship never found. At this moment, she would be more inclined to donate it to a museum and let them deal with it. The sins of her family were duly noted before, during, and after that tragic war. In some ways, it doesn't seem right to benefit from it. And what is going on with Heather? It makes no sense that she would decide to do what's right. Rose ventures that this isn't the last time they will hear from Heather.

When she returns to the swing set, Sally Rose is rocked gently by the breeze and babbles away as if talking to someone she adores. Rose's short-lived relief ends when the hairs raise on the back of her neck. Is someone watching her?

31

VIOLET

It is dusk, and the sunset to the west is an orangey red. This time of evening, they often congregate in the kitchen. Violet is finishing up the dishes as Rose arrives. When Rose tells Violet about Heather dropping the court case, Violet's left shoulder registers a brief yet sharp stab of pain.

"Your shoulder doesn't believe it, either?" Rose asks.

"Evidently not." Violet rubs her arm.

"I knew it," Rose says. "Something isn't right."

"That appeal was a long shot, anyway," Violet says. "But I agree that something feels off about her letting it go."

Violet asks about how things are going with Spud, and Rose tells her about him giving her a birthday card.

"It was symbolic," Rose says. "He was making up for all the missed birthdays."

"That sounds like something Spud would do. He's a sweet man." Violet feels a different twinge this time and not in her shoulder. Is it a pang of jealousy?

"To suddenly have a father I didn't know I had has blown my mind," Rose says. "And now Heather has dropped the court case that I thought we would be dealing with for the next decade."

"Maybe someone is watching out for you," Violet says. "Old Sally always said that our ancestors watched out for us. I'm not sure how true that is, given how she—" Violet stops herself. Her grandmother didn't abandon Violet. She died, end of story.

However, Violet doesn't want the story to end there. She wants to hear her grandmother's voice again and to feel her presence on the beach. But in Violet's dreams, Old Sally won't even look at her. But it seems Violet has a part to play in this, too.

"Speaking of being watched," Rose begins, "I had such a weird feeling when I was in the backyard with Sally Rose earlier. I felt like someone was watching us. It was creepy, but when I looked around, I didn't see anyone."

Violet's arm zings again. One quick zing. She hopes it isn't working its way up to another emergency room visit, though those have been rare in the past. She is thankful she thought to do a protection spell, but do those only work for the inside of the house?

Katie, Angie, and Sally Rose come downstairs. Sally Rose with the slow and steady assistance of Angie.

Violet and Rose exchange a look. Katie is about to learn that she has a grandfather.

"Do you need my help with anything?" Violet asks Rose while Katie and Angie bustle around them.

"Just send good thoughts," Rose says.

Violet says she will.

"Can I talk to you back at the cottage?" Rose says to Katie.

Katie glances at Violet as if to ask if she should be worried. Katie can be supersensitive whenever issues come up with her mom.

"It's nothing bad," Violet says to her.

Katie kisses Sally Rose, who stays in the kitchen with Angie and Violet, and then follows Rose to the cottage.

"Has something happened?" Angie asks Violet.

"It has," Violet says, "but it's something good."

"Good," Angie says. "Life has been challenging enough lately."

Violet agrees.

Angie gives Sally Rose a few Cheerios to eat on the tray of the high chair that she is outgrowing. Angie is a good mom, though Violet never doubted that she would be.

"Where are your girls?" Angie asks. "I've barely seen them this summer."

"They're saying a long goodbye to their high school friends," Violet says.

Angie smiles. "I remember those days."

Violet's conversations with Angie have always been easy.

Spud and Queenie are the next to come downstairs. Congregating seems to be something they do as a household.

"I thought I heard Rose's voice," Spud says to Violet.

"She and Katie just went to the cottage to talk," Violet tells him.

Spud nods and looks out the window toward the cottage. He takes a deep breath, and Queenie kisses him on the cheek. Everyone there knows what is going on except Angie, who will know soon.

"It will be fine," Violet tells him, patting his arm. She used to wish that Spud was her father back when they would talk in Miss Temple's kitchen.

Spud smiles at her, and she winks back at him.

"Key!" says Sally Rose, pointing at the Cheerios. She picks them up one by one to show Queenie, with fingers getting better at grasping small things.

Queenie eats a Cheerio and makes a funny face. Sally Rose giggles. Something about a child's laughter makes everything seem right with the world. Tia and Leisha come in the back door with three friends, part of their usual crew. They say their hellos to everyone and then hug Violet before going into Leisha's bedroom. Violet can barely remember being that young. She has worked at different jobs since she was sixteen. Then she replaced Old Sally when her grandmother finally stopped working for the Temples, and Violet became a housekeeper in a house filled with ghosts.

Yet, Violet's life is changing. She is still pondering Marylou's idea to hold small events at the tea shop and read tea leaves on a more regular basis. A month ago, she would have never contemplated such changes. These new possibilities feel like stepping off a cliff into an abyss. Yet what if they are also an opportunity to fly?

Violet thinks of Old Sally, and a wave of grief rolls in. Waves sometimes take her breath away. Violet misses Old Sally's spirit, as well as her flesh and bones. The ache that comes registers in her chest, not her shoulder. Deep grief revisits her; it seems to have settled in to stay.

32

QUEENIE

"T he usual?" Spud asks Queenie. It is 8 p.m., and they have the kitchen to themselves.

"Let's do it." Queenie gives him a wicked smile reserved for delicious treats.

Spud takes the vanilla ice cream out of the freezer, and Queenie grabs the chocolate syrup and crushed walnuts. Spud unpeels a banana and cuts it down the center. He positions it in the bowl. There is an art to creating a good banana split.

"How are you getting on with Rose?" Queenie sprinkles the walnut bits on top of the chocolate syrup.

Spud shrugs, which is unlike him. He has been quieter than usual since she has been home.

"Rose has welcomed you, hasn't she?" Queenie asks.

"Yes. Absolutely."

"Then what are you troubled about?"

"I'm not troubled. I'm just taking it slow."

"You were never that fast, Mr. Grainger." Queenie playfully leans into him.

He rolls his eyes but doesn't add one of his quick comebacks.

Queenie takes a cherry from a jar in the refrigerator and places it on top. "Another masterpiece," she announces.

They click their spoons together like a celebratory toast and then sit at the table.

For a while, the only sound is their spoons against the bowl that sits between them. Queenie debates whether she should draw Spud out and get him to talk about this new revelation. But before she has time to form a question, Tia and Leisha come into the kitchen, minus the friends from earlier, and begin to banter about the bigness of Spud and Queenie's sundae and then decide to make one of their own.

The four of them chat about the girls leaving for college and how close they'll be geographically, but also on their own. Violet and Jack have done an excellent job of raising them. They are confident, humble, and respectful young women. They are also her granddaughters. A fact that Queenie finally claimed after Iris died. She tries not to focus on the time they lost, and with an *Aha*, she wonders if "time lost" is what's bugging Spud.

"You guys should visit while we're there." Tia's wide smile reminds her of Violet's. Not that Queenie has seen Violet smile that much in the last year.

"We're planning a few trips to see you," Spud says.

The girls name several places they might visit while they are there, none of which Queenie recognizes. After their chat, they return to their rooms with bowls of ice cream. It is quiet again.

"What's going through that mind of yours?" Queenie asks. "You're so quiet. It worries me."

"Sorry, sweet pea," he says. "I don't mean to worry you."

Queenie waits for him to say more, but he doesn't. "Shall we go out on the front porch and look at the moon like we used to enjoy doing?"

Spud agrees, but Queenie thinks he is doing it more for her than for himself. He puts their bowl and spoons in the dishwasher.

Queenie leads the way out to the front porch, where they pull two rockers close. The ocean's blueness has faded to a dark gray with moonlight sparkling on the waves like stars. With periodic ease, the waves clap at the spectacle. The porch is lovely this time of evening. Though their big house is full of people, it seems they have the whole universe to themselves.

"I thought we were going to stop living in the past," Queenie begins. "Isn't that what we decided when we had our long talk? We were going to live in the present and look forward to the future."

Spud nods.

"Talk to me," Queenie says softly.

Queenie has never been a patient person, and she must bite her lip to keep from filling the silence.

"I am so angry at Iris I don't know what to do," Spud says finally. "How could she lie and keep this big secret and not tell Rose and me?"

Queenie has never heard him speak in anger about anyone. She didn't even know if he was capable.

"She betrayed me," he says, his eyes dark. "She betrayed Rose. Why would she do that?"

Queenie pauses, faced with a rare opportunity to defend Iris. "I think she was frightened, to be honest. I think she was a coward." As she says the words, Queenie is aware that she was a coward for years, too, not to tell Violet that she was her mother. "People are so scared of being judged, and I think they'll do anything to avoid it. Even betray people."

Spud turns to look at her. "How did you get to be so wise?"

Queenie chuckles and thinks of Old Sally. "It runs in the family."

"It does, indeed," Spud says.

"But I don't blame you for being angry," Queenie says. "I would be angry, too. Iris could be infuriating. She was the most entitled person I've ever known, on top of being clueless. The world is unfair sometimes. But I guess we've got to be grateful for what we have now, including that this secret came to light with enough time left for you and Rose to get to know one another."

"She's telling Katie tonight," Spud says. "I hope it goes okay. It is a shocking thing to deal with."

"Katie will be thrilled," Queenie says. "I don't read tea leaves, but that's my prediction."

"I hope you're right," he says.

While looking up at the stars, Queenie realizes that Spud's history with Iris doesn't seem to matter anymore.

As night falls, moths dance around the porch lights. The screen door opens, and Katie comes out onto the porch.

"Hi, Grandpa." She smiles.

Spud laughs a short laugh and then stands. He and Katie hug.

"Welcome to the family," Katie says as the hug ends.

"You don't mind?"

"Are you kidding? I feel like I won the lottery."

Spud's shoulders relax, but before Queenie has time to do the same, a rustling comes from the dunes. The three of them turn to look. Queenie reaches for Spud's arm.

"Who's out there?" Queenie calls.

Spud rushes inside to get a flashlight and comes back and shines it into the dunes. Nothing is there.

"Maybe it was a coyote," Katie says.

"I've never seen one this far north on the island," Queenie says.

"Surely it wouldn't be people," Spud says. "Not at this time of night."

"Queenie, have you seen that couple lately that you told me about?" Katie asks.

"Not lately," Queenie says. "But I've been away."

"Maybe it was one of those armadillos," Spud says. "They show up on the island more and more. They root around in the dunes and can make a lot of noise."

"Whatever it was, it was watching us," Queenie says. She may not have the family sensitivity, but she does know when someone is watching her. Maybe it comes from putting up with Iris's cold, hard stares for thirty-five years.

The mystery unsolved, Spud and Katie set a time to talk the next day. Before leaving the porch, Queenie glances into the dunes. The next time Queenie sees Violet, she will ask her how long those protection spells are supposed to last. It may be time to make another batch.

33

ROSE

Katie took the news well of having a surprise grandfather. Rose suspected she would. In Wyoming, Katie's elementary school had a Grandparent's Day every year, and Rose attended to make up for the absence of elders in Katie's gene pool. Queenie wrote in one of her letters that she had told Rose's mother about Katie's birth. But there was no acknowledgment of the matriarchs only grandchild. Not even in her diary.

One time, Rose's therapist, Maggie, in Cheyenne, sat an empty chair across from her one session and told Rose to imagine her mother sitting in the chair.

"What do you want to tell her?" Maggie asked.

To her surprise, Rose was unable to say a word even in an imaginary confrontation. It took Rose weeks before she could express anything to her pretend mother in the chair. Yet finally, Rose had a breakthrough and confronted the woman who made her life miserable more often than not. Rose told her what it was like to grow up under constant criticism and how it felt never to measure up, no matter how hard she tried. Now, Rose feels like she has more to say. Reading her mother's diary has added a new dimension to that empty chair Rose never knew.

Maybe it's time to visit her. Rose hasn't been to Bonaventure Cemetery since her mother's funeral. It also occurs to her that perhaps she shouldn't go alone.

With Max watching *Monday Night Football*, Rose telephones Violet.

"Meet halfway?"

Violet agrees.

They often meet halfway between their houses to sit in the backyard to talk. For that purpose, two Adirondack chairs face west toward the sunset.

It is just past dusk, and the automatic lights have clicked on.

"How did Katie react to the news of her long-lost grandfather?" Violet asks.

"She was over the moon," Rose says, motioning to it overhead. "But I knew she would be."

"Have they talked?" Violet looks like something is weighing on her, but she has had that look since Old Sally died.

"They have. Katie said it went great," Rose says.

Violet nods.

"Can I run something by you, so I don't obsess over it all night?"

"Certainly," Violet says.

"I'm thinking about going to visit Mother at Bonaventure."

Violet pauses. "Wow, that's different."

"Isn't it?" While Violet has been faithful in visiting Old Sally every Sunday for a year, even on rainy days, Rose has not thought once about visiting her mother's grave. Not until now.

"What brought this on?" Violet sits in shadow. The moon has slipped behind clouds. If not for the patio lights, they wouldn't be able to see each other at all.

"I guess I have new things to say to her after reading her diary."

"That makes perfect sense," Violet says.

To Rose's relief, Violet's shoulder seems indifferent to the idea.

"I thought I might ask Spud if he wants to go," Rose begins again. "And maybe Queenie. We all have unfinished business as far as Mother is concerned."

"I will be surprised if Queenie wants to go, but I've been wrong before," Violet says.

The kitchen door opens, and Spud walks out with a flashlight, not even seeing them there. He shines the light into the bushes and grasses around the house. He seems startled when Rose asks what he's doing. She apologizes for scaring him.

"I was just checking the perimeter," he says. "Earlier tonight, we thought we might have heard a coyote in the dunes."

When he comes closer, Spud smiles at Rose, a quick acknowledgment of their life-changing connection.

"Can I ask you a question?" Rose asks him. "I have a kind of weird idea, and I want to run it by you."

"You bet," he says.

"Did you and Katie have a good talk?" Rose asks. She probably won't talk to Katie again until tomorrow.

"We did," Spud says. "I'm thrilled, by the way."

Violet stands to go back inside.

"I hope I didn't run you off," Spud says to Violet.

"Not at all," she answers. They hug and say their goodnights.

"Shall I join you?" Spud asks Rose.

"Please do." Spud sits and turns off the flashlight. A familiar awkwardness returns, but it has lessened in the last twenty-four hours. Rose imagines that, in a few weeks, there may be no awkwardness at all.

"Coyote?" Rose asks.

"Maybe an armadillo," Spud says.

"I passed one yesterday on my way off the island," Rose says. "It was lumbering along the highway like it had the right of way."

"They always look like they're wearing armor from the Middle Ages," Spud says. "But I don't think that's what was in the dunes. Whatever it was, it gave me the heebie-jeebies. That's why I wanted to come out and have a look around."

"Heebie-jeebies?" Rose smiles.

They laugh similar-sounding laughs, and it feels like the most natural thing in the world.

"What's your weird idea?" Spud asks.

The moon winks at them and then slides behind the clouds again.

"I'm thinking of going to Bonaventure to visit Mother, and I wondered if you might want to go with me. Queenie's welcome, too. But it's fine if neither of you wants to go."

"Let me talk to her," he says. "We're in new territory, and I don't want to hurt her again, but I'd love to go with you if Queenie agrees. I have a thing or two to say to Iris."

"And if it doesn't work out, that's fine," Rose says

again. They are still careful of one another, as she imagines all newly discovered fathers and daughters would be at this discovery stage.

Will she ever call Spud anything other than Spud? They stand in the darkness and exchange another awkward hug, but at least Rose can imagine that changing.

Spud turns on his flashlight and is about to walk away when he turns toward her again.

"What's your favorite kind of music?"

Rose pauses to think. "Blues," she says.

"Of course it is," Spud says as if he should have guessed this. "Etta James?"

"And Nina Simone."

Spud nods as though hearing the strains of some distant tune and then says goodnight again.

On her walk back to the cottage, Rose experiences something she hasn't felt since the hurricane. An easy peacefulness.

34

VIOLET

For months after Old Sally's funeral, Violet couldn't bear to look at the Gullah Book of Secrets as it gathered dust on the bookcase in their bedroom. It felt too painful. It was as if the Gullah ways had died with Old Sally. Now that the possibility of reading tea leaves has presented itself, she appreciates that she and Old Sally took the time to create the book. But Violet's resistance is stronger than ever. Not only is she afraid of giving people bad advice, but she doesn't want to do anything to warrant the disapproval of the residents and businesses of downtown Savannah. She has lived here long enough to know this wouldn't be wise.

Before Marylou left the tea shop after her reading, she gave Violet an old-fashioned visiting card with her name and telephone number. She stares at the card on her desk in the back room of the tea shop. Violet is increasingly aware that something needs to change in her life, but is opening the tea shop for special events the change Violet needs? Following Rose's advice, she has tried to surrender to the notion that Old Sally isn't coming back while also teetering between claiming and discarding the Gullah ways. Sometimes she goes back and forth with such speed she makes herself dizzy.

In a moment of courage, Violet dials the number. When she gets Marylou's answering machine, she leaves a message that she has decided to stay open late the first Friday every month for six months as an experiment. She suggests that they talk about the details later.

Marylou returns her call within thirty minutes, sounding thrilled with Violet's decision. She invites her to her house the following Sunday afternoon to brainstorm the possibilities. Violet agrees, but she is already second-guessing herself.

Before ending the call, Marylou asks if she can send a friend to the tea shop later today to have her tea leaves read.

Violet makes several excuses of why this won't work.

"That's a pity," Marylou says over the phone. "She could use your help."

Violet can almost hear the smile in her voice. She is challenging Violet but in a good way.

"Her name is Elizabeth," Marylou continues. "She's a drama student, and she has a decision to make. I think it would be good for the two of you to meet."

Violet pauses, reminding herself that it is the tea leaves that hold the answers, not her. More excuses clamor to be heard. But if Violet has learned anything from her grandmother, Gullah folk magic needs to be used like any other healing art. It is intended to be helpful.

"Tell her to come to the shop at five o'clock. That's when we close, but we can sit out in the courtyard as you and I did."

"Perfect," Marylou says. "I'll tell her."

AT FIVE O'CLOCK, a young woman knocks at the door of the tea shop. Violet has already turned off the open sign and unlocks the door to let her in. They introduce themselves and exchange a firm handshake. Elizabeth looks like a redheaded version of Drew Barrymore. Her long hair is pulled back in a ponytail.

"Marylou said you give tea readings?" Elizabeth's expression is one of hopefulness.

"Occasionally," Violet says, which is the truth and also ambivalent. Violet sits straighter. "Yes, I give tea readings," Violet clarifies.

Elizabeth smiles. It feels important to make a clear choice. Violet finds herself standing taller, and as a result, Elizabeth seems to relax. Violet can understand why she might be an actor. The young woman is expressive and open, with more than a bit of charisma and beauty. She seems together, confident, and not the least bit in need of guidance. But, as Violet knows from looking in the mirror, looks can be deceiving.

"First, we need tea." Violet smiles now, wanting to continue to set Elizabeth at ease. She hands her a laminated list of the different loose teas the shop carries.

Elizabeth studies the list but decides quickly on an herbal blend. Then Violet suggests that Elizabeth find a table in the courtyard and tells her that she will be out momentarily with the tea. While making the tea, Violet calls Jack to tell him she will be home later than usual, not saying why. It is rare for Jack to disapprove of anything she does. He is easygoing, sometimes to the point of irritation. But for some reason, she doesn't want to tell him about the tea readings just yet.

Elizabeth sits at one of the black wrought-iron tables at the shady side of the area. The courtyard is beautiful this time of year, lush from the recent rains. When Violet bought the place, the yard was full of trash, weeds, liquor bottles, and cigarette butts. Her housemates helped to transform it before she opened it. Several tables are nestled in the shade of a white dogwood that holds center stage. Beds of tea roses and English ivy border the brick courtyard. It took two entire weekends to get the outside presentable. The inside of the shop required longer, but Jack and Max were invaluable in helping Violet get it the way she wanted it.

A large window overlooks the front courtyard, a huge selling point when Violet bought the shop. Rose's idea was to have the shop's name emblazoned on the glass with gold and purple lettering, and Queenie suggested filling the excellent window seat with African violets. It is the perfect place for them, and they never seem to stop blooming. Rose periodically takes one home with her to make a still life painting. And if customers remark on their beauty, Queenie tells them that the owner's ancestors were initially from Africa and that African violets are a way to honor her roots.

It was essential to Violet that the terra-cotta pots sit on

bricks that she brought over from the mansion's ruins. A reminder of what she lost, as well as gained.

Violet steps through the door carrying a tray with a teapot filled with steeping tea leaves and a china teacup and saucer.

A small kitchen timer sits on the edge of the tray, set to go off when the tea is ready.

As they wait, Violet asks her how Elizabeth knows Marylou.

"She came backstage at a play I was in," the young woman says. "She was so sweet and encouraging, and we've been friends ever since."

"Marylou can be very encouraging," Violet says, thinking, *Almost too encouraging.*

"We're so lucky to have her here in Savannah." Elizabeth smiles again. A smile that is so dazzling she could be in a toothpaste commercial.

The timer announces that the tea is ready, and Violet directs Elizabeth to drink her tea but not to empty the cup, leaving a little liquid in the bottom.

Elizabeth nods and does as directed. She comments on the deliciousness of the tea.

"Have you had your tea leaves read before?" Violet asks.

"No," Elizabeth says, "though I did have my fortune told in New Orleans once."

"I imagine this is similar," Violet says. "The tea leaves will leave patterns and formations in the cup that have symbolic meanings. Do you have a specific question to be answered?"

"I do," Elizabeth says. "I got accepted by two drama

schools. One in New York and one in LA, and I'm having trouble deciding which one to choose. Both would be amazing opportunities. But I have a boyfriend here, who has a job that he can't leave or doesn't want to." She pauses as though debating how much of her story to tell.

"Do I want to focus on Hollywood or Broadway, you know?" she concludes with a nervous laugh.

Violet doesn't begin to know, but she nods nonetheless. "How wonderful it must be to have found your calling and have the talent to go somewhere with it," she says.

Elizabeth lowers her eyes as if the scene she's in calls for humility. Is having a tea shop Violet's calling? Or might life require more from her?

Violet takes the teacup handle in her left hand and swirls the cup in a counterclockwise direction. Thankfully, the steps are becoming easier for her to remember, allowing a more fluid process. *No pun intended*, she tells herself.

Violet then takes the cup, turns it upside down onto the saucer, and leaves it sitting for several seconds so that the cup's contents can empty fully. Slowly, she turns the cup up from the right.

They both lean in to look at the teacup as though there is magic there.

How can something completely ordinary hold the answers to anything, much less the direction a life might go in?

Violet tells herself that trust is needed, and she does her best to focus. She closes her eyes and silently calls on the ancestors, hoping that Old Sally is somewhere nearby. Behind a veil, perhaps. Then Violet asks that her words to Elizabeth be somehow helpful and that they do no harm.

When Violet opens her eyes, she finds Elizabeth focused on the teacup, her brow furrowed in serious intention. A spattering of leaves and liquid are on the saucer, as well as inside the cup. The sheer number of shapes in the cup is significant and indicates that Elizabeth is going through a crucial phase in her life.

Violet exhales, not even realizing that she had been holding her breath. The tea leaves seem amazingly cooperative today, forming patterns that Violet can understand. Both the east and west sections of the cup are represented. Both directions are indeed in play.

Violet reminds herself of Old Sally's instructions in the Gullah Book of Secrets. She clears her mind of any thoughts, trusting her first impression. It is important not to rush the process—a challenge in her everyday life. After examining the shapes of the tea leaves, she notices their distribution. Then she waits, not forcing an answer but letting it come to her.

"First off, I see a bridge. This symbol reflects a positive journey," Violet says.

Elizabeth smiles. "To which school?"

Violet pauses again.

"The bridge stretches east to west. But I don't think you could go wrong with either choice," she adds.

Elizabeth frowns. Is this not the answer she wanted? Violet reminds herself to stay true to the tea leaves, not the person's expectations of getting the reading. She refocuses, studying the cup. A deeper reading is needed.

"There is also a horseshoe, which means success in choosing a partner and a lucky trip."

"A romantic relationship?"

"It appears to be," Violet says.

Elizabeth bites her lower lip.

"Does any of this make sense to you?" Violet asks.

"It does," Elizabeth says. "Anything else?"

Violet looks at the cup again. "I see a mountain. A powerful friend may have something to do with your decision."

"A powerful friend?" Elizabeth's eyes widen.

"Yes," Violet says.

Elizabeth stands. "It's too long a story to tell you, but I want you to know that the tea leaves have been perfect." She shakes Violet's hand and then opens her purse. "How much do I owe you?"

Still surprised at how fast the reading has concluded, Violet tells her there is no charge.

Both standing now, Elizabeth hugs her—an excited, quick acknowledgment of their time together. She looks like she might fly off past the Savannah skyline if gravity didn't insist she stay on the ground.

"You have no idea how much this means to me," Elizabeth says. Violet nods.

Seconds later, Elizabeth is gone, and Violet sits with the mystery of what just happened. To her, she was saying vague things that made no sense to Elizabeth's presenting issue, but to Elizabeth, it was something that resonated and gave her solace.

Suddenly tired, Violet takes the tray back inside and cleans up the teapot, cup, and saucer. Ava has already left through the back door, and the shop is quiet. Driving home over the bridge, Violet questions how such a simple reading could be of any value. If Old Sally were here, Violet would ask her to explain what just happened. Yet, she thinks she already knows what her grandmother might say. She would tell her that the outcome was none of her concern and that Violet's job was simply to show up and tell Elizabeth what she saw. Having done that, Violet should feel satisfied. Yet without her grandmother's approval, it seems an empty accomplishment.

35

QUEENIE

Q ueenie sits in the back seat of Rose's car, happy not to be the one driving to Bonaventure Cemetery. This time last week, with the news of Rose being Spud's daughter, Queenie had left home for three days, fleeing north. She won't need to do any more driving. After putting over a thousand miles on her car, Queenie's back is still complaining. However, every now and again, life presents something dramatic that warrants some soul searching. Racking up those miles did Queenie some good. It gave her time to discern her priorities. An endeavor she is sure would make Oprah proud.

In the passenger seat of Rose's car, Spud periodically glances at Queenie in the back seat. Is he making sure she hasn't changed her mind about coming along? When he came to Queenie about Rose's idea to go to the cemetery with them, it tested her resolve to get over the fact that Iris and Spud had a child together. She still gets nauseous every time she thinks about it, yet here she sits. Visiting Iris is the last thing she wants to do today, but Queenie hates being left out of things.

Though they have known each other for years now, Spud and Rose act like new friends. They talk about movies, books, and favorite foods. All things that Queenie already knows about each of them. She yawns and settles into the back seat, contemplating a nap, all the while keeping an ear tuned to the conversation.

"Iris never told you anything about me?" Spud asks Rose.

"Not a word," Rose says. "But in her diary, she says she watched me while looking for the resemblance."

"Interesting." Spud looks over at Rose in the driver's seat. Is he searching for the resemblance, too?

Queenie usually doesn't take a back seat to anyone, but this situation seems to call for it. Uniting with his secret daughter is easily the most significant moment in Spud's life. To find out that he has a child decades after she was born changed his world for the better, and of course Queenie wants that for him. His anger at Iris's betrayal is unusual for him, and she hopes that this visit to Iris's final resting place will help Spud with that.

Meanwhile, having seldom seen her husband from this angle, she notices how handsome he is with his white hair, mustache, and tanned skin. Violet used to call him "dapper" whenever he visited the mansion. And even without his bow ties, he is still that. Bow ties Queenie didn't think Spud would ever give up. But he has exchanged one obsession with another, now having a collection of Hawaiian shirts in every color. Today he wears a green and white one with his usual khaki pants. Iris would have made fun of someone wearing that shirt, all the while questioning the wearer's intelligence.

Queenie straightens her blouse and skirt, wondering why she dressed up for her dead nemesis.

Old habits die hard, she tells herself, before vowing never to let Iris's opinion—whether dead or alive—control her behavior ever again.

Queenie probably has crossed this bridge into Savannah thousands of times by now, maybe tens of thousands. Before her little escapade north, Queenie had never been beyond Charleston. Spud has offered to take her on cruises and to all sorts of foreign places. But what most people don't know about Queenie is that she is quite the homebody. She prefers familiar environs.

"Tell me what your father was like," Spud asks Rose, causing Queenie to raise an eyebrow. She could give them both an earful, having known Oscar in the most intimate of ways.

"He was no match for Mother," Rose says. "But he could be kind when he wanted to be."

"He died when you were away at college?" Spud pets his mustache, a habit he's had the entire time Queenie has known him. She wonders if she'll get tired of this gesture someday.

"My junior year," Rose says.

"That must have been very rough," Spud says.

"It was," Rose says. "I realize now that his heart attack was probably alcohol-related. He was a high-functioning alcoholic, but it took its toll."

"It always does," Spud says.

Queenie wouldn't call Oscar "high functioning" at anything. Maybe he was during the daytime when Rose was a girl, but everything was about concealing his drinking toward the end. He ate peppermints to cover up the smell. To this day, Queenie can't smell anything peppermint without also smelling a hint of bourbon in the mix.

To his credit, Oscar dressed impeccably, which convinced people he was doing better than he was. As Iris required, he always dressed for dinner, and he never drank at the table. Not even a glass of wine. He used makeup concealer to dot away the dark circles under his eyes, and he carried Visine in his pants pocket to use periodically to conceal his bloodshot eyes, along with the peppermints. Queenie doubts that even Iris knew the full extent of Oscar's drinking problem.

Toward the end, Queenie tried to get him into his bedroom before eight o'clock because he blacked out most evenings. Otherwise he would fall asleep on the leather sofa in his office. With Rose away at college, and his son, Edward, refusing to be near him, and his friends finally having enough of it, he seemed to be an intensely lonely man. Queenie did her best to keep him company, all the while pretending that Violet wasn't their child. Drunk or sober, the underlying threat of dismissal was ever-present.

"You okay back there?" Rose looks at Queenie through the corner of the rearview mirror. "You're awfully quiet."

Spud looks back and smiles at Queenie as if grateful for her patience.

"I'm fine," Queenie says. "I've been nodding off."

"We'll be there soon," Rose says as she takes the turnoff toward Bonaventure. "Let's just hope it doesn't rain on us. I checked the weather before we left, and there was a fifty percent chance of thunderstorms."

"You never know. Those weather people have been wrong before," Spud says.

Rose agrees.

"It was raining the day of Iris's funeral, remember?" Queenie says. "There was a fifteen percent chance of rain that day."

"It was a downpour," Rose says.

"Cats and dogs," Spud says.

"Cats and dogs and parakeets," Rose says, and she and Spud laugh.

Queenie must resist rolling her eyes, but she has to admit they are cute together.

After they park, Queenie gets out and stretches her back. She should have let this be an outing between Rose and Spud. They need time to be together, just the two of them, so they can get to know each other and be silly if they want to without someone watching their awkwardness.

"How's your back, honey pie?" Spud asks.

Queenie tells him that her back is fine, which is mostly true.

In the meantime, except for their wedding day, Spud is the happiest Queenie has ever seen him. She and Spud walk hand in hand, Queenie's purse slung over her other shoulder. She forgets how lovely Bonaventure Cemetery is with its live oaks draped with Spanish moss and the sandy roads and paths running throughout. This land is full of history, not to mention dead people. Yet, as far as she knows, none of her kin are buried here. Given how they helped build Savannah and keep it going, this seems unfair.

They walk toward the Temple mausoleum, where Iris's bones are laid to rest. As for her spirit, Queenie sometimes wonders if Iris ever truly gave up haunting places. Queenie has a hard time imagining her half sister resting in peace. She wouldn't be surprised if Iris had her bony fingers into things all over Savannah.

"What are you going to do once you get there?" Queenie asks Rose.

"I'm not sure," Rose says. "Now that I have a better sense of who she was, I wanted to visit her."

Queenie holds her tongue. Iris was Iris, no matter what she wrote in that diary. She could be mean and vindictive and manipulative, too. Has Rose forgotten how Iris disowned her? Not to mention lying to Rose about who her birth father was. Nothing in that stupid diary can change the damage Iris left behind.

Spud squeezes her hand as if making sure she is okay. But Iris's final resting place is a bit of a walk, and Queenie's back hurts more. "Will you be paying your respects, too, Mr. Grainger?"

Queenie aims for support, but it sounds snarky.

"I'm here for Rose," Spud says.

But just last night, he mentioned again how angry he was that Iris had lied to him for decades. Queenie thought he'd sooner spit on her than pay his respects. But maybe she was wrong. If she were Rose, she would be furious at Iris, too. Perhaps that will come later.

When they finally arrive at the mausoleum, Queenie walks to one of the benches outside and sits, dropping her purse to the ground. All this walking is more exercise than she usually gets in an entire day. Spud motions that he is going inside with Rose.

Queenie nods, thinking how good it feels to sit for a minute after all that walking.

Because of the threat of vandalism, the mausoleum stays locked. However, a key remains hidden underneath a rock by the pink azalea closest to the door. It has been in the same place since Queenie started coming with Iris every week for thirty-five years. Visiting the dead Temples was a part of Iris's weekly routine and, therefore, Queenie's.

Rose finds the key and opens the door to one of the most prominent structures in the cemetery. The Temple name is etched on the front as if an ancient Roman emperor resides inside. The stone mausoleum is the size of a small chapel or a one-car garage. Once Rose opens the door, Spud follows her inside.

You won't catch me going in there, Queenie tells herself. *Not in a million years.*

Queenie takes a paper fan from her purse and swishes around the humid air, trying not to think about how close she is to Iris's bones. Tiring quickly, she puts the paper fan on the bench and pulls out a Sudoku book from her purse that she always carries with her to the beauty parlor, and starts on the next puzzle.

Dark clouds cover the sun, and distant thunder announces a storm is coming this way. Afternoon thunderstorms are a frequent occurrence in the South in the summertime, and Queenie wishes now that she had grabbed one of the portable umbrellas in the back seat of Rose's car and put it in her purse. Within minutes, the wind picks up, and the Spanish moss dances in the trees. The temperature has dropped by about ten degrees—a welcome change but also an alarming one.

"Is that you, Iris?" Queenie looks up at the darkening sky.

Thunder rumbles again—louder this time.

A hundred yards away, tourists walk quickly down the path while others run. Queenie fishes a plastic rain bonnet from the bottom of her purse and puts it on.

"Do you always have to be the center of attention, Iris?" Queenie seethes her irritation. "By the way, I resent you leaving behind that diary full of secrets and causing another mess for us to clean up."

Queenie imagines Iris laughing. A laugh that was haughty and used whenever Iris had the upper hand—which was always—and delighted to rub it in.

"Spud will never forgive you, you old witch. You should never have lied to him."

Lightning crackles nearby, followed by a rumble of thunder that shakes the ground underneath her feet. The storm is getting closer. Raindrops begin to fall that are the size of silver dollars, just like the day of Iris's funeral. As much as she hates the thought of being inside the Temple tomb, Queenie quickly moves in that direction.

"I'm coming in, Iris," Queenie warns at the door.

With the next lightning crash, she steps inside. Rose and Spud visibly jump when Queenie enters, as though she is an unexpected Temple joining the Great Beyond. Spud comes to her side, taking her purse so that Queenie can adjust herself to the new surroundings. She shakes the rain off her rain bonnet and lays her things on the closest crypt.

"Do they have the air-conditioning on in here?" Queenie asks. "It sure is chilly."

"It's all the stone," Rose says. "This may be the coolest place in Savannah."

The mausoleum is quite beautiful as far as burial chambers go. Two massive stone crypts sit against the side walls with stained-glass windows above them reaching toward the ceiling. Diffused light comes through the windows, offering a kaleidoscope of subdued hues. The most prominent wall appears to have built-in stone filing cabinets, each square marked with a Temple name, the earliest dating back almost two hundred years.

Queenie looks for Iris's name and can't seem to find her.

"Where's her highness?" Queenie asks Rose.

Rose points to the newest crypt underneath Queenie's things. Queenie grabs her purse and steps back, catching herself not wanting to make Iris angry. The ground underneath them shakes again to tell Queenie that it is too late for that.

"Heaven help us," Queenie says, followed by an even louder thunderclap. In unison, they move toward the center of the room and huddle as though awaiting Iris's wrath.

36

ROSE

Weirdly, Rose's visit to the mausoleum feels like a family reunion. She almost expects Old Sally to have made deviled eggs. While Rose was growing up, her mother brought her here several times a year and schooled Rose on the family lineage. The building seems smaller than she remembers, but it is still the largest mausoleum in the cemetery. A fact her mother emphasized with every visit.

"It's like a tomb in here," Queenie says with an exaggerated shiver, causing Rose and Spud to laugh.

"A classy tomb, at least," Spud says.

"The Temples insist on the biggest and best of everything, even when it comes to final resting places," Rose says.

"Some people live in houses smaller than this," Spud says.

The storm rumbles as they remain close together. So close that Rose can smell Spud's aftershave, as well as the onions that Queenie had for lunch.

"For thirty-five years, I drove Iris to this very place every Monday afternoon at four o'clock," Queenie says. "That woman was a creature of habit."

"I didn't come that often," Rose says. "But it did seem that dead Temples mattered more than the living ones."

"We always stopped by the florist beforehand and brought a big bunch of lilies," Queenie says. "To this day, lilies give me a headache and make me sneeze."

Another thunderclap shakes the walls, and Spud holds Queenie closer. He tells them that they are probably in the safest place they could be, and Rose hopes he's right.

"It was odd," Queenie says. Iris couldn't tolerate perfumes or fragrances of any kind, yet she could somehow take the smell of those lilies. I just never understood it."

"Mother was a paradox," Rose says, thinking of the diary.

Spud agrees.

"She was also a royal pain in the backside," Queenie says. "She put those lilies in that vase right over there." Queenie points to an empty gold vase on a pedestal in the corner of the room near the stained-glass window.

"I thought you never went inside," Rose says.

"Iris always insisted I put those damn lilies in the vase, but I was out of here as fast as you could say *deceased*. I'm in here this time because a thunderstorm is right on top of us."

Rose looks around. It has been decades since she has been here. The ceiling is painted a dark blue with gold stars scattered throughout—something that might belong in Florence, Italy, rather than Savannah, Georgia.

"This place is practically soundproof," Spud says.

"Leave it to Spud to be checking out the acoustics," Rose says with a smile. Her affection for him is growing.

"No chance of anyone waking the dead, I guess," Queenie says with a short laugh as if relieved Rose's mother won't be making an appearance. "Although it would be just like Iris to drum up a storm so that we would all have to been in here together, practically bowing at her feet."

While Queenie tends to get more talkative when she is nervous, Rose gets quieter. Does her mother know she's here?

"I mean, if Iris can create a Category 4 hurricane, a thunderstorm must be a piece of cake." Queenie cackles. "Come to think of it, a piece of cake would sure taste good right now."

"I think we've all learned never to underestimate Iris Temple," Spud says. "She was indeed a force of nature."

An enormous thunderclap intercedes, adding an exclamation point to his words.

In unison, they turn toward the stone crypt, a move that seems almost choreographed. While alive, Rose's mother commanded all the attention in a room. It seems she can do that while dead, too.

"Trapped again in a tomb with dead Temples," Queenie says. "I thought after the mansion burned down that I wouldn't have to do this again."

Rose never pictured herself doing this, either. Yet all of her Savannah ancestors are buried in this mausoleum: her parents, grandparents, and great-grandparents, as well as her brother, Edward. On the opposite wall of her mother's crypt is an almost identical one that holds her great-grand-father—another Edward, who was alive when the mausoleum was built. When Rose was a girl, her mother had a crypt prepared for herself that was just as elaborate as her great-grandfather's.

Leave it to her mother to one-up the guy who built this place.

Rose's father is buried here, too, next to Edward, forever held hostage in the Temple family. He was a prisoner, in a way, just like her mother. On the other side of Edward is a place for Rose if she chooses. However, the thought of spending eternity next to her brother makes Rose feel claustrophobic. It would make more sense to have her ashes sprinkled in the Gullah cemetery on the island under the live oaks.

Queenie chuckles to herself and gives Rose a wink. "With all the preservatives they put in things these days, I bet that bucket of KFC is still extra crispy." Her chuckle grows to a cackle that echoes off the stone walls. Rose laughs, too, thankful to Queenie for lightening up the moment.

Spud smiles but doesn't get the reference. Did Queenie never tell him about her mischief before her mother's funeral?

"I admit that, in retrospect, it wasn't my finest hour," Queenie says.

"Given how Mother treated you all those years, it seemed harmless enough," Rose says.

"Could someone please explain?" Spud asks finally.

Rose remembers again that he is her father, as she does dozens of times a day.

Queenie, tight-lipped, looks at Rose as though unable to confess, so Rose fills Spud in about how Queenie placed a bucket of Kentucky Fried Chicken at her mother's feet before the funeral.

His eyes widen, but then he stifles a laugh. "Oh, my," he says.

"She used to leave buckets full of KFC bones pushed under the seats of the town car," Queenie says, to explain further. "All the while, pretending all over Savannah to have a delicate constitution."

"Hence the exotic meats," Spud says, lifting an eyebrow.

"I've eaten enough caribou to last a lifetime," Queenie says. "Not to mention smoked eel and the rest of it."

Spud nods. "Her requests were not easy to find."

Rose sometimes forgets that Spud was a butcher or that Queenie ate formal evening meals with Rose's mother every day for thirty-five years. Rose spent the first twenty years of her life doing the same. Sometimes Sally would hide notes under her plate to keep her amused after Rose learned to read. Messages with riddles or questions she could ponder. Sally made those long evening meals bearable and almost enjoyable.

"I hope Iris can't hear us," Queenie whispers. "We shouldn't have this much fun in a graveyard."

"Funerals and cemeteries often bring out the humor in people," Spud says.

"Maybe it's in knowing that we all have the same fate," Rose says. "We might as well enjoy the time we have left."

For the first time, Rose realizes that Spud is almost seventy, and there are no guarantees about how much time they will have together. The thought of lost time sobers her again.

"I've had enough of this." Queenie opens the door to check on the thunderstorm. The rain is torrential, so she closes the door again. Quiet descends.

"Well, we can either make a run for it and get soaked or wait it out," Rose says.

They agree to wait it out. Settling in, Rose sits on the crypt at her great-grandfather's feet, and Spud and Queenie sit on the stone bench by the door. It's impossible to get comfortable, but Rose tells herself it is only temporary. Queenie pulls a nail file out of her oversized purse and begins to shape her nails. When Rose looks down, she sees acrylic paint on hers.

"Maybe we should create some kind of ceremony while we're here," Rose says.

"You mean like each of us saying a few words?" Spud asks.

"Yes," Rose says, except she isn't sure what she might say, except to ask her mother why she lied to her all these years.

Rose remembers the diary and how her grandparents threatened to disown her if she did anything that might tarnish the Temple name. A threat Rose received, as well. *Disowning* was the most significant consequence leveled at a Temple and always involved money taken away.

All that ownership, only to end up here. Rose looks around the mausoleum. Suddenly a ceremony seems more crucial than ever. "Do you have anything you'd like to say to my mother, Spud?"

"I don't think you want to hear what I'd like to say." Spud's voice is just above a whisper.

"I'd like to hear it if you feel like sharing," Rose says. "I have things I'd like to share, too."

"Me, too." Queenie drops the nail file back into her purse like this party suddenly got interesting.

Spud stands and looks over at the crypt where Rose's

mother resides. "Iris, you should have told me about Rose," Spud begins. "You knew how much it would have meant to me."

Queenie says an "amen" like she's at a prayer meeting at the Gullah church and then waits for Spud to say more. Queenie's support of Spud touches Rose, and she steps closer.

"You could have told me after Oscar died," Spud begins again, turning to look at Rose. "That would have given Rose and me thirty more years of knowing each other. Do you know what I've missed in those thirty years?" He pulls a handkerchief from his back pocket and wipes tears from his eyes. Even though they don't know the details of each other's lives, it feels like his grief is Rose's grief, too. Seeing him cry does something to her.

Queenie takes Spud's hand. She has come a long way from her initial reaction to the news.

"I'm not sure I can ever forgive you for this, Iris. If you have even a shred of decency, you need to make amends."

Rose wonders what he might mean by *amends*, but Spud appears to have finished. He puts a hand on his chest and offers Rose a slight smile before thanking her for suggesting that he say what he needed to Iris. "I feel like a weight has lifted," he adds.

Rose wants to feel lighter, too. She stands and closes her eyes to discern what she needs to say before opening them again and turning toward her mother's crypt.

"After reading your diary, Mother, I now understand how trapped you were by the Temple dynasty," she begins. "But I'm still disappointed by your choices. It was shameful not to tell Spud and me that he was my biological father. Also—" Rose pauses. Is she brave enough to say what she truly thinks? "You were also a coward to only do what people expected of you instead of being yourself, and I think you regretted it your entire life." Rose takes a deep breath and releases it. "Whew. That felt good."

"I've always said Iris lived in a gilded cage," Spud says.

"Well, I lived right there with her," Queenie says. "A thirty-five-year sentence with no time off for good behavior. This bird has flown the coop."

Rose congratulates Queenie for being free, too.

"Is there anything else you'd like to say, Queenie?"

The thunderous part of the storm appears to be subsiding, but Rose can still hear the heavy rain.

Queenie stands and faces the crypt. "When I did my little joyride up the coastline, I talked to you a lot, Iris. You know exactly how I feel." Queenie chuckles. "At this moment, though, I feel sad for you. You had everything people could aspire to, and yet you were still bitter and mean and unforgiving. And by the way," Queenie concludes, "I refuse to believe that you were in any way better than me, even though you believed it to your core."

Silence follows, as though intentionally written into the program of their impromptu ceremony.

Rose pulls her mother's diary out of her purse by the door. "Does anyone have matches?"

Queenie offers a gleeful smile. "I might." She digs inside her baggy purse with no success and then walks over and pours out the entire contents of her bag on top of Rose's mother's crypt. "Finally, we can use this for something useful," she says.

"I've never understood why you carry so much around," Spud says.

"It's how Southern women survive, sweetie."

Rose joins Queenie at the crypt. The first time she witnessed the contents of Queenie's purse was in the hearse on the way to entomb her mother in this very spot, and the contents have grown. A magazine of Sudoku puzzles joins a crumpled rain bonnet, spare car keys, a roll of quarters, chewing gum, a red Swiss army knife, half a Reeses cup, a pumice stone, the nail file used earlier, a pack of AA batteries, eyebrow tweezers, a small sewing kit, a miniature first aid kit, a white notepad, along with several pens with names of different establishments on them, as well as her wallet and a change purse and various receipts.

"That's quite a stash," Rose tells her.

Queenie smiles and then holds up a green plastic lighter that looks like she may have found it on the side of the road somewhere. She sparks the flame. "We're in business," she says.

"Should we do this?" Rose holds up the diary.

"I'm all in," Queenie says.

Then Rose looks at Spud. "I support you in whatever you choose," he says.

When Rose was in therapy, she became good at burning things she wanted to let go of: lists of grievances, letters from people she was no longer in relationships with, and, at one point, her journals full of wounded writings. This feels similar. "While the diary burns, let's let go of all the hurtful things Mother did, and let them float up to heaven with the smoke. My therapist in Wyoming suggested a similar exercise when I was seeing her."

"I feel lighter already," Queenie says with a giggle.

Rose places the book on top of her mother's crypt. It sits upright as if on display, open, and with pages exposed.

The book seems too beautiful to be destroyed. Yet, it has served its purpose. The truth has been revealed.

Rose steps forward and clicks the lighter, placing the flame on the brittle pages. The flames grow quickly, and Queenie opens the door so that the smoke can exit the tomb. The rain has stopped.

Humid air battles with the smoke as they watch the diary burn in silence. Rose imagines all the secrets floating up to heaven, where they can't hurt anyone anymore. She oversees the pages turn to ash, and a blueish flame curls around its edges. The book falls over. They continue to watch as Rose is mesmerized by the possibilities of finally letting go of her mother's hold on her.

While the book smolders, they step outside. The trees drip with moisture, and the resurrection ferns in the live oaks have turned from gray to a vibrant green—resurrected. The storm has passed, and the world around them looks cleansed and renewed.

"Rest in peace, Mother," Rose says, looking back at the Temple chapel. In the next moment, the clouds scatter, and sunlight breaks through the trees.

37

VIOLET

More than ever, Violet wishes Old Sally were here, and more than ever, Violet feels the absence of her. Meanwhile, Violet's shoulder is at it again. A dull pain has grown throughout the day. At times she has wondered if her shoulder was a blessing or a curse.

After double-checking things at the tea shop as she prepares to leave, she checks in with Jack, Tia, and Leisha. Everyone seems fine. The National Weather Service also ensures that no surprise hurricanes are heading in their direction. This morning she even asked Marylou if Elizabeth was okay after their tea reading. Marylou told her how exuberant and grateful Elizabeth was to have a sense of new direction.

"She's telling everyone she knows," Marylou says.

Violet's scalp tingles. "No, it's supposed to be a secret."

"A secret?" Marylou sounds surprised. "But you're good at it. Why would you want to keep it a secret?"

Violet doesn't know how to answer. Perhaps the secret she wants to keep is from herself. Maybe the most important secret she is holding is that Gullah folk magic is in her blood. Marylou reminds her to *Claim it*, which stresses out Violet even more.

When she arrives home, Rose, Spud, and Queenie are returning from the cemetery. From the looks on their faces, it must have been an eventful visit. Queenie and Spud go into the big house. Rose asks if she's okay.

"Can we talk about this later?" Violet asks.

"Of course," Rose says, and Violet goes into the house and changes into casual clothes.

Despite her weariness, Violet takes her evening walk. For most of the way, she looks down, deep in thought. She thinks of tea leaves, the tea shop, and her shoulder, which is like a puzzle she can't figure out.

By the time Violet looks up again, she is at the lighthouse. She breathes deeply and takes in the structure where she spent the most harrowing hours of her life. In the week leading up to the storm, her shoulder gave her minimal warning until it was practically on top of them. At the time, it made no sense, and it makes no sense now. Does this mean her current warning has to do with something bigger than Hurricane Iris? If so, this is a terrifying possibility.

For over half a century, the lighthouse was Old Sally's touchstone. A place she visited daily and spent time inside worshipping at an altar of the past. And Old Sally was Violet's touchstone. Her grandmother's death is a reality that is much more painful than her shoulder.

She wants to yell: *Where are you when I need you?* But instead, she remains silent. Silence being the terms of her surrender. Violet's shoulder gives another scream of pain, confirming her truth.

Turning toward home, Violet passes a mother with a child who is a little older than Sally Rose. The little girl toddles down the beach, chasing a seagull feather that is suddenly airborne. When her shoulder gives a sudden throb, she wonders if one of her daughters is in danger. Violet quickens her pace to almost a run. When she arrives at the front door, she is winded, dripping with sweat, and imagining the worst.

But when she goes inside, Tia and Leisha are laughing in the kitchen. Katie, Angie, and Sally Rose are there, too, and Sally Rose is in the high chair having a snack. Violet hugs each of her girls like she hasn't seen them for years. They comment on her silliness. She is so happy that they are okay; she doesn't take offense.

Sally Rose looks up from a small square of cheese that she intends to get her fingers around. Violet's shoulder stops hurting, a flipped switch. For several seconds she wonders if she imagines things or if her grief is making her crazy.

"Is Sally Rose okay?" Violet asks Katie and Angie.

"Of course," Katie says. "What's wrong?"

While intending not to alarm them, she has done just that. She takes a breath and tells herself to stay calm.

"Has she been to the pediatrician lately?"

"Just last week," Angie says. "She's doing well. Perfectly healthy. Why?"

"Mom, you're scaring them," Leisha says.

"I don't mean to." Violet apologizes. "My shoulder has been acting up, so I'm just checking with everyone."

Their body language changes from tension to ease.

"I'm sure it's nothing," Violet says, not at all sure.

"That shoulder of yours is like a crystal ball," Angie says.

"I wish it weren't," Violet says.

"That must be hard," Katie says, the more empathetic of the two.

"It can be hard sometimes." Violet kisses the top of Sally Rose's head.

Katie and Angie exchange a look as though wondering if Violet is becoming untethered. Perhaps she is.

Sally Rose offers Violet some cheese, and Tia and Leisha announce that they are meeting friends in Savannah in an hour and need to get ready, though they already look acceptable to Violet. Did she fuss this much with her hair when she was their age?

"Is your mom at home?" Violet asks Katie, looking out the kitchen window toward the cottage. Violet could use a friend right now to help her stay calm.

Katie says she is.

Before going to the cottage, Violet checks in with Jack. She finds him with Max and Spud watching sports in the den. Jack gives her a wave, and she comes over to the couch and kisses him on the cheek.

"What's up?" he asks, not taking his eyes from the screen.

"I think I'll go visit Rose since you guys are watching the game."

Jack nods.

Perhaps sports exist to give women a break from their husbands. Not that she and Jack need a break, but it does allow Violet to do other things on certain nights and weekends.

When Violet knocks on the cottage door, Rose seems to

expect her. She invites Violet to sit at the kitchen table, where they do most of their talking when she visits the cottage. Rose seems more upbeat than usual.

"Tell me about Bonaventure," Violet says.

"We burned Mother's diary," Rose says.

Violet doesn't hide her surprise. Rose has mentioned burning the Temple Books of Secrets for years and never gotten around to it. "That must have been cathartic."

"It was. For all of us, I think." Rose looks into the distance as though still watching it burn.

"Queenie and Spud went with you?"

Rose nods and tells Violet the details of their ritual and about how everyone felt lighter afterward. Violet wants to feel lighter, too, and wonders what she might do to create a similar feeling.

"How's your shoulder?" Rose asks.

"It flared up on the beach a little while ago, but now it's better again," Violet says. "Makes me want to scream."

"Why?" Rose asks.

Violet pauses. "I'm not sure," she says. "At first, I thought it was about Tia and Leisha. Or the parents of this little girl I saw on the beach. Now I'm wondering if it's about Sally Rose."

"Sally Rose?" Rose turns serious. "Why would you think that?"

"I'm grasping at straws, Rose."

"Where were you when your shoulder set off the alarm?" Rose asks.

"Near the lighthouse. I'm probably overthinking it. I do that sometimes."

"Join the club," Rose says.

"What do you think I should do?" Violet genuinely

needs advice. "I hate pain. It makes me feel vulnerable and crazy, especially when I know it means something is going to happen."

"I can't even imagine," Rose says. "Why don't you take a hot bath and try to get some rest. We can talk more about it tomorrow."

Violet thanks her. Rose has had a big day, too. They are each trying to figure out where they fit in the world.

Rose's reasoning helps to calm the unreasonable part of Violet. She will try not to think about her shoulder anymore tonight and what it is trying to say to her. From her experience, it's when she forgets about it that the answers come.

After her bath, Jack's game is in the fourth quarter, and she goes to bed without him, thankful for a bit of time to think. She has given Marylou the go-ahead to opening the tea shop one Friday a month to poets, writers, and musicians. The tea shop clientele is primarily white, but she wants to welcome black people to the events, both as talent and audience.

While some residents of old Savannah have wandered in from time to time, the shop has attracted students, people who live and work nearby, and tourists. Since the hurricane and Old Sally's death, Violet must admit she hasn't had any ambition to do more. Getting through the day has been challenging enough.

Yet Violet stands on the threshold of doing these new things and feels paralyzed. Now she is contemplating reading tea leaves. She remembers what Marylou told her about Elizabeth telling everyone she knows. It seems her secret is already out.

38

QUEENIE

Katie and Angie ask Queenie to watch Sally Rose while they have an appointment in Savannah with their couples therapist. Queenie is honored. Usually, they ask Rose, her actual grandmother, but Rose has an eye appointment scheduled for the same morning. Something about the child makes Queenie feel like a grandmother. As a baby, whenever Queenie held Sally Rose, she melted right into Queenie's heart and has stayed there ever since.

After Katie and Angie leave for their appointment, Queenie puts the fancy stroller in the car, and they drive down to the small boardwalk on Dolphin Island to take a stroll. Even though she is two, Sally Rose still loves her stroller and begs Queenie to let her ride instead of walk, pretending she's a baby instead of a toddler. Queenie pretends to be younger than her age, too, though it seems increasingly harder to pull off.

When they get home, Sally Rose insists on getting in the stroller again, and Queenie pushes her throughout the downstairs part of the house, pretending they are a race car approaching the finish line. Queenie is easily winded, and they end up on the front porch, where she locks the wheels in place. She double-checks that the lock is working, as well as the little seat belt. These actions ensure that Sally Rose doesn't take one of those famous Australian aboriginal walkabouts down to the shore that Queenie read about in the *National Geographic* in the dentist's office.

It is only then that Queenie realizes her bladder is full. Rather than roll Sally Rose into the downstairs bathroom with her, she pushes the wicker basket full of toys that stays on the front porch to within arm's reach of Sally Rose so that she can play with them while seated in her stroller. Sally Rose's reaction to the toys is a squeal, followed by, "Da, Key," her way of saying thank you.

"Now, don't go anywhere," Queenie says to Sally Rose. "I'll get you a snack to have while we're out here."

"O's," Sally Rose says, short for her favorite dry Cheerios straight from the box.

"I won't be long, love," Queenie says and darts inside.

The house is empty this morning except for Queenie and Spud, which is a rare occurrence. Spud is upstairs reading a book about jazz history in his favorite chair by a sun-filled window. That book has mesmerized him for weeks.

While emptying her bladder, Queenie hears Harpo, Katie's dog, barking upstairs. She can't deal with a dog right now. She finds the Cheerios in the cabinet and puts them in Sally Rose's favorite bowl. It has an orange giraffe painted on the bottom. She also cuts her some apple slices and cheese and fills a sippy cup with water. Queenie wishes she had timed herself because even she is impressed with how quickly her excursion into the house has gone.

"I have your favorites," Queenie says when she returns to the porch. She puts the snacks on a nearby table and peeks her head around the stroller, and her body freezes. Where is Sally Rose? Queenie bolts upright as adrenaline jolts through her body. She yells for Sally Rose as if she has just wandered off, an impossible prospect given that Houdini would have trouble escaping the harness they put in those strollers.

Queenie runs into the house, thinking that maybe Katie and Angie are back early and have picked up Sally Rose on their way into the main house, and Queenie has missed them, but their car is still gone.

"Oh, my heavens," Queenie says, feeling frantic. She yells for Spud. It reminds her of one of the primal screams she did while driving up the coast and trying to forget that Iris and Spud were intimate and had a child together once upon a time. But this moment doesn't call for blowing off her frustration. This situation is immediate and dire.

Wearing his reading glasses, Spud looks down at Queenie from the top of the stairs. "What's wrong, honey?"

"I can't find Sally Rose."

Spud rushes down the stairs as fast as a man in his sixties can go. He holds Queenie's shoulders and looks frantic. "When did you last see her?"

"We had a nice walk, and she was outside on the front porch in the stroller. I ran in to go to the bathroom. I was gone for two seconds."

"Okay, okay. We'll find her." Spud softens his expression and tells her everything will be okay. "She couldn't have gone far," he adds.

"Maybe Katie and Angie came back early and took her

upstairs?" Queenie knows full well that their car is still gone. She is not making sense. "Maybe she's at the cottage with Rose," she adds, though she knows full well that Rose is in Savannah today, too.

"We're the only ones in the house," Spud says.

A sound comes out of Queenie's mouth that she's never heard before. A cross between a wail and a scream rises in volume. "Spud, what are we going to do?"

"Let's go outside and look around," Spud says. "Maybe she got out of the stroller and just wandered off."

"But she was buckled in. I double-checked. You know how adamant Katie and Angie are about making sure the clasp is closed."

Queenie questions again if they are home. Maybe they found Sally Rose on the porch alone and are teaching Queenie a lesson. She calls out their names, asking if they are here.

Spud leads the way outside. They circle the house and then go up the driveway calling Sally Rose's name. They search the dunes in front of the house and walk to the shoreline, looking left and right. The only children on the beach are older and with their parents or are teenagers with other teenagers.

"What do we do now?" Panic rises again in Queenie's voice. She feels physically ill.

"We'd better call the police," Spud says.

"Police?" Queenie says, not wanting the situation to warrant law enforcement. "Maybe Jack took her someplace. He likes to take her for rides."

"Jack is running errands today," Spud says. "And Violet is at the tea shop. And Rose is at the eye doctor."

"How about Max?" Queenie asks.

"Dental appointment, I believe," Spud says.

Queenie wonders what's up with all these appointments. *Is everybody falling apart?* "You think we should call the police?" She catches herself being grateful that Sally Rose is white and not black.

Spud says they should, and Queenie picks up the kitchen phone to dial 911 and tells the operator that their baby has gone missing. The operator says that they will send out a car right away.

After she gets off the phone, Queenie's heart is beating so rapidly she wonders if she is having the beginnings of a heart attack. She goes back outside to the front porch and examines the stroller again. She tries not to touch anything in case the police want to take fingerprints.

"There's no way she could have gotten out of this herself," she says aloud to herself.

It is only then that Queenie spies a white piece of paper near the stroller that the wind may have moved. The words are typed in all caps.

DO NOT CALL THE POLICE, OR WE WILL KILL THE CHILD. WE WILL CALL YOU THIS EVENING WITH INSTRUCTIONS.

In the next second, Queenie leans over the porch railing and vomits into the oleander bushes. After expelling more of her breakfast, she wipes her mouth and goes inside with the note. Rose has just returned home, and Spud is telling her what is going on. Rose looks as upset as Queenie feels. Her eyes widen, and she is full of questions. Queenie shows her the note that Spud reads over her shoulder.

"Oh my God!" Rose covers her mouth as if stifling a scream.

"But you already called the police," Spud says to Queenie.

"You've got to call them back," Rose says. "We can't let anything happen to her."

Spud's somberness has grown to a new level.

Queenie dials 911 again, not knowing what she'll say exactly.

"I'm so sorry," Queenie tells the operator. "I called you a few minutes ago to tell you our little girl was missing. But we just found her playing in the dunes." Queenie apologizes, telling the 911 operator to please not send anyone out to the house. She then apologizes again before hanging up.

Spud exhales as though he had been holding his breath.

Meanwhile, Queenie announces that she's about to be sick again and rushes out to the front porch, leaning over the railing as before to expel the remaining bits of her breakfast. She isn't sure she will ever be able to eat scrambled eggs again. Her mind is like scrambled eggs, too. She has no idea what to do next. The thought of sweet Sally Rose with someone who might do her harm is too much to bear. More than anything, she hopes the little girl isn't frightened. But how could she not be? Queenie is terrified for her.

Rose brings Queenie a wet washcloth while Spud repeats that everything will be okay, but he doesn't sound as convinced as he did before.

"I shouldn't have left her alone, even for a second," Queenie says to Rose.

"We can't be paying attention one hundred percent of the time," Rose says. "I've done the same thing." Rose's statement is an act of incredible generosity, given Rose's only grandchild is missing and no thanks to Queenie. They exchange a quick embrace as if to fortify each other, but Queenie's knees are quaking.

"We need to try to find Katie and Angie," Spud says.

The three exchange looks as though already imagining Katie and Angie's horror when told what has happened.

"We need to get everyone home," Queenie says. "Then we'll talk about what to do next."

"I agree," Rose says. "But Katie and Angie need to have the final say."

"I'll call around and find Max and Jack," Spud says, taking the phone book out of the kitchen drawer. He heads upstairs to use the bedroom phone, which is their private line.

"I'll call Violet at the tea shop," Rose says.

"And I'll call Katie and Angie's therapist's office," Queenie says. "They left a number on the notepad by the fridge."

When Queenie dials the therapist's office, an answering machine picks up. Queenie leaves a message that she is trying to get in touch with Katie and Angie and ask them to call home. She tries to sound calm, even though *calm* is the last thing she feels, and the message is urgent.

"Weren't they going out to lunch after their session?" Rose asks Queenie.

"They were," Queenie says. "But they didn't tell me where. Do you have any ideas of where they might have gone?"

"Maybe River Street," Rose says. "I'll ask Spud to call restaurants, too." Roses leaves to go upstairs.

In the meantime, Queenie returns to the porch as though returning to a crime scene—her crime being to step away from Sally Rose for two minutes while she went to relieve herself. A wave of guilt rolls in like a tidal surge. Two minutes was just enough time for someone to walk up to the porch and take her.

Queenie's memory flashes to the tall man with the long beard she saw in the dunes weeks ago with a woman. Could those two have been plotting to take Sally Rose all this time? Queenie has watched enough crime shows to know that the storyline often highlights someone who has nothing to do with the crime. Nobody in these dramas is as they seem. But without clues, Queenie has nowhere to go.

Rose finds Queenie on the porch. "Violet is on her way. I didn't tell her what the emergency was, only that it wasn't about her girls. I didn't want her to panic and drive too fast over that bridge."

"Did Spud reach Max and Jack?" Queenie asks.

"He was able to contact Jack at the Home Depot as he was checking out," Rose tells her. "Max is still unaccounted for. I think he was going to our attorney's office after the dentist. And Tia and Leitha are at their friend's house in Savannah until later this afternoon."

They are right to get everyone home, except maybe Violet's girls. They might as well stay where they are.

"What do we do now?" Queenie asks.

"I truly have no idea," Rose says. "We need a divine intervention or something."

"We need Mama," Queenie says.

Rose agrees.

Rose sits with Queenie in the kitchen as they try not to go into a full-fledged panic.

"To not let the police handle this feels dangerous," Queenie says, "but I imagine the person who took Sally Rose is serious about their threat."

"We have to assume," Rose says.

"I'm not sure I could live with myself if something happened to Sally Rose."

"Let's not get ahead of ourselves," Rose says. "For now, we just wait."

Spud comes downstairs to report that he hasn't been able to find Katie and Angie at any Savannah restaurants. "I had no idea there were so many," he says. "But nobody seemed to fit the description I gave them."

"They could be anywhere," Queenie says, feeling queasy again.

"Well, I'm not giving up," Spud says. "I'll keep calling." He kisses Queenie on the cheek and goes back upstairs.

"I heard on television that the first twenty-four hours are crucial in child abductions," Rose tells Queenie.

Queenie moans.

"We can't go there, Queenie. Once everybody gets home, we'll brainstorm what to do next."

Every second that Sally Rose is gone is terrible news, and Queenie isn't sure how having a plan will help that. They must wait for the kidnappers to contact them. Until then, everything is out of their control.

39

ROSE

Unable to watch Queenie fret any longer, Rose knocks on the door of Queenie and Spud's bedroom. He tells her to come in. "Any luck?" Rose asks.

"None so far." He sits on the bed with the phone and phone book, crossing restaurants off his list.

"This is horrible, isn't it?" Rose's voice shakes.

Spud looks at her, his eyes full of compassion.

"It's important that we stay calm," he says. "As soon as I find Katie and Angie, I'll go back downstairs to help console Queenie. It's just quieter up here for calling noisy restaurants."

Rose nods and sits on the bed. Watching Spud talk is easier than watching Queenie pace. What is unspoken between them is that if something happens to Sally Rose, Queenie will never forgive herself.

While Queenie's natural response is to throw up over porch railings, Rose has a different reaction. She wants to kill the kidnappers with her bare hands.

"When do you think whoever took her will call to give

instructions?" Rose is already thinking about how they might pool their resources to pay off the demands.

"The note said this evening," Spud says. "Who knows when. But we'll be here, and we'll do everything they ask."

Rose looks at her watch. It is almost three o'clock. Katie and Angie didn't plan to rush back because they probably told Queenie to put Sally Rose down for a nap.

She tries to imagine what her life would have been like to have a dad like Spud instead of the one she had. Perhaps she wouldn't have turned to alcohol to cope as her father did. Or maybe she would be more trusting that everything will work out okay—a trust that isn't about inaction but is an active faith in life that it will prevail.

Spud calls another eating establishment in downtown Savannah. He describes the two women who may be having lunch there who have an emergency at home. No luck again. But on the second call, he says, "They were there?"

Rose walks toward him.

"They just left. Katie and Angie are on their way home," Spud says after he hangs up.

"I'll tell Queenie," Rose says.

"I'll go with you." His smile says, *We'll get through this*, and Rose wants to believe him.

Jack and Max have made it back, and Queenie is in the kitchen, filling them in.

"They're going to want money," Max says. "A lot of it." He puts an arm around Rose and asks how she's holding up.

"I'm not," Rose says. "I want to commit homicide, and I'll do anything I have to do to get our granddaughter home safely."

Max squeezes her shoulder as if to remind Rose that she's not in this alone. Rose has always appreciated Max's calmness during a crisis. They had many on the ranch. And while Rose may appear calm on the outside, on the inside she is not only furious, she is on the verge of having a panic attack. She tells herself to take deep breaths.

"The good news is I found Katie and Angie," Spud says to those gathered in the kitchen. "They just left the restaurant. They'll probably be home in the next thirty minutes."

"That's good news?" Queenie's expression is one of full-on dread.

"Maybe we should do a more extensive search," Jack says to everyone gathered. "I know she's not lost, but there may be clues."

Max agrees that's a good idea, and Spud asks if he can go along. The three men leave by the front door just as Violet walks in.

Violet greets the men, holding her shoulder. "What's going on?" she asks, walking into the kitchen. "Rose, you sounded so serious over the phone."

Violet looks at Queenie, who looks at Rose.

"What's happened?" Violet asks again.

"Sally Rose is missing," Rose says.

Violet gasps. "What do you mean she's missing?"

"Someone has taken her," Rose says.

It is Queenie, sitting at the kitchen island, who tells Violet the details. She repeats the story, including rescinding the 911 call after finding the note.

Rose hands the note to Violet from the kitchen counter.

Violet reads it and covers her mouth as though stifling a scream.

Violet asks about Katie and Angie.

"They'll be here any minute," Rose says.

The room grows silent as they imagine Katie and Angie's reaction. Her only child's precious baby has gone missing.

"I only left for a minute," Queenie repeats, her eyes filling with tears.

Violet places her hand on Queenie's.

"My shoulder kept warning me," Violet says. "But I couldn't figure out what it was. I even made one of Old Sally's protection spells."

"I remember," Rose says.

"I spread it all over the outside of the house," Violet continues. "All the doors and windows. But it didn't do any good. It never occurred to me put it on the porch or the steps leading up. I just put it on the door."

"You couldn't have known," Rose says.

"Couldn't I?"

"No, you couldn't," Rose says. "Blaming ourselves isn't helpful," she adds. "Next, we'll be blaming each other."

Violet turns to walk out the door again.

"Where are you going?" Rose asks.

"I need to talk to Old Sally," Violet says. "I'll be back as soon as I can."

Minutes after Violet leaves, another car pulls up on the gravel driveway. It is probably Katie and Angie. Rose feels herself stiffen. They come in the kitchen door, carrying a doggie bag of leftovers. Both are smiling. Their outing must have gone well. When they see Rose and Queenie, they stop.

"What is it?" Katie asks. "What's happened?"

Her voice is calm, and Rose tells them that someone

has taken Sally Rose and will call later tonight. Katie, who has always been emotionally mature and skated through her teen years without an ounce of drama, sinks to the floor sobbing. Angie, Queenie, and Rose rush to her side.

They repeat reassuring words. But Rose can't remember when she has felt this helpless. She holds Katie tight, not knowing what else to do. But then she thinks of Old Sally and recalls the scariest part of the hurricane when they lost all hope of surviving.

"Remember at the lighthouse when Old Sally told us to keep the courage fires burning?" Everyone turns to look at Rose as though the moment still burns in their minds.

"We need to build a massive courage fire now," Rose says. "We need to gather all the kindling and strength that we can. We'll get through this. We can do hard things. Just like we got through the hurricane."

Everyone agrees. But Rose anticipates that it will take everything the housemates collectively have to keep that fire going.

40

VIOLET

O n the way to the cemetery, Violet scolds herself for not putting more graveyard dirt around the house —best sprinkled at midnight when the soil is the most potent. After Violet's protection spell, life grew calm for a time, and Violet lacked the imagination to see that they might need more. But like a mother knows to check on mischievous children that suddenly grow quiet, Violet should have guessed that all that quietness was building up to something loud.

Violet sits on the bench under the live oaks near Old Sally's final resting place. She catches her breath, unsure what to do next. After the anniversary of Old Sally's death, continuing to come every week felt too painful. Anniversaries are often magical times, primed in mystery. She had thought perhaps Old Sally would show herself then, and when she didn't, she forced herself to accept that her grandmother is gone forever, disappearing behind a veil that Violet is not allowed to see through.

It doesn't help that her dreams at night continue their

search. Violet will visit places that Old Sally has just left. Or she will find Old Sally's sandals at the front door in a dream, but upon entering the house, Old Sally is nowhere to be found.

However, with Sally Rose missing, Violet feels the urgency to connect with Old Sally even more. Violet must try one more time. She stands at Old Sally's grave.

Violet imagines the opening between the two worlds. A portal, perhaps. A veil. A thin place, as her grandmother called it.

Can you hear me?

Violet pauses, doubling her intent.

Sally Rose is missing, Grandmother. Someone took her. They've threatened to hurt her if we involve the police.

Katie and Angie must be home by now and in complete panic. When she thinks of Sally Rose, the pain in her shoulder causes her to wince.

We need your help, Violet says to Old Sally again. *We're so scared for her. Please. We need you.*

Violet needs her, too, but that feels selfish now. As lost as Violet has been in the last year, she also knows something is changing. For the first time in ages, Violet is hopeful that she may be finding her way. The tea readings in the courtyard seem to be part of it. This morning, she scheduled three for next week. Elizabeth told a friend, and that friend told a friend. The tea shop will also be open next Friday evening. Her life has been closed for over a year and is opening again. But that means nothing until they have Sally Rose back.

Violet pleads more, not only to Old Sally but also to the ancestors. The sound of waves fills the silence. Violet flashes on an earlier scene of Sally Rose passed over Old

Sally's grave in the Gullah ritual. Old Sally possessed a deep love for Sally Rose. They connected in an other-worldly way as if they had met each other before. Old Sally would help them if she could. But can she?

Closing her eyes, Violet rocks her upper body and asks for Sally Rose's safety. She will return home soon and join the others. But first, she must ask the ancestors and the spirit world again to help. After finishing her plea, she opens her eyes.

In the next second, a bluebird lands on the top of Old Sally's stone marker.

Violet freezes, not wanting to scare it away.

The bird turns its head and looks at her. It is indigo blue—Old Sally's favorite color.

Is that you? Violet asks without speaking.

The bird sings. A short trill followed by a long O. At that moment, it is the most beautiful sound Violet has ever heard. The bluebird remains perched on Old Sally's marker and looks around as though curious about why it was summoned.

Violet reaches into her memory for what Old Sally told her about songbirds. Singing on a doorstep implies that company is coming. Is this cemetery a doorstep into another world?

Violet tries to imagine what "company coming" might look like regarding what has happened to Sally Rose, but her mind can't seem to make sense of it. She knows not to take the message literally. It is a sign of a possibility. At its best, it might mean that Sally Rose will return soon. At its worst, it could be that the kidnappers come to the house.

The bluebird flies off into the live oak. Violet searches for the flash of blue, not wanting to lose it. The blue flickering through the tree has a backdrop of gray Spanish moss. It goes higher and higher, from limb to limb. Then it glides to the grasses in the dunes and then onto a piece of driftwood on the beach. It turns to look at Violet and sings its song again.

A vision begins like a dream playing out in front of her. Violet sees Old Sally walking up the beach. Younger. Her body healthy. She doesn't look back at Violet, who now stands at the edge of the Gullah cemetery. But she is intent on going somewhere.

Her grandmother doesn't speak in the vision, either, yet Violet somehow intuits the message. Old Sally is on her way to the lighthouse, and Violet must go there, too. It is there that Violet will find what she seeks. Then the image fades, and the bluebird flies back to the live oak in the cemetery. As soon as it disappears, Violet rushes back to her car. She must tell the others and go to the lighthouse.

41

QUEENIE

In the kitchen, Queenie nibbles on saltines, her stomach still queasy. The group debates the wisdom of not calling the police. Jack and Max want to involve them, and Queenie and Spud don't think it is a good idea. Rose can't seem to decide. They spend an hour presenting both sides and getting nowhere. It is a horrible choice to have to make, but Katie and Angie have the ultimate decision. They choose not to telephone the authorities in fear of further endangering their child. With that, the debate ends.

While the women wait in the kitchen, the men drive around Dolphin Island, searching for anything out of the ordinary. Finding clues to where Sally Rose has been taken seems a longshot, but Queenie can understand their need to do something.

Meanwhile, Katie cries off and on, and Angie remains stoic. Queenie guesses that underneath her seeming lack of feeling, Angie is shattered. Queenie can't imagine what it is like for either of them.

Queenie sits near the telephone, waiting for the kidnappers' phone call, even though it may not happen for hours. Not knowing is the worst. She remembers stepping out of that lighthouse after Hurricane Iris had turned up the coast and finding her world changed. She didn't even know if they would have a home anymore. But homes are one thing. The possibility of losing an innocent and vulnerable child is tragically worse. Queenie would trade her almost-used-up life for Sally Rose any day.

Queenie wonders out loud how things are going at the cemetery with Violet. Does Violet think that Old Sally is going to start talking to her again? "It seems if Mama could help, she would already be helping," Queenie says to no one in particular.

Dazed, Katie looks up. "Violet went to talk to Old Sally?" She seems to find the thought hopeful.

Queenie answers in the affirmative, grateful that even though she was the one they left in charge of their child, Katie and Angie have not unleashed their upset onto her. In a way, this makes her feel worse. She wishes they would get furious with Queenie instead of taking the high road. After all, she is furious with herself.

"Anybody hungry?" Queenie asks, going to the pantry for more saltines.

It doesn't seem that anyone is, but Queenie opens a can of soup. It is nearing dinnertime. Not that Queenie feels like eating. It is unlike her to get sick to her stomach. That was always Iris's forte. Queenie must admit she has a bit more compassion for her half sister now.

Seconds later, Violet bursts through the front door. Everyone automatically stands. Even with all of Violet's struggles in the last few months, she is the one they count on to stay steady, the heir apparent to Old Sally. Albeit a reluctant one in Queenie's opinion.

"I think I know where Sally Rose is," Violet says.

"Where?" Queenie asks.

Katie, Angie, and Rose rise from the table.

"The lighthouse," Violet says. She seems so confident, and Queenie is hesitant to question her. Yet, she decides to, anyway.

"What makes you think she's at the lighthouse?" Queenie sounds more like Iris than she intends.

"Old Sally told me," Violet says. "Well, actually, a blue-bird told me, and I saw Old Sally walk toward the light-house, and I knew I was supposed to follow her."

The group's initial hopefulness fizzles like a wet fire-cracker.

"That seems a little too easy, doesn't it?" Queenie says.

"You want it to be hard?" Violet and Queenie rarely disagree, and they exchange a look that has their entire history in it.

"Let's go get her," Angie says to Katie, taking her hand.

"Wait," Violet says. "We need to be smart about this."

Katie asks what she means.

"Violet means that we don't know who is with her or if they have weapons or anything about what these people are capable of doing," Queenie says. Then she turns to Violet and tries to say as nicely as she can, "Maybe you wanted to see Old Sally so badly that you imagined her walking toward the lighthouse."

Violet narrows her eyes. "That's a possibility, but do we have anything else to go on?"

Uncharacteristically, Queenie feels the urge to pick a

fight with Violet. But if she's honest, she's really upset with herself.

Violet stands at the kitchen island, her hands resting on the polished counter. "Maybe it was Old Sally. Maybe it is my imagination. But I think it's worth checking out."

"Feel free," Queenie says, with a snarkiness second only to Iris. Her stomach gurgles, and she feels like she might throw up again as her self-loathing hits its peak.

She pauses, telling herself to get a grip. Queenie apologizes to Violet for being out of sorts, admitting that she has never been so scared in her life.

Violet accepts her apology and says she understands. She sits at the kitchen table with the rest of them as though rethinking her suggestion.

The men return. It is rare, of late, to have everyone in the kitchen at the same time. Besides Violet's girls, who still have no idea what's going on, the only person missing from their current clan is Sally Rose. With this thought, Queenie's stomach lurches, and she runs to the downstairs bathroom. When she returns, the conversation has advanced.

"A car was sitting at the back of the lighthouse when we went by a little while ago," Spud says.

"What kind of car?" Queenie asks.

"Small import," Spud says.

"Could just be someone parking there to walk on the beach," Jack says. "People do it all the time."

They agree it could be nothing. However, Queenie suggests that they should go and explore, though she is not volunteering. And she wouldn't want Spud to go, either. These people might be dangerous—Jack and Max suggest calling the police again.

Different people offer to go to the lighthouse to check it

out, and the kitchen gets loud with everyone offering their possible plans. Only Violet is silent. They debate who should stay and answer the phone, whether Katie and Angie should go. If it's the men, should they take weapons? And how would they get there without alerting the kidnappers? Not to mention what they should do when they get there. Then they circle back to whether or not they should get the police involved. The conversation is going nowhere, and the room gets louder and louder as they speak over each other. They appear to be in total disagreement for the first time since they have all lived together.

Spud stands next to Queenie, asking her over the din of noise if she is okay. Queenie says she's been better. She doesn't mention how she morphed into Iris momentarily and became a royal pain in the backside with her one and only daughter. The noise crescendos as Violet slips out of the kitchen, grabbing something from the front closet before walking out of the door.

42

ROSE

The phone rings at six o'clock, and the cacophony of voices goes silent. Since Rose stands closest to the phone, she asks if she should get it.

Katie nods, and Rose picks up the phone.

"Hello?"

It is a male voice from what sounds like a public phone—Rose can hear voices in the background. "Two million by this time tomorrow. I will call tomorrow to tell you where to drop it off. If you contact the police, she's dead." He hangs up.

Rose repeats what the man said to the others, and Katie begins to sob.

"Did he say anything about Sally Rose?"

"Nothing," Rose says, and she didn't even think to ask. Not that she had time.

Seeing Katie's pain feels unbearable. Tears threaten to come while Rose tells herself to stay strong. She will have time to fall apart later. After Sally Rose is home, safe and sound.

"But we don't even begin to have that kind of money," Angie says.

"I've crunched some numbers," Max says to Katie.

This phrase is something that always made Rose and Katie laugh on the ranch. Max was forever "crunching the numbers" for every family purchase bigger than a toaster, telling them whether they could afford something or not. Those days of money struggles are over for the most part after selling the ranch and getting the stipend from her mother's inheritance, but two million is still a lot of money. Banks don't even keep that much in their vaults. How can they possibly pull that amount together in twenty-four hours? They are defeated before they even start. But that doesn't stop the men from trying to problem-solve with a Hail Mary pass.

"We'll need to pool our resources," Max says, looking around the room.

Spud nods, as does Jack, as though they have been crunching numbers, too.

"We've got properties we can leverage," Spud says, giving Katie a reassuring look.

Max told her once that Spud's inheritance from Rose's mother was a gold mine. Prime beach properties in Hilton Head go up in value every year.

For these last few harrowing hours, Rose hasn't allowed herself to think of the worst-case scenario or the best for that matter. As a girl, when bad things happened, she always ran to Old Sally. But Old Sally isn't here any longer, and for the first time, Rose truly understands how hard this last year has been for Violet. The world seems a gentler, more manageable place with Old Sally in it, and Rose

knows that Old Sally would do whatever she could to keep
Sally Rose safe. In this world or the next.

Rose looks around for Violet. With all the talk of
money, she seems to have stepped away. Rose doesn't
blame her. The kitchen is chaotic and full of discussion
about getting the money together quickly to pay the
ransom.

In the meantime, Rose walks back to the cottage to find
the small burlap sack that Old Sally gave her for protection. Rose sniffs it to conjure up the person she wishes was
here. Then she opens it carefully to examine its contents.
Inside are a small, gnarled root, a marble-sized pearl, and a
piece of fabric in indigo blue. It is a mystery to Rose why
this combination of objects holds power to protect, but she
trusts Old Sally. Rose squeezes a prayer into it and puts her
hand close to her heart. Then she walks back toward the
big house, slipping the small sack into her pocket.

"We need you," Rose says aloud. She looks up as
though Old Sally resides in the sky. She remembers her
mother's diary, now a pile of ash in the Temple
mausoleum. Nurturing the Temple legacy came at a high
cost to the matriarch, who seemingly had everything. In a
world where money equals power, some people will do
anything to get it. Even kidnap a child. With three hours of
daylight left before darkness descends, Rose wraps her
arms around herself as though the day has suddenly
become cold. But in truth, she is trying desperately to hold
herself together.

43

VIOLET

Violet stands by the shore, the lighthouse in view. She pulls her hat farther down on her head in case whoever took Sally Rose might recognize her. The hat is Old Sally's. She wears it now, replaying in her mind the vision she saw on the beach in front of the cemetery. It was a message from Old Sally. Violet is certain of it now. She's not sure why she let Queenie's doubts sway her. Old Sally did everything except make a motion for Violet to follow her. If her imagination is playing tricks on her, she likes these tricks.

It is also entirely possible that no one will be at the lighthouse, and it will have been a chase of the wild-goose variety. But Violet must try, anyway. It is the first time in a year that Old Sally has felt even the slightest bit close.

Meanwhile, Violet studies the large white structure in the distance. She pretends to be a tourist, someone seeing the lighthouse on Dolphin Island for the very first time instead of someone who grew up here. It looks as it always does—deserted. From here, Violet can't see if the lock is still on the door. She needs to get closer. If the lock is still there, it is empty, and she can go back to the house and help with planning what to do next.

Visions aside, to think that the kidnappers might take Sally Rose to the lighthouse seems almost too far-fetched. But stranger things have happened, like having a bluebird and her dead grandmother point the way.

Violet climbs the steps leading up to the lighthouse as memories rush at her from when Hurricane Iris came ashore. She pushes them away. She can only handle one trauma at a time. When Violet gets to the top step, she sees that the lock is off the door. Her heartbeat accelerates as she contemplates going inside, and her shoulder sends a quick, intense warning that danger could be ahead.

Violet inches the door open, trying not to make a sound. A metallic, musty smell rushes to greet her that is familiar from other times spent here. Metal stairs wind up the center of the structure onto a circular observation deck, where the obsolete beacon reigns. A radio plays softly upstairs, and a backpack sits at the bottom of the steps as though someone refused to lug it up the stairs. Next to the pack sits a bottle of cough syrup for children and a sticky spoon.

Inside the backpack Violet finds a fake beard and two hats. Several snacks and bottled waters are inside, too, as well as a road map of the United States. While her heart races, the rest of her body feels frozen. Time passes at a glacial pace. Violet doesn't have a plan for what to do if the kidnappers are inside. Except panic.

The vision of Old Sally returns. She has her back to Violet and slowly climbs the steps to the beacon. Violet hasn't been up these stairs since the storm, and the memories are so disturbing she grips the handrail until her knuckles are white. But she must follow. Sally Rose needs her. On the first step, her body trembles. She takes another step, and another, carefully making as very little noise as possible. With each step, her legs feel like weights are attached. It doesn't help that she is trying so hard to be quiet. However, she is not alone. The ghostly image of Old Sally waits at the top of the stairs, her back always to Violet like the dreams she has had for weeks.

Violet follows and stops right behind her grandmother, feeling as though she has climbed Mount Everest. Whether real or an illusion, Violet is grateful for her presence. Sweat drenches her, and her palms are clammy. The radio plays hits from the '80s. From here, Violet can see onto the circular observation deck that surrounds the beacon. All the windows remain broken from Hurricane Iris. The sea breeze whips through the top of the lighthouse, making a slight humming sound.

Old Sally now stands near the center of the beacon in spirit form. Below her is a folded blanket. On it lies Sally Rose, sound asleep. At the far end is a woman, about Violet's size, facing the back of the lighthouse watching for someone. She taps her foot to the soft music. Violet can't see her face, but her long hair looks familiar.

"Heather?" Violet asks.

The woman jumps and turns to face Violet, wearing a startled expression.

"How did you get here?" Heather looks at Sally Rose and then back at Violet. She takes a step forward, and then stops as though thinking better of it.

Violet's eyes stay fixed on Heather, wondering if the woman will try to grab Sally Rose. Heather takes another step in that direction, but stops again, as if a wall has suddenly erected between her and the child.

Memories rush forward of Violet at fourteen, earning extra money by helping her grandmother with a Temple party. She stepped into the garden for some fresh air and suddenly Edward, Rose's older brother, was there. Violet remembers the garden peepers singing their song as Edward pulled her into the garden shed and cornered her. His smile announced his entitlement and his willingness to take her against her will. Violet now confronts his daughter, Heather. A daughter he didn't even know he had. Yet she carries the same arrogance, though a more wounded version. That night so long ago, she bit Edward's hand when he covered her mouth to silence her, and she got away. Violet will do whatever she has to do with Heather, too. She clenches her fists.

Violet inches closer, noticing again how much Heather looks like Miss Temple—the big eyes, the pinched nose, and an attitude that life has cheated her somehow. Heather looks older than she did when Violet first met her on Queenie's wedding day. Their only other contact was before, during, and after the hurricane. It was then that Violet surmised that Heather was not the least bit courageous but a broken, frightened girl. Heather had been dealing with grief, too. Her mother had recently died and before she passed Heather found out her father wasn't just a sperm donor, but Edward Temple from Savannah.

"Did you plan all this by yourself?" Violet asks, remembering the "we" in the ransom note.

Heather's shoulders relax as though she no longer sees the point. "My brother helped me, but it was my idea. He couldn't plan his way out of a closet."

Heather's surprising confession is without any hesitation. Violet remembers seeing Heather and her brother in the tea shop before the storm. Were they planning a way to get Temple money even then?

Violet inches toward Sally Rose. She is sound asleep, with evidence of red cough syrup around her lips. Heather must have wanted to keep her sedated and quiet. Violet's concern is about the dosage and how much syrup Sally Rose was given.

"Where's your brother?" Violet doubts he will be as agreeable as Heather. She seems complacent, or perhaps resigned, and hasn't made a move for the door.

"He's out making the call for the ransom request," she says. "He'll be back any second." Heather offers a crooked smile, watching to see if Violet is frightened. But Violet doesn't have the luxury of being scared. She needs all her wits about her to figure out how to get Sally Rose out of there.

"Why did you do it, Heather?" Violet's first thought is to distract her so that maybe she can grab Sally Rose and make a run for it.

"Surely it's obvious." Heather scoffs and looks out the window again.

In the background, the radio plays the song "You're No Good" by Linda Ronstadt. It strikes Violet as odd that Heather would listen to an oldies station. She's barely twenty. But the song seems the perfect backdrop for the occasion.

In the meantime, the vision hasn't left. The shimmering image of Old Sally still stands a few feet in front of Violet, facing Heather. A part of Violet is calm like her grandmother. But then a chill raises the hairs on the back of Violet's neck, and another ghostly figure appears. Miss Temple stands facing Old Sally. Heather doesn't seem to notice, but Violet sees them vividly. They look like two enemies in a standoff, facing a final battle.

Old Sally and Miss Temple exchange words, but Violet can't hear them. They seem to be coming up with a strategy as they look at Sally Rose and then at Heather. To Violet's surprise, her grandmother and her former employer appear to be working together. They discuss more, and then Old Sally nods. They agree. If Violet didn't know better, she would think that Miss Temple is making amends. Then Miss Temple looks toward Sally Rose and nods at Violet. Now is the moment. Without hesitation, Violet steps forward and lifts Sally Rose into her arms, a heavy rag doll from a hefty dose of children's cough syrup. Violet repositions her, laying her head gently against Violet's shoulder.

Heather continues, "I'm the daughter of a Savannah Temple and have absolutely nothing to show for it. Do you think that's fair?" When Heather finally turns, her eyes flare when she sees the baby in Violet's arms, followed by a flicker of surprise. Yet she makes no move. Violet wonders if it is because Miss Temple, in her ghostly presence, appears to be blocking Heather from Violet and the child.

"You're right," Violet says to Heather. "It doesn't seem fair that you have nothing to show for being a Temple."

Violet's statement appears to weaken Heather more.

"You people have so much," Heather begins, "and who knows how much that sunken ship will be worth to you if somebody ever pulls it up."

Heather looks out the window again. Her rescuer is long overdue.

"I imagine you still miss your mother, too," Violet says, moving slowly toward the stairs. "You only lost her a little while ago."

Heather's lips tighten.

"I know how grief can change a person and make them do things they've never done before," Violet says. Although, to her credit, she hasn't resorted to kidnapping someone's child to make some cash. "My grandmother's death has been devastating."

"That old lady died?" Heather asks.

"A year ago," Violet says.

She remembers now that Old Sally met Heather and, in fact, had warned Violet to be careful, that something wasn't right with her.

Meanwhile, Miss Temple and Old Sally stand between them. A shield between the baby and Heather. Violet's senses are on alert. If Heather's brother returns and tries to take Sally Rose from her, Violet isn't sure what she will do.

"You think I don't know what you're doing?" Heather asks without turning around. "Just stop acting like you care about me and get out of here."

With that, the spell is broken, and Old Sally and Miss Temple fade into nothingness. Any unfinished business between the two spirits appears finished. Violet doubts she will ever understand what just happened, although it seems that Old Sally and Miss Temple were on the same side. Both wanted to protect Sally Rose.

Carrying the child in one arm and gripping the metal handrail, Violet rushes down the stairs, taking one sturdy step after another. For a moment, she remembers the water climbing when Hurricane Iris came ashore, but the past has no role here anymore. The present moment is all that matters.

After Violet makes it down the stairs, she pauses to ensure Heather's brother isn't coming around the corner. She opens the squeaky door, and a rush of freedom comes in with the salty air. In the distance, she hears a car arriving. Violet runs down the sandy concrete steps toward the beach, carrying Sally Rose. She then labors through the high sand that grabs her shoes, slowing her forward movement. People are nearby taking walks and wading into the surf. She doubts Heather's brother will risk chasing after her.

Sally Rose is still sleeping.

"We're going home, little one. You're safe." Reaching the shoreline, Violet stops periodically to catch her breath. Her arms ache. Violet looks behind her every few steps to make sure she is telling the truth. In a few minutes, Violet and Sally Rose will be home.

Without Old Sally, Violet would have never thought to go to the lighthouse. Her only regret is that she didn't get to see Old Sally's face. It was just like in the dreams. However, her grandmother showed up when she needed her most, and to Violet's astonishment, so did Miss Temple.

Violet walks fast toward home, feeling more empowered and grateful with every step.

44

QUEENIE

W hen Violet walks through the door carrying Sally Rose, Queenie screams and cries happy tears. Katie runs to greet her, with Angie close behind, and they take Sally Rose from Violet's arms. Violet collapses inside the door, and Queenie goes to her, holding her steady, as the others give Katie and Angie room.

"They gave her cough syrup to make her sleep," Violet says. "I don't know how much."

Angie rushes into the kitchen to call their pediatrician. Queenie overhears her asking if they should take Sally Rose to the emergency room or if she wants them to come there.

While Katie holds a sleeping Sally Rose, Queenie takes the little girl's hand and says a silent apology for letting this happen.

"She'll meet us at the hospital," Angie says, hanging up the phone. "It's just a precaution," Angie adds. "She'll probably just wake up on her own in a few hours."

To Queenie, this sounds like something a pediatrician

might tell a hysterical parent. Who knows what the truth is?

"Do you want us to come?" Queenie asks.

Katie says not to but promises to call as soon as they know anything. Within seconds they are out the door and on their way to Savannah.

"It's smart to check her out," Spud says to Queenie, who is wiping her tears on a dishtowel by the kitchen sink. Rose takes the other end and wipes a few of her own. Even Max and Jack have not managed to stay dry-eyed.

"She's safe now," Queenie says. For the first time in hours, she doesn't feel nauseous.

"I hope you can forgive yourself now," Rose says to Queenie. Spud agrees.

To Queenie, this is a lovely idea, but she isn't so sure she can. Nor will she be able to breathe easier until the doctor pronounces that Sally Rose is okay.

Meanwhile, Rose sits at the kitchen table like a deflated balloon. Violet is quiet, too, and appears distracted and deep in thought.

It is then that everyone asks Violet how she pulled this off. When the details emerge, Queenie has never felt prouder. When Tia and Leisha come home in the middle of it, the whole story begins again. It occurs to Queenie that this story is something that will follow Sally Rose her entire life. She will tell it to every significant person she meets.

It seems unbelievable that it was only two hours ago that the kidnapper had phoned requesting two million dollars before they would return Sally Rose. Now, thanks to Violet, their worries are over. The quickness of the resolution makes Queenie a bit giddy, as well as relieved.

"Heather and her brother took Sally Rose," Violet says to the questions about the kidnappers.

When Violet talks about Heather plotting the deed, Queenie and Rose exchange a look that says, *We knew that woman was bad news.* In all of Queenie's imaginings of who might have taken Sally Rose, she did not once imagine Heather. Why would she? But now that Queenie thinks about it, why didn't she?

Max calls the police and tells them about the kidnapping and who was behind it. Two officers will come out to take statements. Hopefully, they will be issuing warrants for Heather's and her brother's arrests.

"They're probably long gone," Queenie says to those still gathered in the kitchen. She knows what it's like to run away.

"I'm sure they'll catch them," Rose says.

"Let's hope so," Queenie says. "It doesn't sound like they were very smart kidnappers, thank heavens. I just hope Sally Rose is okay."

Within an hour, two detectives arrive and ask Violet a bunch of questions for their report. A squad car was sent to the lighthouse, but Heather and her brother were nowhere to be found.

When the phone rings again, it is Queenie who answers it. Katie tells her that Sally Rose just woke up and that she is going to be fine.

Queenie repeats the news to everyone waiting, and a cheer goes up that hurts her ears. Jack and Spud even open a bottle of champagne in the back of the fridge left over from Queenie and Spud's wedding. They drink a toast to Sally Rose's safe return, Rose having a ginger ale.

Several people talk at once again, but the conversation

has lightened considerably. Their youngest family member will be fine, and life will carry on. Now, Queenie is trying to figure out what is going on with Violet since she returned from the lighthouse. She acts as though she has seen a ghost.

45

ROSE

Two months after the kidnapping, Rose and Spud drive to Savannah to drop Rose's painting of the Gullah cemetery live oak at Violet's Tea Shop. While Sally Rose recovered quickly, the adults have taken much longer to get over the trauma, if indeed they have. Once-in-a-life-time events take a while to process. As a result, the painting took much longer to complete, as well. With tonight being Violet's first Friday night event—postponed until now because of the kidnapping—Rose wanted to surprise her with this new addition to her walls.

Rose parks Max's truck on the narrow street outside the tea shop to deliver the new painting. Hazard lights blinking, a No Parking sign in clear view, Rose doesn't plan to stay long, and she is grateful Spud is there to help.

They maneuver the large painting out of the back of the truck and into the courtyard. Spud opens the door with one hand as the bells jingle to announce their arrival. Ava smiles a greeting as Violet delivers two coffees to a table near the window. Other than that one table, the place is empty.

Since the kidnapping, Violet seems younger and more content and frequently carries around the Gullah Book of Secrets to study.

They lean the painting against the brick wall near the violets in the window. Earlier that day while Violet was out, Max installed a hanger based on Rose's specifications and Ava was able to keep it a secret. Violet greets her, and they exchange pleasantries while Rose begins to unwrap her surprise. As she rips into the final layer of kraft paper surrounding the canvas, she tells Violet to close her eyes.

Rose clears the final wrapping away and then tells Violet to open her eyes again.

Violet gives Rose an enormous smile that she hasn't seen in ages.

"Oh my, it's gorgeous," Violet says.

"You like it?" Rose asks.

Violet stares at the tree as though taking in the wholeness of it. Her eyes reveal the beginnings of tears. "It's amazing, Rose."

"I told her the same thing," Spud says, smiling. "I'm so proud of her."

Rose's eyes turn misty, too.

"Shall we?" Violet says, eyeing the wall behind them.

Together Violet and Rose lift the painting and put it on the hook. Rose adds some final straightening while Spud and Violet stand back to get a good look.

Their smiles are the reason Rose paints. Sharing her art is Rose's way of offering a tiny bit of healing to the world.

They sit for a few minutes, asking Violet how the evening is shaping up.

"Marylou and Ava have handled everything," Violet says, filling them in on the details.

Rose takes note of how different Violet seems. Taking risks, like tonight, seems to suit her, and her tea readings in the courtyard have a nine-week waiting list. However, a mystery remains about what happened at the lighthouse when Violet rescued Sally Rose that Violet still hasn't shared. But the days and weeks afterward seemed to produce a slow awakening of some kind in her. That's the only way Rose can think to describe it.

Spud looks at his watch and reminds Rose of her blinking hazard lights outside and their early dinner reservation.

After the kidnapping, Rose and Spud began to meet once a week, just the two of them, to get to know each other better.

As they stand at the door, they wish Violet the best of luck and promise to return by seven o'clock.

"We don't want to miss anything," Rose says.

"There may not be anything to miss," Violet says, showing her first hint of nervousness. "What if nobody shows?" she adds.

Rose assures her that will never happen. "All the people who love you will be here," Rose says. "If the rest of Savannah chooses not to show up, that's Savannah's loss."

Within minutes, Rose and Spud make their way across town to a favorite restaurant. To celebrate these occasions, Spud wears a colorful bow tie that he brought out of retirement. A red one with yellow polka dots. It makes the experience seem festive.

"I don't think I ever told you how impressed your mother was with your early paintings," Spud says. "The ones you did at Smith?"

Rose pauses, taking this in. "She never said a word. I assumed she hated them."

"I told her that you probably thought that," he says. "Iris could be stingy with her praise."

The diary opened Rose's eyes to another side of her mother. A side that Rose was glad to know. But Iris Temple was Iris Temple. For a woman who seemingly had everything, she was indeed very stingy with her praise, as well as her love.

"The point I'm making, I guess, is that Iris didn't have a heart of gold, but she did have a heart," Spud continues. "Even if she seemed incapable of expressing its desires at times."

"Why are you telling me this?" Rose asks.

He hesitates. "I do have a motive, actually," Spud begins. "I want you to know that I loved your mother, and she loved me, so you were created with love."

His face momentarily blushes, turning as red as his bow tie.

The more she gets to know him, the more aware Rose is of Spud's innate kindness.

"I hope Queenie gives you the love that Mother wasn't able to," Rose says.

"Oh my heavens, yes." Spud smiles. "Our marriage is better than ever. I hit the jackpot with Queenie."

They laugh.

"Queenie is more than special. She's one of a kind." He blushes again and then whispers across the table: "I love her with all my heart."

"I know you do," Rose says. "I love seeing her this happy."

Spud's brow furrows. "The kidnapping took a lot out of her. She was shaky there for a while."

"We all were," Rose says.

"I hate to think we almost lost that little angel." Spud straightens his bow tie as if to remind himself to keep his composure.

Their dinner arrives, and they dive in to enjoy their meal. As their empty plates are taken away, their conversation deepens again.

"Tell me about Heather," Spud says.

"My brother, Edward, never acknowledged her existence," Rose says, "and she had a single mother who struggled to raise her. Then after she died, Heather found out that her absent father was quite wealthy."

"I was so surprised that she and her brother pleaded guilty," Spud says.

"I think they were going for leniency after being caught trying to leave the country," Rose says.

They pause while the waiter brings two decafs and a piece of cheesecake that they will split between them.

"Change of subject?" Spud asks.

"Sure." Rose appreciates the ease with which they have come to speak to each other.

"Violet seems much happier these days, doesn't she?" Spud says. "I was worried about her there for a while. She was so sad. But it seems she's had a breakthrough of some kind."

"I've noticed it, too. *Breakthrough* is a good word."

"I must confess, Rose, I don't know much about Gullah

magic. I'm just an old white man who has lived in the South my whole life."

"But?" Rose asks.

Spud smiles. "But. Do you think Old Sally helped Violet find Sally Rose? I mean, I want to believe it. And I'm so glad it happened. It just seems so fanciful."

Rose agrees that it might seem a bit far-fetched.

"But I am open to the possibility." Spud smiles.

"If I hadn't grown up around Old Sally, I would probably think it was impossible," Rose says. "But she taught me that there's an invisible world out there, along with a visible one. It's a world that people don't see that can be equally as dramatic and even magical."

"Well, I love that there are people who think that way," Spud says. "And I'm all for Gullah folk magic if it keeps the people I love safe."

Rose touches his hand across the table and wonders if someday she might want to call him Dad. Not once did she call her father Dad. It would have been too personal for the Temple household. So, in a way, this term of endearment feels like it might only belong to Spud. Yet it seems too soon to cross that bridge now.

Spud asks the waitress for the check. He refuses to let Rose pay her half. They leave the restaurant and walk to the car. In fifteen minutes, the music is supposed to begin at Violet's shop. If Violet's fear is realized and nobody comes, they will go into damage control and sit on the front row with the rest of their household cheering on Violet and the event.

Now and again, the surprise renews, and Rose realizes that Spud is her father. It never occurred to her that at this stage of her life, there could be more surprises. Not big ones like this one, anyway. Rose remains grateful that she has so many people to love and who love her.

They walk down the street in silence from the parking lot two blocks away. Their footsteps sync up on the sidewalk. For the longest time, Rose felt like she didn't belong anywhere. As a girl, she didn't fit with the Temples, and then while living on a ranch in Wyoming, she didn't feel like she belonged out West. Then after she returned to the Savannah area, she wasn't sure where she fit, either. But it turns out that Rose is where she belongs. Savannah is her home, and she is with her Sea Gypsy sisters, her people.

Rose is proud of Violet for taking this huge risk tonight and feels a tad envious. She wonders what she might risk and what she might call on her courage to do. The answer comes quickly and clearly.

"I enjoy our time together, Dad," Rose says to Spud.

Spud stops on the sidewalk and turns to look at her. "I enjoy our time together, too, daughter." His voice catches with emotion.

They embrace as if realizing the momentousness of the occasion. From now on, it will never be a question of where Rose belongs. They have each other.

46

VIOLET

A few people trickle in. Violet looks over at the new painting hanging on the wall and thinks of Old Sally. On the drive into Savannah, Violet realized that tonight is a full moon. She imagines that old oak now in the cemetery lit with shadows, the waves of the tide lapping against the shore. Violet may never see her grandmother again or hear her voice, but Violet has the Gullah Book of Secrets. Violet's Gullah ancestors still have plenty of things to teach her, and she wants to claim everything that is hers to claim.

It is a big night at the tea shop. A jazz duo will perform, a female vocalist and a bassist whom Spud had heard and highly recommended. Violet even advertised the event in the Savannah newspaper. Violet had run home to change clothes earlier and then drove over the bridge toward Savannah for the second time that day. It occurs to her that people can be bridges, too. Marylou is one of them. She encouraged Violet to read tea leaves and has helped Violet expand her vision beyond her old, careful way of living.

Within minutes, the tea shop is as full as Violet has ever seen it, and Ava is putting out additional folding chairs that they rented just in case. Violet greets everyone at the door. To her surprise, she recognizes a few of Miss Temple's friends. A mixture of old Savannah society is here to listen to the music, along with young people in various shades of white and brown. Violet takes a deep breath and smiles, proud of herself for creating this place for people to gather.

Among the guests are people for whom Violet has conducted tea readings. Periodically, they catch her eye and smile or wave. Elizabeth is there, the young artist trying to decide between drama schools. She wears a Big Apple T-shirt, so Violet imagines she has made her decision. Violet remembers Queenie's wedding, where Old Sally stepped aside so Violet could step forward. It felt then that her grandmother was passing the mantle. It took two years for Violet to finally accept it, including the secrets held by the tea leaves. Violet will never apologize for—or hide—her Gullah ancestry again. She just won't. With that commitment has come a clarity of purpose. Violet will be of service to Savannah and the surrounding areas in whatever way she can.

Rose and Spud arrive and sit with Queenie, Max, Katie, and Angie at two tables pulled together. Sally Rose sits nearby in a booster seat. Rose kisses Sally Rose on the cheek, and Queenie wraps an arm around Spud as though finally allowing herself to relax into his love. Jack sits at a nearby table with Tia and Leisha and several of their friends. Everyone Violet loves is in this room.

Well, almost everyone, she says to herself, thinking of Old Sally.

Marylou sits at a table near the front, looking elegant and pleased. A white-haired gentleman sits next to her; this is her son, Ralph, who isn't at all as Violet imagined him. He is short and stocky with black-rimmed glasses. At the door, they shook hands and exchanged small talk. Violet wonders if he is aware that one of Violet's tea readings is why Marylou is still in Savannah.

The jazz duo is fabulous. At intermission, Violet and Marylou find each other and go out into the courtyard, where it is quieter.

"It's a total success," Marylou says.

"I couldn't have done it without you," Violet says.

Marylou smiles. "Sure you could have. You just needed someone to give you permission."

Violet would like to believe this is true.

"You look so different tonight," Marylou says. "You look practically radiant."

Has she ever been called *radiant*?

"I think I've finally made peace with myself," Violet says. "After Old Sally died, I put away the Gullah part of me and pretended it didn't exist. It was the only way I could bear her loss. But I seem to have found that part of me again."

Marylou claps as though giving Violet an encore. "I'm so happy for you," she says. "Keep it up."

Violet thanks her. If not for Marylou, she wouldn't have tried that first reading of tea leaves, and it may have been years before she had the courage and inclination to open the tea shop to events.

As intermission ends, Violet returns to the counter and

leans against the back wall to watch. The musicians set up in the front window, and to the left is the new painting.

Just a few short years ago, at this time on a Friday, Violet would have prepared Miss Temple's dinner and be standing in the grand dining room, a mere servant. Today, Violet stands in a tea shop that she owns. A shop filled with not only satisfied customers but friends and family and fantastic music.

In the next instant, Violet's shoulder tingles, but not in a painful way. The sound of the music fades, and an image slowly comes into view.

Violet gasps. Standing in front of the live oak painting, facing her, is Old Sally.

Is that you? Violet asks in the way her grandmother taught her.

For the first time in over a year, the veil between them lifts, and Violet hears the words that Old Sally is thinking.

It be me, child.

Tears rush to Violet's eyes, and she looks around to see if anyone else is seeing what she is seeing. But everyone is watching the musicians.

I thought you'd deserted me, but I see now that I was the one who abandoned you, Violet says. *I'm so sorry.*

While soft jazz plays in the background, Violet's grandmother beams courage at her from across the crowded tea shop as though she couldn't be more pleased. Violet puts a hand to her heart, soaking it in like a thirsty flower.

Heaven be full of forgiveness, Old Sally says with a smile as Violet catches her first glimpse of the ancestors who came before her.

November 2021

Dear Reader,

In early 2020, I began to write a new historical fiction novel set outside of Charleston. Book three of the Wildflower Trilogy, *Daisy's Fortune*, had come out a few months before and had been a joy to write. Yet, I wanted to develop new characters and a new story. Then came the pandemic and my creativity went into survival mode. To make the best of this extreme situation, I created a Resilience Dispatch—daily words of encouragement about resilience—that I posted on my blog and my Facebook Author page. As a former psychotherapist and a writer of novels for over twenty-five years, I know a few things about resilience. Initially, I had planned to keep going with these dispatches until the pandemic was over. Little did I know how long this virus would be with us.

When I began to feel my creativity reemerge later that year, my priorities had changed. I turned instead to my love of something familiar—the characters I had created in *Temple Secrets* and *Gullah Secrets*. During the ongoing pandemic, I wanted to spend time with Old Sally, Queenie, Violet, and Rose. I needed their wisdom, their views of life, and their courage. With that, I began to create an unexpected and somehow necessary third book in the *Temple Secret* series which became this book, *Tea Leaf Secrets*. Writing more of the story of these strong women was like preparing a feast of southern comfort food, minus the calories. I hope this book gave you comfort, as well.

During my writing career, I have created several stand-alone novels and two trilogies: The *Wildflower Trilogy* (*The Secret Sense of Wildflower, Lily's Song, Daisy's Fortune*) and now the *Temple Secrets Trilogy* (*Temple Secrets, Gullah Secrets, Tea Leaf Secrets.*) It has been my great honor to create these stories and characters. It has also been a privilege to get to know many of my readers. Thank you so much for reading my stories, spreading the word, and passing my books along to people who may enjoy them. In the meantime, stay well, be brave, and keep reading!

With every good wish,
Susan Gabriel

ACKNOWLEDGMENTS

I am so grateful to the members of my writing team who were an enormous help in getting *Tea Leaf Secrets* out into the world. It is my good fortune to be surrounded by people who have great expertise in their different fields.

Anne Alexander handles the business end of everything I write, and I hate to think where I would be without her. My daughter, Krista, is my historian, who researches details for my books, answers my questions, and finds interesting tidbits about Savannah, Charleston, Gullah magic, or the mountain lore of the Blue Ridge Mountains. My first readers are invaluable and do a fantastic job at catching things that I miss and providing suggestions to make what I write a better story. They are Kimberly Wohlford, Cheryl Groeneveld, Betty Bessette, and Maureen McGough. My exceptional copy editor is Christine Langone.

Many thanks to Holly Adams for the superb narration of my audiobooks, and to Lizzie Gardner who creates the lovely book covers.

Where I am most fortunate is with my many readers. A special thanks to those who contact me through my website (www.SusanGabriel.com) or on Facebook (Susan Gabriel, Author) to tell me that you loved my stories and that they have made a difference to you in some way. Thank you for helping spread the word by telling friends and taking the time to write reviews on Amazon, Audible, iBooks, Barnes & Noble, Goodreads, etc. And thank you for your sweet comments on my blog or Facebook Author page. Your encouragement means the world to me.

ABOUT THE AUTHOR

Susan Gabriel is an Amazon and Nook #1 bestselling author who lives in the mountains of North Carolina. Her novel, *The Secret Sense of Wildflower*, earned a starred review ("for books of remarkable merit") from Kirkus Reviews and was selected as one of their Best Books of 2012.

She is also the author of *The Wildflower Trilogy (The Secret Sense of Wildflower, Lily's Song, Daisy's Fortune)*, *Temple Secrets Trilogy (Temple Secrets, Gullah Secrets, Tea Leaf Secrets)*, *Trueluck Summer*, and other novels. Discover more about Susan at SusanGabriel.com.

OTHER BOOKS BY SUSAN GABRIEL

THE WILDFLOWER TRILOGY

The Secret Sense of Wildflower

Named a Best Book of 2012 by Kirkus Reviews. Small southern towns have few secrets in Appalachia, 1941. When thirteen-year-old Louisa May "Wildflower" McAllister is targeted by the town's teenage bully, she may need more than her "secret sense" to survive.

Lily's Song

A mother's secrets, a daughter's dream, and a family's loyalty are masterfully interwoven in this sequel to The Secret Sense of Wildflower. A compelling tale set in 1956 Appalachia that captures the resilience and strength of both mother and daughter, as secrets revealed test their strong bond and ultimately change their lives forever.

Daisy's Fortune

Tennessee, 1982. Wildflower McAllister returns to the small mountain town that stole her innocence and cast her out. Can she stop a harrowing legacy from spreading to another generation? If you like strong women, generational tales, and the power of family and the land to heal, then you'll adore this compelling finale to the Wildflower trilogy.

Available in paperback, hardcover, ebook and audiobook.

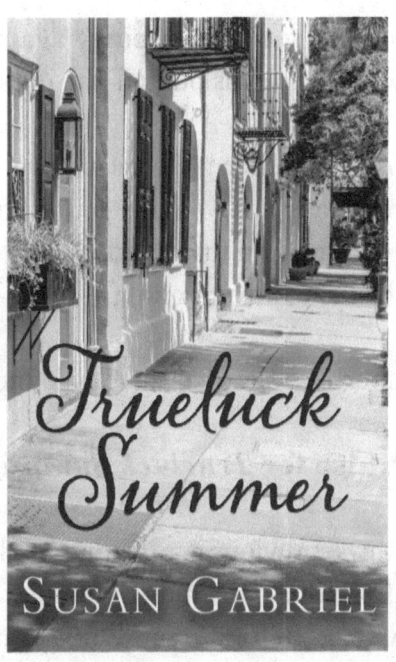

Trueluck Summer

SUSAN GABRIEL

A hopeful grandmother. A sassy young girl. Their audacious summer stunt could change their southern town forever.

Charleston, 1964. Ida Trueluck is still adjusting to life on her own. Moving into her son's house creates a few family conflicts, but the widow's saving grace is her whipsmart granddaughter Trudy. Ida makes it her top priority to give the girl a summer she'll never forget.

When a runaway truck nearly takes her life, Trudy makes fast friends with the boy who saves her. But since Paris is black, the racism they encounter inspires Trudy's surprising summer mission: to take down the Confederate flag from the South Carolina Statehouse. And she knows she can't do it without the help of her beloved grandmother.

With all of Southern society conspiring against them, can Trudy, Ida, and their friends pull off the impossible?

Trueluck Summer is a Southern historical novel set in a time of great cultural change. If you like courageous characters, heartwarming humor, and inspirational acts, then you'll love Susan Gabriel's captivating tale.

Available in paperback, hardcover, ebook and audiobook.

Praise for *Trueluck Summer*

"Having read three previous captivating books by this author I was afraid this book may disappoint. In the first chapter I knew I was in for a treat. Once again, I fell in love with the richly drawn characters. I could not wait to find the time to read this treasure. The courage shown by these characters portrays how real change evolves. It is a book you will not forget!" - Cheryl Quinn

"*Trueluck Summer* is a thoughtful, excellently written adventure. I am a big fan of Susan Gabriel's books and this one may just be one of her best. She brought Charleston and the characters to life. I felt like I laughed and cried with Trudy, Ida and Paris. Was scared with them and proud of them. I will reread." - Molly

"WOW what a book. Even though it is written about what was going on in the southern states in the late 1950's, unfortunately it still exists. I have read several books by this fantastic writer, and thought each one was the best, until I read the next one. It is truly a book worth reading and then look forward for her next book. Great job Susan Gabriel....this historical fiction really shows what it was like in that time period." - Ro

"Just finished *Trueluck Summer* and I loved it. Such an important message for these troubled times...Not only was the subject matter of the story poignantly written, the aura brought back so many good memories from my childhood during this era." - Joan Meyerhoefer Roddy

"Simply fantastic!! The emotions of this story are as relevant today as in the timeframe in which the story was written. I didn't want it to end and hope there may be a sequel in the future that will continue the fascinating story of the characters." - Mary

"This is a coming-of-age story, for all ages. A story of the 60's when not only people in that era had difficult choices to make, but of a country, stretching and becoming more, finding its footing as much as any adolescent. If you didn't live through the sixties, then this book will speak to you of things on a large scale, and on smaller ones. It shows you the sweeping changes, and the fear that people battled as they dealt with all the volatile situations. The book has heart. And soul." - Loretta Wheeler

ALSO BY SUSAN GABRIEL

Temple Secrets Trilogy:

Temple Secrets

Gullah Secrets

Tea Leaf Secrets

The Wildflower Trilogy:

The Secret Sense of Wildflower

(a Kirkus Reviews Best Book of 2012)

Lily's Song

Daisy's Fortune

Trueluck Summer

Grace, Grits and Ghosts: Southern Short Stories

Seeking Sara Summers

Circle of the Ancestors